MARKED

the sequel to *TRACKED*

JENNY MARTIN

DIAL BOOKS

DIAL BOOKS
An imprint of Penguin Random House LLC
375 Hudson Street
New York, New York 10014

Copyright © 2016 by Jenny Martin

Printed in the United States of America
ISBN 978-0-525-42871-8

1 3 5 7 9 10 8 6 4 2

Text set in Perrywood

FOR MY GRANDMOTHER
JOY JOSEPHINE,
WHOSE SPIRIT FUELS PHEE

MARKED

the sequel to *TRACKED*

CHAPTER ONE

I DON'T SLEEP MUCH ANYMORE. MOST NIGHTS, I GET THREE or four hours of real shut-eye. Maybe five. If I'm lucky, and exhausted enough, I don't even dream. No nightmares, just a quick, merciful blackout.

I'm not lucky very often.

Today, I wake up disoriented. I roll over and haul myself up. I sit on the edge of my bunk in the field barracks, and my body twitches, forgetful. Every cell in me thinks I'm back in our old apartment in Capitoline.

I suppose it's no wonder. Here, my bed's just as narrow and lumpy as my cot at the Larssens'. The concrete floor's just as bare, so it's easy to forget I'm on another planet altogether. That I'm on Cyan-Bisera, at a rebel camp, instead of back home on Castra. It's only after a few rapid blinks, a hazy sweep of the tent . . . the tiny kick of adrenaline, that I remember. Cash is gone. My uncle James is gone, and right now, I don't have a home at all.

What I have is a rebellion. A handful of Cash's allies and friends, hiding out in the middle of the Strand, amidst an impossible forest of giant white poppies, their stalks as thick as trees. Here in our little valley, under a quiet moon, we hold our breath and wait for war.

It's the waiting that consumes me.

I sit in the cool darkness, and I sense it. War *is* coming. There's no denying that now. I've watched the feeds. And not just the official news, but the bootleg footage the flex net hackers send us. You can see it in the raw clips of soldiers, putting down the riots in Capitoline. The people wanted answers after my disappearance. Instead, they got sirens and boot stomps and beatings and screams. Fifty-six million miles away, my planet teeters on the edge between martial law and chaos. And Bisera—Cash's home—isn't far behind.

So I roll up, awake before sunrise, and play the familiar game, even as my feet first hit the soft grass outside the tent. As I walk to the showers, I imagine my enemy. It doesn't matter that Charles Benroyal is on Castra, and that we're millions of light-years apart. I scrub my face, and he stands in his penthouse in the Spire. I drag a comb through my black tangles, his tailors fit him for a new suit. I brush my teeth, he signs a contract. I zip into refugee blues, he prepares another ten thousand soldiers. But when I pull on my boots, the vision becomes more than a game. I know, even as I tighten the laces, that Benroyal is looking for us. Looking for *me*. I'm not just the street racer turned circuit star, the girl who ran away. I am the pawn who slipped through his fingers, and there will be a price to pay. King Charlie will see to that.

Clean and dressed, I head for the center of camp. The pre-dawn sky is caught between light and dark, and it's like I've stepped into a blank world that's waiting for color. Mismatched uniforms move across the makeshift court-yard. Soldiers head for the bunks to sleep after a night's watch. The day crew hustles toward the mess hall, and I fall into the drift.

Even in the chow line, you can read the quiet tension—the little ripples of movement, as formal units break apart and rebels sort themselves into predictable groups. It's mostly Biseran volunteers here. Cash's people outnumber everyone else three to one, and they answer to Captain Nandan. Among the rest, there are a few Castran ren-egades like me, and a handful of Cyanese friendlies. But even after fighting side by side, it's an imperfect alliance. People still tend to cling to their own—their friends and family, reminders of the country they came from. Thrust together, we get along. Mostly. If nothing else, at least we have a common enemy.

I scan the crowd. Among the familiar faces, I see the one that matters most. Bear is a dozen yards ahead, and I rush to catch him.

"Hey," I say. "Wait up."

He stops. His voice is as gray as the sky. "Morning."

When he turns, the crowd breaks around him, forking like a river against a rock. I scan his face. The shadows under his blue eyes, the careless spikes of blond hair. He is six-five, two hundred forty pounds of exhausted.

I frown. It's not even a question. "You picked up another shift."

"Hank was short-handed. Someone's got to man the watch towers."

"You can't keep doing this, Bear. You can't burn every daylight hour in a simulator, then run patrol all night, and still have time for physical therapy."

"I don't need physical therapy anymore."

"Maybe not, but Mary says it's still a good idea to take it slow."

He answers. "You don't have to worry about me, Phee."

I read the subtle shift in him. Polite. Formal. Painfully neutral. That's the deepest cut. To watch the way he relaxes—honest grins and gentle swagger—with everyone else.

"I know," I say. "It's just—"

"My back is fine. I'm fine. Everything is fine."

There's no point in pushing Bear. At the moment, ours is a fragile truce. For a dozen years, our shadows were attached, but when I took the circuit deal and signed with Benroyal, everything unraveled. After I fell for Cash, all the seams so carefully stitched—by time, by friendship, by love—were pulled apart. Now there's only one knot left, tied up in duty. So I'm quiet, unwilling to test the cord.

Zaide, another would-be pilot, joins us. Like Cash, she's Biseran. They share the same dark skin, sharp smile, and golden eyes. Bear angles her way, and just like that, he's at ease again. I stand in his shadow as they talk over the day's work—flight simulations and squadron duty and gear inspections. All the things I won't be doing, since Hank won't allow me to train at flight control. Unlike Bear, I haven't become an officer.

"You up for two more runs in the sim?" Zaide asks him at last. Bear nods.

"Find me after drills," she says.

They trade salutes as she walks away. I force a smile and wave, even though I'm glad to see her go. Bear's not the only one who can play polite and formal.

We're just stepping back in line when a noise takes me by surprise. The whir of vacs overhead. The tang of burning fuel sap overpowers the almond-sweet haze of the poppy fields and I tense. Even though this happens nearly every day, and Cyanese aircrafts deliver supplies from the west all the time, I can never get a grip on the unease. Most of us barely survived the ambush that drove us here, the one that nearly killed Bear and took Cash. We might have escaped Benroyal, but he's left us plenty of scars.

I don't relax until all three vacs touch down, their engines dying to a less-than-deafening hum. The usual blue and silver stars painted on their cargo bay doors tell me that these *are* Cyanese aircraft. *Stand down,* I tell myself. Bear's eyes soften, but he doesn't reach for me or tell me it's okay to exhale. He doesn't know the rules. The little routines I keep just to survive here. The Pearl Strand is supposed to be our thousand-mile strip of safety. Between two countries, it's both no-man's-land and holy ground, a refuge for renegades and monks. But I don't *feel* safe. Not anywhere, not since the ambush. So I do what I have to do to get by.

I avoid shadows and sharp sounds. I steer clear of the north end of the field range, where the echoes of practice fire land hardest, like dull, knuckled jabs against old bruises. I keep moving all the time, to chase off the constant fear of getting cornered and captured. The bustling launch yard is the worst, because I can't completely avoid it. But no one can know how it gets to me, how the hot whir of landing aircraft drags me into a blinding, black-brained pit of nausea. If I could just keep a lid on it, I could get past this on my own. I know I could.

A few deep breaths, and Bear and I fall back in the chow line. We make it all the way to the mess hall doors, when the wind picks up and a jolt of chatter pulses through the yard. I look up again. As the sun rises, another vac speeds our way, a black streak against the blooming sky. This one is nothing like the others before it. It's not Cyanese military or anything else I recognize. The sleek box hurtling toward us is unmarked, and from the sound of the shouts around me, it's coming unannounced. From the east, where our enemies have been lying in wait.

Benroyal. Another attack.

Panic thrums in my veins. Bear reaches for me, but I break away. Automatically, I lunge through the crisscross of soldiers on high alert. Even as my legs carry me to the nearest guard station and my hands seize a weapon, I'm outside myself. The powerful rifle slung over my shoulder should be heavy at my side, but I am lighter than air, a senseless engine charging.

I have a sense of movement around me. Dully, as if through a locked door, the sound of shouted orders and charging weapons reaches me. *Incoming transmission. They have a landing code. Hold your positions. Wait for my order.* But the shriek of the airborne vac rings so much clearer. The sight of it, hovering over camp, presses like a blade and it's the only thing I can actually feel now.

Around me, my comrades respond, their eyes fixed on the lone aircraft. I'm still pushing my way through when one of them turns and commands me to halt. I hear Zaide, shouting my name and begging me to stop. But I cannot kill the motor inside me. Pumping harder, I swing right, past the courtyard, toward the first line of stalks, where the poppies begin to encroach. The rifle thumps my shoulder as I race up the nearest stalk. As I climb, again and again my body slams into the blunt, tree-knotty buds, but I keep going, until my fingers are slick with nectar and sweat and blood.

I reach the top, the last viable foothold. But I'm close enough now. I don't even have to be that good of a shot. Shaking, I anchor myself, the barrel of the rifle leveled over the waxy, white bloom of the poppy. I power the gun, dialing it up to maximum charge. A second later, the vac begins to descend, but I have it in my sights. With this much heat, only two or three shots will take it down.

From the ground, more voices call to me, but the memories in my head are so much louder. I hear the sound of enemy transmissions, right before the ambush. *Razor, this is Gold Lion . . . Target is designated. Eyes on. Eyes on. Eyes on . . .* A thousand eyes *were* on us, ready to strike and scorch and kill. I'm there now, back at that rendezvous stand, and it's happening all over again. In my head, I hear the swarm of IP fighters. Artillery fire. Screams, after the IP attack from above. They shoot Bear in the back. They shoot Cash. He is wounded and he is gone and there is nothing left.

No. This isn't happening right now. I twitch, then wipe my forehead against my shirt. Blinking, I try to focus, but it's useless because I am trapped in a bad dream with claws long enough to reach me here. I sight the lone vac once more. My finger hovers over the trigger.

They're coming for us. They're coming and they won't stop . . .

I hear the shouting again. One voice rises over the rest. "PHEE!"

My eyes sweep the ground. Below, more than forty feet down, Bear is calling to me. Beside him, a dozen rebels bark at me as the vac lands without incident. Hank rushes to the root of my perch. "Stand down, Van Zant!" he calls. "That's an order!" He's trying to wave me down, but it's Bear who draws my gaze.

Calmly, he looks up. I'm paralyzed, my hand tight

around the rifle. His voice isn't hoarse and pleading. There's a steady lilt of command I've never heard before. "Come down, Phee. Come down. It's okay."

Over and over, he says it, until the words take hold and I start moving down. Halfway, I start to sway. The panic drains away, leaving me clumsy and hollow. I'm practically sliding from thorn to thorn. Still, Bear keeps talking, coaxing me to the ground.

Lightheaded, I lose my grip too soon. I drop the rifle and fall the last few feet, but I'm caught up in strong arms. I close my eyes, and this time, the bad dream is gone.

"It's okay. I've got you," Bear whispers.

CHAPTER TWO

IN THE INFIRMARY, I SIT ON THE EDGE OF A COT WHILE MARY rolls a bio-scanner over me. Hal records my blood pressure on the flex screen in his hand. Of course, they elbowed their way through the uproar and pulled me out of Bear's arms like I was a soldier critically wounded in battle. Only there was no battle, unless you count the one inside my head.

In seventeen years, I've bugged out more times than I can count, but I've never short-circuited like this before. Back me into any corner, push me to the edge, and I can fight my way through. Under pressure, I perform. It's the one thing I *can* do. Or could do.

I don't know anymore.

Bear ducks in to check on me, but Mary shoos him out.

For once, he doesn't protest. No longer my satellite, he seems almost relieved to go his own way. *You asked for this,* my heart nags. I don't like the way my stomach twists when he leaves with a casual nod.

Mary returns to the cot. She tucks a strand of gray-blond hair behind her ear, then presses a damp cloth against my forehead. I want to curl into the crook of her arm like I'm six years old again, awake after a nightmare. Instead, I take the compress and edge away.

"What happened out there, Phee?" she asks.

"Nothing."

"Running off like your hair's on fire? Hauling a rifle forty feet up and taking aim at a random civilian vac doesn't seem like nothing to me," she says. "Seems an awful lot like something."

I think about how to reply, but all the possible answers seem as loaded and dangerous as the gun I held in my hands. I can't tell my foster parents how far I've slipped. How lately, I wake up in the middle of the night, drenched in cold sweat. How my throat tightens every time I hear an airborne engine. Worst of all, how more and more often, I see Cash's face in the crowd, even when I know he's gone. To say the words out loud is to open all the doors. I need them to stay shut.

So I don't say anything. When I shrug, Hal kneels in

front of me. The gesture is protective and fatherly, so perfectly *Hal* that I can't bear it. "It's normal to feel afraid. After what you've been through."

The tremble starts to build in my jaw, and I clamp down hard before it reaches my lower lip. "I'm not afraid. I overreacted. I misunderstood orders. That's all."

Mary frowns. "Phee, we need to deal with this."

"There's nothing for *us* to deal with." I stand up, turning my back on her. I hate the sound of my own voice, so high and tight. I head for the exit. "It won't happen again."

I rush through the open flaps of the infirmary tent. And that's when I run into the pilot.

The stranger's skinny and shortish, still trussed up in a helmet and flight gear, and she nearly knocks me over. I stagger back, but she doesn't say sorry or excuse me. Instead, her bark is parched and serious. "Are you Phoebe? Phoebe Van Zant?"

My real name, first and last. Hardly anyone here uses it. Like it or not, to almost everyone I'm still *Phoenix Vanguard,* Benroyal Corp's ex-racer. The pretentious alias is just one more thing that sets me apart and makes them wary. Despite everything, my Sixer ties—the fact that I once drove for the corporates on Castra—haven't done me any favors with the band of rebels who're fighting against them.

The pilot's impatient and asks again. "Are you Phoebe Van Zant or not?"

Hal approaches, stiffening up. I sense he's about to move between me and this jaw-jacking runt, but I step up first. "Who wants to know?" I ask.

"It's *me*," the pilot says matter-of-factly. "You weren't expecting my arrival?"

I skid past annoyed, landing at defensive. "I don't know you."

The stranger pulls off the helmet, and I realize "me" is a dark-eyed, dark-haired, slim-limbed, sweat-soaked girl, surely no older than I am. "My name is Miyu Yamada."

Mih-Yoo, she pronounces. *Me*.

"Hold up, you're—"

"I'm Grace Yamada's daughter," she says. "And I have a message for you."

Stupidly, I blink at her.

"We've been sending coded transmissions for the past two weeks," Miyu adds. "Perhaps you didn't receive them? Is Hank Kinsey here? I was told Hank might know how to intercept them."

"Hank is . . ." I pause, completely flustered. "He never said anything about getting messages. I don't know."

She sighs, then flashes a prim little smile. I get the distinct impression that she'd like to roll her eyes, but that she's been taught that kind of thing is completely beneath her. The way Miyu sizes me up isn't exactly rude, or arrogant. It's as if she simply knows her place in the world. And I guess when your mother's company controls every Sixer bank from here to Castra, you *own* that place, even when you're dressed like a scruffy vac pilot.

Mary springs on Miyu. "What kind of message? Who knows you're here? How did you know where . . ." The second she trails off, I see what's left her mouth hanging open.

Hank approaches, but he's not alone. Behind him, at least a dozen fully armed Cyanese soldiers march our way. I don't recognize any of their faces, but the way these men and women tower over everyone else tells me all I need to know. So many silver stars, stitched into formal dress blues. Not a worn-out, stubbly chinned rebel among them.

No, these guys are official, pressed and polished.

Hank's arguing, trying to get them to halt, but they brush him off, which is a sight to behold in itself. Hank is no small man, but these men and women are all seven-foot-tall, golden-haired, jack-booted giants. So easily, they outpace him. And they are headed straight for the infirmary.

Too late, I see that they are headed for *me*.

Miyu steps aside; her shrug might as well say *Hey, don't look at me, I just got here*. Before she or Hal or Mary or anyone else can say another word, two of the soldiers—a Cyanese man and woman—flank us and take me by the arms.

A third soldier, one with an elaborate bird of prey embroidered over his heart, moves out of the pack. He must be Hal's age, or close enough. There is no gray at his temples, or deep lines on his face, yet there's something in him that speaks of weary time, long-stretched. He is different from the others, and it's not just the thread of his jacket.

"Ms. Vanguard?" he asks.

The shoulder-length waves of his hair shine a deep gold, and his eyes are a dark, dark blue—a color stolen from battles at sea, all smoke and drowning and night. I drop my chin, focusing on the white-winged barden stitched into his coat.

When I don't answer, he tries again, "Or would you prefer 'Ms. Van Zant'?"

I hate the alias Benroyal chose for me, but I decide to let it go. "Either is fine."

"I'm Commander Larken," he says.

"Commander Khed Larken," Hank adds, catching my eye.

Khed. I'm certain I've heard that name before.

"Would you accompany me to the armory, Ms. Vanguard?" the commander asks calmly.

Hal stands behind the tight circle of soldiers. "Does she have a choice? Is all this really necessary?"

"If you'd be kind enough to excuse us," Larken says, ignoring Hal. He looks at me. "We've come for Phee's hearing."

Once, maybe two years ago, when I first scored a spot on Fat Benny's crew, I took a race out in the boonies west of Capitoline. Bear and I didn't know what we were in for, and we ended up getting completely off course, on the far end of Piper Dunes. I will never forget the dip in the road, the one I never saw coming.

The thing is, you hit a ramp fast enough, and it's like the world opens a trapdoor. A second after the bottom drops out, you soar. Suddenly, you're flying and your stomach hits the roof of your mouth. When your rig hits the track again, you know the jolt's going to crack your jaw.

Standing in the doorway of the infirmary, I'd just begun to sense the fall. But now, getting marched across the courtyard, catching the heat of a hundred stares as they lead me toward the armory, I'm barreling off the edge of the dock.

Our escort turns Hal and Mary away, but Hank stays at my side as we sweep toward the biggest brick-and-mortar building in the whole camp. "This is standard procedure," he reassures. "They just want to ask a few questions. Nothing to worry about."

But when we reach the armory, and the soldiers usher us inside, I know Hank is sparing me the truth. This isn't a friendly, fact-finding meet and greet. This is an inquisition.

We step into the concrete-floored building. On any other day, I'd see a barely organized warehouse, jam-packed with supplies and armaments and everything else we don't have room to stow in the mess hall or infirmary. But it's all vanished. Not ordered or tidied up. *Gone.*

Except for one empty chair, which has been placed in the center of the room. And I can rusting well guess who it's for.

As for everything else, all the rows and piles and boxes of powdered milk and magma launchers and vac engine parts have been inexplicably swept away. Must've been a good day's work for at least a dozen soldiers to clear everything out. The emptiness is more than spooky. It's as if the rebels decided to call it quits.

Hank stays close as the guards escort me farther into the room. By the far wall, a dozen more Cyanese officers stand in quiet formation. Around the lone chair, they've created a wide-arcing ring marked by a six-inch band of mirror-polished metal. The band's smooth-edged and flat. A shimmer flickers through it, like it's alive. Like it's not really metal plate at all, but a narrow stream of liquid light. It's then I stop moving.

If I let them push me into that chair, their questions will test all my locked doors. They will want to know about the ambush.

I don't want to go back there.

One of the soldiers touches my elbow, and I stiffen. Doesn't matter that I know I'm overreacting. I pull every muscle taut and try to ride it out.

Hank reads the tension in me, but says nothing. Commander Larken towers over us, and as he leans down to look me in the eye, it seems to take a lifetime to stoop low enough. "I stand with you," he says.

Bidram arras noc.

He doesn't say them in Biseran, but these are old words. Powerful ones. And Larken speaks them in the most honorable way, exactly the way Cash would. If panic were venom, *these* are the right words to draw the poison from my heart. For a second, I close my eyes and remember Cash's face, the fierce nobility in it. This same nobility lives in Larken. He is the kind of man Cash will become . . . if he's still alive.

"I know what you've been through." Larken pauses. "What you and your friends have done for this rebellion."

"So why am I here?"

"There are others who need to hear your story. Will you speak to the Skal?"

"Who is that?" I ask.

"*We*," he corrects, "are the nine. The sovereign council of Cyan."

Of course. *Khed*. My mind reaches back to a conversation long ago, one with Benroyal. He'd tried to school me, listing off the names of ancient emperors and royals, but at the time, I wasn't interested in his little history lessons. *Alexander the Great. Khed II.* Now I wish I'd paid more attention. Larken is more than a soldier. He's one of Cyan's leaders, from a long royal line.

I turn on Hank, and mentally, I'm already clawing his eyes out. I cannot believe he didn't tell me that the Skal—the rusting high council of Cyan—was planning this hearing. But before I can open my mouth to growl at him, Larken gestures toward the chair.

Hank's eyes plead. *Please do this. Please.*

Quietly, I leave the edge of the circle and follow Larken to its bull's-eye center. I sit in the chair. They stand beside me.

"Phoebe Van Zant," the commander calls out. "Present for official hearing."

My name rings like a signal. An eye-blink later, the armory disappears.

CHAPTER THREE

THE RING ON THE FLOOR EXPLODES; A THOUSAND BLADES OF light pierce the air and search every surface. For a moment, I'm blinded. When my eyes adjust, the pinpoints arc and crisscross, slicing through each other faster than my vision can track. The air vibrates. It's not something I hear. It's something I feel in my sternum.

And then the thrum is gone. When I stand again, I'm trapped in a stone-walled chamber. Larken and Hank are still here with me. A ring of carved thrones surrounds us.

I look at the council members sitting in them. Some are dressed in ordinary clothes. A few wear uniforms, like Larken's. All wear capes, though: heavy, map-colored cloaks that speak of different provinces. One is a deep, silky green, another gray, brown, magenta . . . somber shades trimmed in fur or braid-work or barden feathers. My eyes trace the circle, and it's pretty much hard looks and stony lips all around.

At last, I spy the ninth council throne. There's a cloak here too, resting on its arm, but the chair is empty. A huge, ugly, splintering gash mars it. Instinctively, I touch the scar at the nape of my neck. It's as if the sight of the broken seat made it throb.

"It's all virtual?" I ask Larken.

He nods. "Multi-dimensional streaming. MDS."

We call it "slipstreaming," but on Castra, immersive sim tech is corporately controlled, and the Sixers jack the price up, selling "slip time" by the second. Growing up, virtual holidays weren't exactly in our price range, so I've never experienced slipstreaming outside of quick, walk-through ads. Here, on this scale . . . it's pretty amazing.

I goggle at the high windows and vaulted ceiling. "Nice. Hard to tell none of it's real."

"To the contrary, Ms. Vanguard. This hearing is very real."

I snap, looking for the voice. One of the council—a gray-eyed, gray-robed man—has spoken. He's not the oldest in the circle, and he's not the youngest. That place surely falls to Larken. But Gray's eyes are the sharpest. The cold, spittle-lipped trill of his voice tells me he's the one I should fear.

An older woman next to him answers with a dismissive

wave. *"Parabba."* From the impatient lash in her tone, she's either invoking his name or cussing him out. "We haven't even started, and you're already throwing daggers."

Across from them, another woman interrupts. "Precisely so, Agna. Shall we proceed, Commander Larken?" She is beautiful. Luminous, and so pale you'd think she'd just spent the last year trapped in ice. But there's a terrifying edge in her shine too.

"Yes, Vilette," he says, bowing respectfully.

"By all means then." Vilette raises an eyebrow, then smooths out her moss-dark robe. "Let us speak plainly, that she may understand."

Larken straightens. "I call the Skal to order."

They answer in unison. *"We are the Skal-rung, the nine, the host of Cyan. We tend the coast, the mountain, the plain, and the tower. We defend all therein."* There's a weary reverence in the words.

"And we stand?" he prompts.

"We stand as one."

"And we fight?"

"We fight as one."

"And we fall?"

"We do not fall, nor fear. We do not shrink."

Then, silence. I've witnessed something private and sacred, and now the quiet burns.

Larken takes his place beside the empty throne, but the sight of him beside the broken seat makes my gut twist. It's then I know. It wouldn't matter if he were really there, in the tower with the others. It wouldn't matter if the throne were unmarked. Larken doesn't *sit* on this council. He doesn't, because the wood-splintered scar can't be repaired. He will never quite belong.

Gray Eyes clears his throat, then jerks his chin at Vilette. "Well now, you're the one harping about wasted time. Are you going to get on with it? Ask questions or not?"

She ignores him, her eyes still fixed on me. "Tell us how you came to the Strand."

"I don't know where to start."

"Start at the beginning."

"What do you want to know?"

"Everything."

I blurt the first things that come to mind. "My name is Phee. Phoebe. My circuit name was Phoenix. I drive. I crewed for Benny Eno in Capitoline. I live . . . I *lived* in apartment 533, 4911 Mercer Street South. I've been arrested once. I've wrecked three rigs. Tommy Van Zant is my father."

I stop. I've run out of easy things.

Other members of the council press for more. "What about your time in the Spire? You drove for Benroyal?"

"We need to know about the tracker," another demands.

"What happened to Prince Dradha?"

"Tell us about the attack."

I don't need to look up to know they're still staring.

Larken shifts, and gives an encouraging glance. He is soft-eyed and compassionate. But I don't know what the rest of them want from me. I don't understand any of this.

"I can't . . . I don't know . . . I blacked out." I stumble. "When I woke up . . . I don't remember." *Lies.*

"You remember nothing?" Gray Eyes prods, his eyes hateful and disbelieving.

I look away. "Why am I here?" I ask quietly. Six months ago, I would have roared.

"You dare to question the Skal?" he spits. "You're here because the tracker in your neck brought an army to the Pearl Strand's edge. Because you bungled a mission we were foolish enough to support. The blood of a Biseran prince is on your hands! You brought on that attack, and now—"

"That's enough, Parabba," Larken growls, but the damage is done. A murmur ripples through the circle. I strain for the thread of their whispers, catching only a handful of words.

Unreliable. Unstable. Liability.

To Gray Eyes's left, another councilor speaks up. "How can we be sure she didn't know about the tracker? Or that she's telling the truth?"

The old woman, Agna, barks out a laugh. "You must be joking. Look at her. This wisp of a girl? If she's Benroyal's spy, I'm the prime minister of Castra."

A few guffaws. More than a few nods. An inch of breathing room.

But Parabba is far from finished. When he sits up, it's like watching an old hound snap to attention.

"Oh no, she's not a traitor. No, it's worse than that. She's a fool. Nothing more than a reckless simpleton."

I bristle. "I'm not a—"

Teeth gritted, Parabba cuts me off. "A few precious years of peace, hard won, between our world and yours. And you've brought Benroyal and his whole forsaken army to our doorstep. You cost us the Biseran prince and ruined our plans." He points a crooked forefinger at me, then looks to the council, scanning each member in turn. "Mark my words, she brings disaster."

Vilette shakes her head. "Benroyal's grown too powerful, and she's not to blame for his bloodshed. And we cannot abandon these rebels or hand her over to him."

"We should never have gotten involved," Parabba growls. "We should never have armed those rebels and provoked the Sixers. The treaty between Cyan and Bisera is fragile enough."

Larken turns, squaring up against Parabba. "Bisera was our strongest ally for over a thousand years, before the Sixers swarmed this planet. Benroyal and his kind are to blame for the tensions and the treaties and the whole sap-stinking Thirty Years' War. They're the ones who want to keep us divided. And if you can't see clearly enough to remember that, Parabba, then you're the bigger fool."

The old man rises from his seat, shutting him out. "Here is what I see: Every day that we harbor this girl and shelter her friends in the Strand brings us closer to war. They will come for her, and then they'll come for us. Benroyal. The Sixers will swarm our borders until Cyan's rimmed in blood. I will not break the peace with Castra and Bisera for this!"

"No, you won't break peace, Parabba." Larken sighs. "You'll keep it until we're too weak to bleed at all."

"I'll not take judgment from the likes of you. Your grandfather was a madman, and your father was a disgrace," Parabba roars. "Khed IV, indeed. Spawn of a treacherous line. Don't talk to me about blood."

The council erupts. Half the circle springs up. Everyone's talking all at once and waving arms and shaking fists. Bickering in their language and mine, they fight to be heard.

"Parabba's a fool—"

"—can't afford another war."

"—can't afford to cower."

"If we stay out of—"

"—let the Biseran deal with this."

"Send her back. Send them all back."

Every shout breaks like a wave. Inside, I'm fighting to keep my chin above the surface, which seems to rise an inch every second. I am too insignificant, too paralyzed, too rusting *powerless* to do anything to stop this.

I look up into the hologram's illusion, and see the windows of the tower. The sills seem to narrow, shrinking the threads of light streaming through. Outside the chamber, a burst of wind shrieks. It whistles, rattling the glass. My ears twist the gusts into faraway cries.

Cash. My father. James. They are dead and screaming.

My chest tightens and there's no more noise. Just the black, soundless throb of my heart as it shoves the words up my throat and into my mouth. Each one tastes like a withered match. I can't hold them in anymore.

"ENOUGH. That's enough!" I shout. They stop. Hands frozen in mid-gesture, mouths slack with surprise. Larken is waiting for something. So I give it to him. To the whole rusting council.

A deep breath, then my voice is a strange, deep crackle.

"I sat here and listened to all of you promise to stand and fight together as one. You swore an oath to defend your world, but it's all just words. Cash believed in you, and trusted you. He risked everything."

"Prince Dradha is dead," Parabba says. "His rebellion is a failure, and we've risked enough on rabble-rousers."

"You've risked *nothing*," I snap.

"Careful, girl." Agna's eyes narrow, searching me. "You go too far. We've done much to aid the young prince's cause."

"And look what has come of it," Parabba scoffs. "Oh yes, your great plan to push the Sixers back. I warned you all, and now they're practically marching at the border!"

Another burst of outrage. Again, I shout to be heard. "Don't you understand? This is what they want!" When they quiet, I add, "You might as well be signing one of Benroyal's contracts. You're taking his deal."

That scorches them well enough, but I don't let up. "You are. You're playing into King Charlie's hands, move by move."

Parabba shakes his fist at me. "You little . . . you insolent pawn, how dare you—"

"*I'm* the pawn? You all sit in your tower, silent, while King Charlie reaches for your world. You sit back while his armies patrol the Gap and guard the drug labs and keep the slave labor in line. You say, *Poor Castra. Poor Bisera. That'll never be Cyan.*" I turn slowly, meeting every pair of eyes. "But you want the truth? If you keep fighting amongst yourselves, with the rebels, with Bisera, you're finished. Benroyal will take you apart piece by piece. Gut you like a salvage rig, from exhaust to engine. The way I see it, you've got two choices. You can make peace with your deal, or you can quit jaw-jacking at each other, and stand up to the Sixers."

Agna guffaws. "You can't be serious, girl. Are you suggesting we simply declare war, at your word, and start a revolution?"

An old spark flares, fed by defiance. "Do whatever you want. Send me back. Extradite me into Benroyal's hands. I don't care. All I know is, I'm not taking his deal anymore. You can all stay there and sit in your tower. But me? I'm not going down without pushing back."

CHAPTER FOUR

IN THE END, THEY DISMISS ME. THEY CUT HANK AND ME FROM the circle, all but shoving us out the armory doors. Honestly, I'm relieved. Rust if I want to stand around while they finalize my extradition.

Miyu is waiting for us, helmet in hand. "I trust that went well?"

Hank chews on an answer, poking around in the turf with the toe of his boot. "It could've gone more smoothly."

"Let's just say," I reply, "if my goal was to dig my own grave, I overshot. There's a hole big enough for all of us now."

"I see." Miyu gestures toward the far end of the launch yard, where her vac's grounded. "In that case, maybe you'll welcome my news and come aboard sooner than later."

I take a step back. "Come aboard?"

"I told you. I have a message for you."

Hank is impatient. "About that. I got your transmissions. You said you'd be coming, but you never said why. What exactly do you have to say?"

She looks at me. "Your uncle, James Anderssen. He left something for you. In a vault, in the city of Manjor. Before he disappeared, he made my mother promise to keep everything you'll need to access it. It's critical that you come with me. She sent me here to see to this myself."

"Manjor? In Bisera?" I gape. "What did he leave for me?"

"I thought you already knew." She's as taken by surprise as I am. "I'm talking about your inheritance."

"I've seen the feeds. Benroyal looted the company. Locus is frozen now. There's nothing left."

"No." Miyu shakes her head. "Locus Informatics is gone, but the fortune isn't."

"What?" I gasp.

"He left it for you. James left you everything."

Hank and Miyu and I find the Larssens in the infirmary.

"You okay?" Hal asks me.

My nod's a little shaky. "For now. Where's Bear?"

"He's working the launch yard. Regular patrol," Mary says. I don't reply, but raise an eyebrow as she slides a tray of bloody instruments under the sterilizer panel.

"Emergency appendectomy." She tilts toward the curtained patient area, where the air smells like heat and disinfectant. "Captain Nandan's boy. He'll be fine."

My foster mother says it casually, like this kind of procedure's nothing. I know better. "Thought you didn't handle the knife. Back home, you always referred surgeries to someone else."

"And who, exactly, would I refer patients to now? There's no one else here with better medical training than Hal and me. The boy needed his appendix removed, so I did it. The scar won't be pretty, but he'll live to show it off."

When Mary crosses the room, Miyu and Hank move out of her way.

Mary shoves a pile of clean linens into my arms. "We do what we have to do to save a life or preserve a limb," she says. "Sometimes we fail, and sometimes it's not enough, but the gamble's worth taking. I don't fear the hard choices, Phee."

When I don't answer right away, she adds, "Fold those, please. Then stack them on the shelf. The one below the oxygen cells." Then she crosses the room again, stopping at the sink.

For a second, I nearly slip into my old role of clinic assistant. Then Hank clears his throat, and I remember why I hustled through the door in the first place. Our fate's twisting on the hook, yet a few words with my foster mother and I'm completely derailed. I start to drop the crisp whites onto a nearby gurney, but Miyu steps in and takes over. She's a quick, efficient folder. Mary's going to like her.

"I don't have a lot of time," I begin. "The Cyanese council . . . I don't know what they're going to do. They could be coming for me any second."

Immediately, Hal moves to my side. Mary's still at the sink, but I see the muscles in her shoulders pull tight.

"And what did they say?" she asks quietly, her back still turned.

Hank answers before I have the chance. "They discussed the rebellion. They questioned Phee, and to say she spoke her mind, that'd be putting it mildly. Now they're weighing their options."

Mary shifts, not quite turning around, her hands still anchored over the lip of the sink. Slowly, she nods.

"If it comes to it . . ." Hank looks at me. "I won't let them take you. One way or another, by reason or by force, I'll convince them to let you go on your own. And I'm not standing by while the Cyanese deliver you or anyone else, gift-wrapped, to Benroyal. If we have to, we'll cover your exit. You can leave with Miyu or—"

"I'll take them," Miyu says quickly. "I've got plenty of room, and I can get them back over the border quietly enough."

"How soon can you be ready?" I ask.

"How fast can you pack? I've already refueled, and the vac is on standby."

"Is there another option?" Hal asks. "We can't just leave the infirmary. What about all our patients? What will you do if we're gone?"

"We've talked about this," Hank says, looking at Hal, then Mary. "You knew this day might come."

They say nothing, and for a moment, the room is so still, as if it's holding an exhale. But I can already taste the anger. It builds, a hard little knot in my throat. "Wait. You all *knew*? About the hearing?"

"I'm sorry," Hank says, far too calmly. "We didn't want you to worry. We thought the council visit might turn out to be nothing. It would've just upset you."

"You knew the Cyanese were coming for me? And you didn't bother to tell me?"

Finally, Mary turns and faces me, silencing Hank with an upturned palm. "This was my doing, Phee. I made the decision. If we'd have told you, you would have—"

I close the distance between us, almost shouting. "I would've what, exactly?! You think I can't handle—"

"I think you're not yourself!" Her eyes flash hot and her jaw's set. "I think you're shaken up. The ambush wounded you much more than you're willing to admit, and I think that if we'd have told you the Cyanese were staging a hearing, for all we know, you would've run off and gotten yourself . . ."

She trails off, studying me. My jaw is clenched too, just hard enough to keep me glassy-eyed but tearless. I was so scorched at the council. At all their backbiting and indecision. But this is so much worse. Somehow, Mary is the bigger betrayal.

She knew. She kept this from me because . . .

"You think . . ." I can't say the rest out loud.

You think I'm fragile.

"I think you're human," she answers.

The infirmary doors fly open.

It's Bear, bursting in like a thunderclap.

"Captain's looking for you." Panting, he looks at Hank. "They're leaving. Tonight. Packing up all their gear and preparing for launch."

"Who's leaving?" Hal asks.

"The Cyanese. Two of their three vacs are ready for takeoff. I heard them give Nandan their heading. They're going back to Raupang, their capital."

The third vac. They must be leaving the last escort for me.

"I have to go," I blurt, moving toward the doors. "Hank, we don't have much time. How long do you think you can stall them?"

Bear stands in my way. "Stall who? What are you talking about?"

I read the change in him, even as he asks. His eyes, his body language, the mixture of confusion and fear on his face—he's already shifted into defense mode.

For a second, in my mind, I spin it all out. Hank will do his best, but they won't cut me loose or leave things to chance. They'll take me by force. The Larssens will fight it, and Bear . . . if he doesn't fall, he'll follow, another prisoner. The Cyanese officer will send us on our way, back to Castra, back to Benroyal. There will be no apartment in the Spire for us now. No custom rig to parade around the track. No, I'm certain King Charlie's prepared another prison for me. If he lets me live at all.

I can leave now. Alone, for the Larssens' sake. They can stay, protected in the Strand, even if I can't. Better to take my chances with Grace Yamada's daughter than be taken alive at Parabba's word.

"There was a hearing," I finally answer.

"A hearing?" Bear's still taken aback.

37

He didn't know. A hot-needle flood of relief rushes through me. No betrayal in him, as if there ever could be. I nod. "They questioned me, and argued. They're divided about the rebellion and whether they should support it any longer. Well, mostly, they seem divided about me. I think they're going to extradite me back to Castra."

Bear shakes his head. "No. I mean, are you sure? I just spoke with Captain Nandan. The Skal's going to send real support, more troops and supplies than before. Two battalions here by next week, and I heard more are on the move. They'll be on the border, just west of the Strand, at the ready, in case things escalate too quickly."

"That can't be," Hank says, but he's already pulling on his headset. "Shield One, this is Broadsword, come in?" He wanders off, and for the longest moment, we're frozen as he checks in with headquarters.

"Say again?" he says. He listens, then finally answers, "Copy. Out."

Dumbstruck, he pulls the headset off again and returns, staring at us. "You can all stand down, at least for now. No one's going anywhere."

CHAPTER FIVE

EVERYONE ON BASE IS IN HIGH SPIRITS, AND UNDER THE PALE
poppy moon, the bonfires are roaring. Bellies are full and
eyes are hazy with nectar-laced hooch, distilled in the barracks two tents from mine. Every glass is clinking, filled to
the brim with rosy certainty. For the first time, in all the
laughter and gossip and talk, my name doesn't shrink in
suspicious whisper. For once, it's spoken in ease.

I stick downwind, at the lonely end of the blaze. Far
from Bear, who's on the opposite side, surrounded by fellow pilots. Zaide's not there, and I'm ashamed to feel so
relieved. The rest, they laugh and lean in and tip back their
glasses. Sober, Bear's the calm center of it all, and I'm lost. I
wish I knew how to elbow my way in, to get past the wall
of drunken chatter to reach him.

"Excuse me."

I clench up, spooked to find Miyu at my shoulder.

"Apologies," she says, staring into the fire. "I didn't mean to—"

A flock of officers pass behind, jostling us. Miyu and I nearly knock heads, and I shift to keep my balance as they crowd Captain Nandan, hanging on his every word. It's not just the usual gang, a bunch of Biseran ex-military like himself. I recognize one of Hank's Castran recruits, and at least two of the Cyanese soldiers from this afternoon's hearing. Finally, the huddle settles down. Thankfully, a few paces beyond us.

Miyu finishes her thought. "I didn't mean to startle you."

"You didn't," I lie, forcing a tight smile. "But keep working on it. You're almost there. Next time, you might even waylay me. Put me right on the floor."

Miyu's nowhere near amused. It's as if her to-do list's a thousand miles long, and I'm just slowing her down. She reaches into her pocket and pulls something out. "Here," she says, thrusting it my way.

I look down. It's an envelope, folded in half.

"What is it?" I say, reluctant to take it.

"I promised I'd give this to you. It's from Mr. de Chevalier."

"Auguste? My team manager? I mean, he used to be . . ."

She nods, and I run my thumb along the smooth angle of the sealed flap. It's heavier than it should be. There's more than a note inside. "Is he okay?"

Too near, Nandan's group erupts. Someone's told a joke and half of the rest roar approval. I flinch, unprepared for the burst of manic laughter.

Miyu tilts into my line of sight. "You all right?"

I shake off the vague sense of unease. "You were saying . . . Auguste?"

"He doesn't work for Benroyal anymore. He was fired after your last race."

"And my crew?" I swallow. "Gil and the rest?"

"Gil bounced back. He's crewing for Agritech now, and some of the others, I think. But Mr. de Chevalier . . . he's had a hard time."

Every word's a dagger sunk in my chest. I abandoned my circuit team, knowing full well there'd be a reprisal. Maybe I had to, but it doesn't make it any easier to hear it. "How did you get this?" I study the small envelope.

"Grace looks in on him. She sends someone, from time to time. He asked her to take this and deliver it, should an opportunity arise."

"So he knows I'm alive? Does he know I'm here?"

"I don't know what he knows."

Captain Nandan steals my focus. I can't block out his voice. He starts in on the Cyanese officer beside him, jaw-jacking about how his own ancestors were the first to settle the Strand. *Built the oldest monastery here, just a stone's throw from that ridge,* he says. *The ruins still stand.* It's a story the rest of us have heard a thousand times.

I sigh. Miyu shifts uncomfortably. I look back at the message in my hands.

"Perhaps I should leave and let you open it," she says. "Give you some space."

The breeze shifts, and my lids flutter, stung by the hot billow of sparks. "No," I tell her. "It's fine." I turn the envelope over, smooth side up, and my heart beats wildly. In the glow, I read the steady, flourished script.

Ma chère

I open the envelope, careful not to leave more than the smallest tear. Inside, there's a folded piece of paper. As I open it, a scrap tumbles out. I snag it in my palm as the laughter around me turns to simmering talk. Nandan's still droning on about the monastery.

"What is it?" Miyu asks, staring at my catch.

At first, I don't recognize the thick, silky fabric. But after flipping it over, I see what Auguste left for me. Benroyal's racing logo, the Phoenix-winged patch sewn into my old racing uniform. My *first* uniform, black and sleek and nearly indestructible. The one I wore at Sand Ridge Speedway, when I scored my first win.

When I was still whole and brave and fearless.

I hold up the patch, almost touching it to my lips. I inhale. I can still smell the dead heat of the speedway, the smoke of my wreck in every stitch. I glance down at the paper, now unfolded. Again, Auguste's spare and elegant scrawl.

La légende

He'd called me that once. But most often, I was his "Spitfire Girl." I doubt he'd say the same, if he saw me now.

Shaken, I tilt away from Miyu. I can't help it. A tear tries to well up in the corner of my eye. Miyu's kind enough to let me be. Wordless, she slips away with a gentle nod.

I step closer to my share of the blaze and tuck Auguste's gift into my pocket. My mind lets go; I drift out and lose sight of everyone else. As the flames climb and crackle, I stare into them, until the heat kisses my cheeks and stings my eyes. Fingers of smoke reach out before twisting into the night sky. So many stars above the haze. I see Cash there, in the glimmer dark. I always see him. My hand over his, blood seeping through our fingers.

There's a vicious snap as a piece of kindling shifts. I startle like it's a gunshot.

I squeeze my lids until my heart stops racing. My breathing slows, and I sink into invisible grief.

I stand by the fire for a long time, even as most of the soldiers and their families trickle away, their tired faces still candle-bright and hopeful. Behind me, a soft hiss as an ember's trampled. A deep, warm exhale. I turn, and Bear is at my shoulder.

"Funny," he says. "No matter where we go, trouble finds us."

There's a glimmer there, in his eyes. A little piece of us, still shining.

"Trouble finds *me*, you mean." I pull on an old smile. "If you were smart, you'd stay away. Ditch me altogether."

He's quiet, and suddenly I'm wrecked. The Bear I used to know wouldn't hesitate. *Never,* he'd declare. *I'd never leave you.* But I'm not sure I know this boy—this man— standing beside me. He turns up the collar of his jacket, scaring off the evening chill. When he finally grins, it takes me by surprise.

"Maybe," he says. "Can't say."

I huff. Just a little. "Can't say? Well, for sun's sake, don't reassure me or anything."

"Hmm . . ." He strokes his chin, smiling even wider. "Ask me again tomorrow."

I laugh, on edge. This new, cheeky self-assurance, I don't know what to do with it.

Our eyes meet, and I mark the smaller things; the hundred little changes in him. How much shorter his hair is these days. Military cut, perfectly trimmed. But even clean-shaven, he can't quite lose the day's-end shadow of dark blond whiskers. They roughen him up, sharpening his once gentle face.

He coughs when the breeze sends another cindery plume our way. "Earlier, I stood in the chow line with Yamada's daughter, Miyu. She seems all right."

"Oh?" I strain to keep my voice light. "And what did you two talk about?"

He ignores my question. Looks me dead in the eye. "Have you decided?"

"Decided what?"

"Are you going with her, or staying here?"

Bear makes it sound like a critical fork. As if choosing one forever excludes the other. "Manjor isn't so far. Wouldn't take more than a few days to get there."

Just the idea makes him sigh. *This* look, I know. This is my pacer, trying to talk me out of a rust-fool route.

"What?" I shrug. "Why shouldn't I?"

"It's not safe in Manjor. You realize how many IP troops have moved into Bisera since the last race, right?"

"I know that. But we're talking about my inheritance, Bear. James probably left me the better part of a fortune."

"That's right. A *Sixer* fortune. Bet the money's all tied up in trusts and stocks and you'd have to deal with corporates and contracts and never mind the risk of leaving the Strand right now."

"We could do a lot of good with those kinds of credits."

"We need more than credits. We need allies, and training, and time. We need a safe place to regroup." With both hands, he points at the charred ground. "*This* is what we need."

He is so sure, and it's the biggest change of all. This absence of uncertainty. We have traded places.

"I know you think I'll always follow you, but I can't keep doing this. I can't."

"Bear, what is wrong?"

"You wanted me to leave Castra. You begged me to join this revolution. Well, you know what? I have, Phee. I'm not going to Manjor. Not when I have a job now. Flight command's clearing me for duty in two more weeks. I'll have my own fighter and I'll get assigned a copilot . . ." He trails off, like he's too strangled to get the last words out.

Copilot. Partner. I've been replaced. Rust, how the notion cuts me to the heart. We stare at each other, both trying to mask our wounds. I am jealous; he is furious and impatient. I swear, he practically growls at me. "I just don't understand why you'd even consider crossing that border again. Not when . . ."

"When what?"

He pauses a second too long. He looks me in the eye again, before finally spitting it out.

"Not when there's a billion-credit bounty on your head."

I am too distracted to push through the forest of poppies and climb tonight. Instead, I skirt the stalk-line, running my hand along the tangle as I pass. This will be the first night, since arriving, that I've abandoned my nightly ritual of visiting the highest blooms. *Getting above,* finding that place where I can whisper to unfurling petals and all-knowing stars. But I don't have the energy to spare, not when I'm this furious. I'm exhausted, but there's no way I'm going to bed.

At headquarters, Zaide lets me in, no questions asked. But inside, when I ask to see the direct feeds from Castra, the rest of the night crew tries to turn me away, giving me some bull-sap about protocol and how I'm not an officer, and how I'm not supposed to be in the communications room at all, and how about I wait until the morning, when they can check with Hank first. But I won't leave, and just when the shift leader's about to call Hank, Commander Larken steps into the hive.

While everyone else salutes, fists over hearts, I gape at him.

"You didn't leave," I say.

"I'm staying for the time being." He says it likes it means a thousand years. And the way things are shaking out, I'm afraid he might be right.

Zaide clears her throat. "Commander Larken, Van Zant would like to pull up some direct feeds, and they were just explaining Lieutenant Kinsey's orders. No one but officers are allowed in HQ. Should I call him? Perhaps he'd want us to make an exception?"

"That won't be necessary." He raises a hand. "I'll take care of it."

She takes a step back, affirms. I'm not sure why she'd stick her neck out for me, but I'm grateful.

"Thank you," Larken adds. Zaide shoots me a sympathetic look, and I try a little harder to hate her less. No, that's not fair. I don't hate her. I only hate the space she occupies. This is what it's come to: I resent her, the way Bear resented Cash.

When she and all the rest get back to work, Larken turns. "Come with me."

I follow him to a flex glass table, one normally set aside for intercepting and filtering feeds. We take it all in: the official news from Castra, and raw footage from friendlies—hacker groups like BitReaper and the Fist. For weeks, Hank's kept an eye on communications; no one gets new data in or out of our little valley without clearing it with him first. Sure, we can access transmissions, but HQ screens them. All this time, I thought Hank was protecting the rebellion. Now, I see, he was also protecting *me*.

Leaning over the table, Larken signs into the system, disables half a dozen applications, then pulls up a single screen. "Should be able to pick up a few direct feeds from here," he says, stepping aside. "Find me when you're done."

After he leaves, I sit in the chair. I stay up all night watching the screen, staring at feedcast after feedcast. Zaide brings a cup of coffee, but I leave it, cold and untouched. I don't need it to stay awake. The rage is enough.

Back home, I used to avoid too much screen time. Working at the Larssens' clinic and racing for Benny kept me plenty busy, and even when I had the time, I never saw the point in watching anything but circuit racing. On Castra, the news is always depressing, and scripted Sixer shows are nothing but subtle propaganda.

But there's nothing subtle about what they've done to me. My family. Hank and a dozen other rebels. To millions, we're now a pack of bloodthirsty terrorists. Castra's Most Wanted.

Sure, I've seen most of it before. We knew Benroyal

would make us outlaws. But I never expected this latest spin on the story.

It's been three months since the prime minister's disastrous public statement, and I guess Benroyal's smooth-talking strategists got to work. To say they perfected damage control is an understatement. I watch the old feeds, and see the first story break. Then another and another and another.

New Evidence in Vanguard Disappearance.

Circuit Racer Linked to Bombings.

Phoenix Vanguard: Accomplice or Mastermind?

Dradha Presumed Dead, Assassinated by Ex-Racer.

Then, the most recent story. The perfect final blow. False footage of me, supposedly recovered from the ambush. The angles are all wrong, and the action's choppy. The fiery chaos looks all too real, and I could almost believe they actually captured this, then and there, during the attack. Except in this new "footage," there's a new Phoenix Vanguard. A slick, digitized copy of me. Same eyes, same hair, same black racing uniform, but there's a gun in her hand.

I tense, my nostrils flaring.

I stare at the screen. Through hopeless smoke, my ringer stands over a kneeling victim, posed to look like Cash. You can't see his face; he's mostly out of frame as she raises the barrel.

It isn't the jump cut to barren ground as she fires that turns me inside out. It's the crack of the bullet and the sound of his body dropping. The angry churn in my gut curdles into a full-on case of the shakes. One grainy clip, and they've erased who I am. They've hijacked my identity. But I don't stop. I push past the nausea and keep watching. I don't move or make a sound until I see the last feedcast, recorded only hours ago.

Riot in Biseran Capital.

There's a procession, streaming through the Biseran capital. Thousands have gathered for a beloved prince. When the people surge in the streets, fists raised for their Evening Star, I die with them. They cry out for my blood, and I break, biting down on a sob.

I log out and shut it all down. When I finally check the time, I see I've missed the sunrise.

CHAPTER SIX

ZAIDE'S NO LONGER IN THE COMMUNICATIONS ROOM, BUT HER day shift replacement tells me where Larken's gone. As the sun climbs, I find him outside camp on the Hill of Kings. He sits on a rock at the top of the silt-veined slope, surrounded by the tombs of his ancestors.

Despite the stubborn flocks of barden and the crusty layers of bird drip on every grave, on this planet, there is no ground more sacred. For centuries, the Cyanese and the Biseran buried their leaders on this height. As angry as I am, I don't have the right to raise my voice here. Quietly, I sit beside him. "Why do you let them stay here?"

He doesn't tilt my way. Instead, he shrugs. "Let who stay?"

"The birds."

He ignores my question. "Did you find what you were looking for at headquarters?"

I don't answer at first. Instead, I squint into the morning sun, so bright it makes my eyes water. I listen to the birds. Their cries knit into one scratching, fluttering shroud of grief-song. The sound is oddly comforting. "He's taken everything from me," I say. "My home. My birth parents. Cash. But at least I had my identity."

"But you were never Phoenix Vanguard. Not really."

"That's not what I mean. I thought once I escaped, he couldn't touch who I really am. But now . . ."

He takes a breath, as if to speak, but I'm not finished yet. "You know what the bounty on my head is? One billion credits, as of last week."

"And you're surprised? I'd have thought you'd seen that coming."

"I figured he'd smear my name. But I didn't expect him to put a gun in my hand and make me Cash's killer. Millions of people think I did it, Larken. I don't know how to fight this."

Larken doesn't react. Instead, he stares into the bright haze. When his eyes settle on a single distant, open-mouthed crypt, it's like he can see into it, reading some dead man's invisible approach. "My grandfather Khed II rests there."

"Parabba mocks you for it."

"And he isn't completely wrong. My grandfather *was* insane. Imagine a thousand years of peace, between Cyan and Bisera . . . he helped to destroy that. He plunged us all into the Thirty Years' War."

I pause. The only history I've been taught is the version sold on the Sixer feeds. "What happened?"

"The old man marched across the Strand. Tried to invade the Gap, and the Sixers rushed in to 'protect' it for Bisera. Cyan and Bisera haven't been the same since."

I look up at him. "Living here, I think I get it now. It's not just two countries . . . it's more like old friends, torn apart."

"Old friends . . . and families too."

I raise an eyebrow. "Your family?"

"The war dragged on and on. We were blamed for so much. The conflict, the destruction, even the assassination of His Majesty King Mohan."

"But Benroyal and Cash's brother, Dakesh—they were the ones who murdered his father. It wasn't—"

Larken cuts me off. "Yes, but my grandfather sneered at Bisera's loss. In public, he acted all too pleased to see Cash's father gone. He should have denounced the assassination; at the very least, he should have offered some token of sympathy. Instead, he fueled the rumors, making it so easy to pin the lie on us. And my father . . . he couldn't handle the pressure or the shame. He gave up his title. Locked himself away in his country estate, abandoning my mother and me. After that, we never fit in. Not even when the Skal finally came to its senses and put an end to my grandfather's madness."

"Your throne, the one with the scar—"

"The council guard cut the old man down, right there in the tower. They left his chair, as a reminder." Bitterly, he smiles. "Forgive me, if I'm not eager to sit there and take his place."

"Larken, that's horrible. But they have to know none of it was your fault."

A shadow passes over him and for a second, I swear he's a hundred years older. "They know I'm a madman's heir, and a coward's son."

The air's quiet and thick; it's an effort to suck in a breath. I have no title. I will never sit on a throne or lead a people. But I know what it's like for Larken, to be abandoned.

"After my father left, my mother bargained to hold our place on the council. I took my father's seat. But we were never really accepted," Larken adds. "The damage had been done. It was too late."

"But you stayed behind," I let slip. "You could have followed your father and run away."

He doesn't answer. He doesn't have to. That deep sense of duty—it's written all over him. For a moment, shoulder to shoulder, we sit in silence. He eyes the shifting flock of barden. "You asked me why we let the barden stay," he says at last. "But they were here first, and they'll be here after we're gone."

I sigh. "And that doesn't bother you, on your own holy ground? The barden stink. They drip all over the place."

"They also keep the hill clear of things that slither and crawl. They eat pesky groats and wendel, and even their drip serves a purpose. It kills the weeds and fertilizes the poppies." He's too diplomatic to let it show, but there's a slow-blooming smile on his face. "And if the birds seem to prefer roosting on Parabba's family crypt, and a little extra falls on his ancestors, who am I to argue?"

I cough, choking on a bit of laughter.

Larken straightens, and a little of his reserve returns. He's the commander again. "They stick together, this flock. Drive them away, scatter them a thousand times, and they will migrate back, drawn to each other. They do not surrender. They do not give up their ground."

I'm quiet once more. I close my eyes. My city, Capitoline, is light-years away, but I can almost feel its desert fire in the sun-glazed air. "I've done everything but hold my ground, Larken. I abandoned my world, and my people.

These past three months, all this time . . . I've just been hiding out."

"You can call it hiding out, but maybe it's building strength," he says. "After my father died, it took a long time to find my way. Sometimes, it takes a while to recover. You have to make the choice to come back from it. Come back a little stronger . . . a little wiser . . . and you can show them what you're made of. Show them who you really are."

I freeze, uncertain.

"Or not," he adds. "You could just let him define you."

My fists begin to curl at my sides, but even as my temper flares, I know that I'm angry with myself, not Larken.

"How?" I ask. "You're the military strategist. How do I take my identity back?"

"Engage your enemy," he says, as if the answer were obvious.

"What do you mean?"

"First, you've got to choose a suitable battlefield. Second, launch an offensive. Quickly, before the enemy has the chance to read your position."

I blink. "Are you saying I should leave the Strand?"

"I'm saying you have options. Remember: The wisest victors act, rather than react. They know when to strike, rather than defend. So you can wait for Benroyal to make the next move, or you can make one of your own."

Larken stares me down, so I turn away.

"Don't wait too long, Phee." He stands. His final words fall heavy on my shoulders. "You decide. Don't let him choose your battleground."

CHAPTER SEVEN

I NEED A SHOWER AND SIX HOURS STRETCHED OUT ON MY bunk, but instead I walk down to the launch yard to find Bear. As soon as I duck into the flight ops tent, Hank waves from his seat on the command platform, then points me in the right direction. "He's in sim one," he says. "If you don't mind standing by a sec, he's finishing up."

I eye the giant gray sphere while I wait. I'm told it's the largest, most state-of-the-art flight simulator on base, and Bear's logged about three billion hours in it since we arrived in the Pearl Strand. He's bound and determined to become a Tandaemo fighter pilot, and I can't blame him for aiming high. Tandaemo are worthy aircraft. More agile than regular vacs, they're capable in a dogfight, and can still handle vertical takeoffs and landings.

And unlike other fighters, they're set up with two flexible command seats, which can alternate as gunner and pilot positions. At any given time, either partner can switch tasks or take over completely. Which explains the fighter's name: Tandaemo is a play on the Cyanese word *tan,* which means "twin," and *daemo,* which means "bird of prey." Not a bad way to describe such a sleek, dangerous vac.

Finally, another officer hands Hank an oversized flex screen, and after looking at Bear's latest sim score, he enters an exit code. I hear the pressured pod door hiss as it opens. Hank and the other officer stand up to leave.

And then I'm alone with my former best friend. Bear unbuckles and pulls off his helmet, and I catch the rarest glimpse of joy as he sits in the pod's left command seat. He doesn't spy me yet. His face is flushed and his ice-blue eyes are all lit up. It's the happiest I've seen him in ages.

He looks up as he rises from the com, but the sight of me presses him back into his seat.

"Hi." I swallow. "I figured you'd be here."

He nods, and I watch the joy slide away. A shadow passes over him, his jaw sets once more. This is the Bear I've come to know best in the last three months. He says nothing, and suddenly, I'm not ready to have this conversation.

"Perfect score today?" I ask.

"Almost. I missed one target. Or technically, my artificially intelligent copilot missed one. It's a lot harder to run this kind of sim alone."

"But you'll have a partner soon?"

"A copilot? Yes."

Too many seconds of silence hang between us. My eyes sweep the pod; I look at everything but him. "Tell me what you love about this."

"The fighter vacs, you mean?"

"Flight school. The simulator. All of it. Tell me."

"You really want to know?" he asks. He's surprised. Lately, we've only seen each other in the clinic and in the mess hall. I've never sought him out here before.

"I really want to know."

"Then," he says, beckoning me into the pod, "instead of telling you, how about I show you?"

I climb in and sit beside him. Bear hands me a helmet, and I buckle into the second command seat. When the pod door closes, we're pinned down in darkness, the slow sigh of his breathing the only sound. A moment later, the sim comes to life, and I'm dazzled by false sunlight through pretend windows, and the sharp glow of a dozen holographic com screens. Bear swivels toward one and enters a code to launch the sim.

"I'll pick an easy one. We'll have to handle evasive maneuvers over the mountains, but we won't have to land under pressure. I'll fly. You can be my gunner." He gestures at the weapons console, with its lone mechanical control, a throttle-like trigger stick. "I'm betting it won't be that hard for you."

He smiles. Already he's relaxing again, falling into the rhythm of his work. "Flight ops, this is Talon One, reporting for Mission: Karkoun."

"Copy that, Talon One." Flight ops is a silky-voiced, female AI. "Initiating simulation six-six-three."

"Interesting choice for a call sign," I tease Bear, ignoring the pang in my chest. Our first rig, the one I sunk at the docks.

"I've got a better one for you," he answers mischievously. "Flight ops, I have new data."

"Standing by, Talon One," she says. "Go ahead."

"Call sign for number two seat is Short Stuff," he replies, a grin plastered over his screen-lit face.

I scowl at Bear. I should've known. It's his favorite nickname for me.

"Copy that," the computer says. "Welcome aboard, Shorts Tuff." Bear cackles over the wire.

"Seriously?" I kick, but his steel-toed boot's just out of range. I swivel hard in my chair. Bear reaches out to stop me.

"Easy there," he mocks. "Or we'll have to lock your com

seat. And I might need you to swing around once the sim gets up in the air."

Which is exactly what's going to happen in about ten seconds.

"All systems are go, Talon One," flight ops warns. "Prepare for takeoff."

I clench up at the sound of a hydraulic gasp as the com seat platform locks into place. Screens count down the last few seconds before liftoff. The platform jerks, and suddenly every surface vibrates with movement. The launch cycle presses me into my seat, and the way g-forces seem to ripple through me, I'd swear we were blasting into the sky.

The most primitive patch of my brain takes over, delivering familiar orders. Release adrenaline. Endorphins. The bliss-terror cocktail that floods my system every time I buckle into the driver's seat. Worse than a junkie, I've been chasing moments like this for half my life. In a rig, you get an eye-blink, a half-second jolt after you pull a speed trigger. Your heart bursts as you rocket forward. But the bullet-arc of the launch seems to stretch out so much farther. Just when I'm sure I can't get any higher, I *am*. And then the teeth-rattling lift is gone, and we're stabilized, racing smoothly. We're . . . *flying*. I glance at my copilot and think to myself, *I get it, Bear. I really do.*

His hands are on the controls. His eyes sweep the false

horizon, then focus on the screens. "You make it look so easy," I say.

"It's easy when you're flying with flight ops. The system can do a lot on its own, given the right parameters. But you can't always rely on auto-pilot. If there's any kind of systems failure, or signal disruption . . . airspeed, energy-to-weight ratio . . . it's all on us. You can't ever count on coasting, Phee. You've always got to be ready."

Silent, I nod. In the past three months, Bear's recovered from a bullet to the back and become a pilot. What have I done with the same number of hours? Marched the perimeter, laid some brick, and swept some floors. He has grown beyond me.

"Flight ops," he calls out. "Ready for briefing."

"Copy. Affirmative," she answers. A floating grid map appears. "Your mission is to penetrate hostile airspace over the Karkoun mountains, drop supplies to target, and return to base. Pilot Talon One, you will manage fighter position and employ evasive maneuvers against enemy fire. Gunner Shorts Tuff, you will monitor airspace and dispatch enemy fighters at will. You have twenty-eight minutes to complete your mission. Over."

"Copy."

"Out," flight ops signs off.

And with that, we begin. I'm mystified as Bear effortlessly keeps an eye on airspeed and altitude. One touch to a screen or tilt of the center stick, and he easily manages the high-speed pitch and roll. A few prompts appear on my own screen (I think my com seat must be set for "novice"), but I catch on quickly enough. I'm to watch the defensive grid for approaching hostiles. If I see any, all I have to do is aim, and pull the trigger to blow them away. In the sim, Benroyal's IP fighters shoot disruptive pulse fire, but they're also equipped with tracking missiles and charged magma artillery. I'm not sure what kind of heat we're packing.

"What am I firing? Pulse fire or—"

I'm cut off as Bear pulls us into a steep climb, then into a gut-churning spin. It takes me a second to figure out that I'm upside down, caught in a high-speed maneuver. A loud alarm pierces the fog.

"Warning," flight ops says. "IP signatures detected. Hostiles in pursuit."

Just as quickly as we flipped, we spiral again. I don't know how Bear keeps his head in the game and his hands on the flight controls. I've raced my share of rigs at more than two hundred miles per hour and crashed half as much, but this flying thing? All the blood's gone to my head, and it's screaming *Which way is up?*

"Three fighter vacs at seven o'clock. Get on it, Phee!"

Bear says something else through the headset, but I'm

too bugged out to catch it. *Dig in, Van Zant.* My eyes loll back, then I curse and force them to focus. *Get a grip.* I zero in on my targeting screen and reach out for the trigger stick. The feel of it in my hands anchors me. Bear engineers another plunging turn, but this time I'm ready for the swing. When the first hostile slips back on my screen, I'm on it. When I tilt to follow the target, it's as if I'm riding the gun barrel, poised to rain down heavy fire.

The alarm doesn't let up, but I tune it out and pump the trigger once, twice, three times. I miss by a mile. The careless pulse fire does nothing to stop the IP fighters. Relentless, they loop back around in hot pursuit.

"Hold steady. You have to pull and hold it for a missile lock!" Bear shouts. "When your target blinks, let go!"

We nearly take a direct hit, but Bear manages to keep us out of range. He dips, slowing down, until the fighters have eclipsed us. This time, when they appear on the targeting grid, I take Bear's advice. A four-second squeeze, and we blow the first fighter to bits. It takes two other stomach-turning sprints to get into position again. I hammer the second fighter, ripping it out of the sky. Through my headset, the sim rewards me with a satisfying crack, and we weather the aftershocks of a fake explosion. It's too easy to forget this isn't real.

The third fighter isn't going down so easy. It rockets

ahead, moving over the drop zone. "Target in range," flight ops alerts us. In the midst of combat, the monotone calm of her voice is jarring. "Air drop must occur below one thousand feet."

"We won't make it," Bear says. "I've never made a successful drop without dispatching all hostiles first."

Sim or no sim, it pains me to let him down. "You've never had me on the trigger," I say, forcing a confident edge I don't really feel. "It's not too late. Sweep down. Attempt the drop. I've got your back."

He takes me at my word and manages the descent. I swear, my stomach climbs into my throat as we fall. I've always known Bear as a brilliant navigator, but I'd never bargained he could play so fast and loose.

I prepare for another evasive move, but the enemy fighter's pulled ahead. It's racing toward our drop zone. I strain to get a better glimpse of the ground. We are in the Karkouns now. The rebel camp's below us. As we close the gap, the hostile vac slows down again. The enemy fighter's playing a new game. We are no longer his target.

And I have been here before.

A rain of enemy pulse fire strikes the edge of the camp. The screens blink, illuminated by the hit.

"Warning," flight ops says. "Abort mission. Return to base."

My throat tightens and I'm paralyzed, my hands in a stranglehold around the targeting stick. When I don't let go, missile after missile blazes forward, misfired into the air. I hardly notice. My eyes are fixed on the ground, and I watch as the enemy fighter obliterates the camp.

Memories of the ambush rush in, and all the locked doors fly open at once. A dry heave twitch builds in my gut. I have to get out of this harness. Get out of this sim. I am here and not here. I can't handle this.

"Phee, are you okay?" Bear asks. He sounds so far away.

An ear-splitting alarm sounds as I unbuckle and fumble with the com seat harness. My screen flashes with orders. *Simulation Incomplete. Re-Engage Safety Restraint.* I ignore the warning, but when I stand up, I can't tell if the platform is still shifting or if I just can't find my feet. One exhale gallops after another, and I sink to my knees, desperate to catch a deeper breath. A sob is crouched in my wind pipe, and I'm determined to hold it in.

"Flight ops," Bear barks, swiveling toward me. "Sim Over. Rapid Shut Down."

For a moment, I'm alone in the dark. No more sirens to cover my gasps. But then Bear's hand falls on my shoulder. At his feet, I heave, shuddering like a helpless mess. My chest burning, my mind whirling, my whole body contracting, I'm pulled toward the black edge of tunnel vision.

The white-knuckle fog seems to last forever, and when it finally lifts, I am past light-headed. I am empty.

The emergency pod lights power up and I'm exposed. There will be no denying the panic attacks after this.

Mercifully, Bear waits. He doesn't try to pick me up or put me back together. And when our eyes meet, the quiet kindness sends a fresh stream of tears down my face.

I shift, angling toward his seat. Bear leans until our foreheads touch. "You'll get through this," he says.

"I don't think I can."

"You will."

"He's gone, Bear."

In the space of a breath, he is on the floor, beside me. I reach for him like a child waking up after a nightmare, and without a word, he takes me in, scooping me into his arms and holding tight. In the crush, there's relief. Between us, there's no more anger. Only forgiveness. I've been so afraid and alone. I'd forgotten how much I've missed my best friend. How starving I've been for all that he is.

For a long time, we are silent. Then Bear shifts. His lips find my forehead, my eyelids, my cheeks, my temples, and I am too relieved, too comforted to resist. Tenderly, he searches out every wound and heartbreak. When at last, his mouth seeks mine, I welcome the gentle press. His kiss is slow and lush, as weightless as compassion. I drink it in, the touch of his soft lips and sandpaper jaw.

Once, I pushed Bear away for wanting this. But things are different now. *We* are different.

"Stay," he says, kissing me again. "Stay in the Strand."

I feel my resolve slipping away. But when we come up for air, I force the words out. "I can't. At least, not yet. I have to figure things out and find out what James left for me."

"We'd be the best fighters the rebellion's got," he whispers against my cheek. "Fly with me. Be my partner."

It'd be easy to appease Bear. I could forget about Manjor and send Miyu back alone. I could throw my arms around this new life and never look back. It's not hard to picture him and me, taking down IP vacs. Even more easily, I imagine us together. His body, warm and close. But then I think of Cash, and of other kisses; another embrace, not so long ago.

Somehow, I know deep down inside that I'm not ready to forget him. And trying to ignore the pain by losing myself in Bear . . . that isn't healing. It's hiding.

Maybe Bear is the one for me. Maybe we are meant to fly, side by side. But I won't know for sure until I can stand on my own. Slowly, I pull back, staring into his eyes. "I think I want this," I say. "But Benroyal murdered my father and my uncle, and he still has my mother. I can't just turn my back on that and keep hiding out here."

"How can you say that, when we're gearing up for war? There's more than one way to fight him," Bear protests.

"I know. And I've got to find my own way to fight. I need this, Bear. I have to go to Manjor."

Bear doesn't answer. Instead, he sighs, reaching for me. This time, he lingers, as though he's memorizing the shape of us. Ours is the sweetest kiss, the bitterest kiss, the one that tastes most like good-bye.

"I can't follow you this time, Phee."

"I know."

I shatter as he pulls away.

CHAPTER EIGHT

IN THREE DAYS, MIYU AND I LEAVE FOR MANJOR. IT'S DARK, and I lie on my bed. I close my eyes, but I can't rest. I long to get lost in the white-noise gutter of the wee hours, but sleep won't come. So I sit up, then head outside.

I walk around the camp to outpace the thought loop in my head. Every half-lit, terrifying thing I've ever seen or imagined unspools in my brain. Sometimes, a flash of light—a good memory—claws its way through the cold sweat and I can stop to take a breath. But it takes so much energy to sustain that patch of warmth. Sometimes, it's just easier to surrender and keep moving. One more lap around the armory, and I'll be tired enough. I won't imagine the rebel corpses. I won't see Cash bleeding where we left him. My brain will shut off. I'll collapse.

I pass the infirmary. Soft light spills around the doorway. I hear the low buzz of a sterilizer panel, an air purifier's churn and puff. If I close my eyes, I could be at home, in the Larssens' clinic. In the night, the soft blue hum's an invitation.

I step inside.

In the patient area, Hal sits in a high-backed chair with his head lolled to the side. I suspect he's on call, uncomfortably catching a moment of shut-eye. Hal's patient is either asleep or unconscious on the cot beside him. One of the Biseran rebels. The young man's face is beaded with sweat; a spiderweb of wired sensors are attached to his temples, arms, and chest. The flex monitor clipped to the cot supplies a steady beep . . . beep . . . beep. But there's no sign of blood or bandages. I wonder what he's doing here.

Across the room, there's an empty, white-sheeted gurney. Quietly, I climb onto it and lie down. Curled on my side, I watch Hal. Even now, asleep, his forehead's pinched with worry. This is where Bear gets it. He is a guardian, through and through.

"Phee?" a voice whispers.

I look up. Mary is sleepy-eyed, dressed in her favorite raggedy scrubs. "Awake as ever," I say.

She sits on the edge of the gurney. Brushes a few flyaway strands from my face, then rests her scrubbed-rough hand on my arm. I let the warmth of it sink in. I memorize it and file it away, because neither of us are tender creatures. "Who's the patient?" I ask her.

"You know Zaide?" she answers. "The lieutenant in communications?"

I nod again.

"The boy's her brother. We're trying out stim therapy, to see if it helps him."

When I squint in confusion, she elaborates. "Aram's a recovering sap addict. Stim's a new approach, something we've learned from the Cyanese, but from what I've seen, it's pretty effective."

"How's it work?" I ask her, shifting to give her more room on the gurney.

"We hook him up, and give him a programmable serum that zeroes in on certain areas of his brain while he's unconscious." She frowns, struggling to explain. "Stim therapy allows us to stimulate, or in this case, de-stimulate his nervous system. It's like turning the volume down, or turning part of it off. Short intervals, so that the mind has a better chance to recover. Sometimes we can reverse the damage. And even when we can't, patients have an easier time building new neural pathways. It's a real second chance for addicts."

I think of my mother, locked away in the Spire, imprisoned by the crumbling walls of her own mind. A pang of remorse needles me. I should've taken her with me when I had the chance, and I can't let it go. "So he'll be okay?" I ask Mary.

"Hopefully." She sighs. "These things take time. Some things heal more slowly than others."

I look away when her hand touches my forehead. Gently, she tries to smooth the furrow in my brow. "There are other therapies we've learned from the Cyanese." She pauses. "There's one I'd like you to consider. I've been working on it."

My throat dries up even though I'm burning to answer.

"It's not weakness to care for yourself," she prods. "If you can't, how can you care for anyone else?"

I swallow hard. "I don't know where to start."

"You can start by admitting you're wounded."

Instinctively, my body wants to curl into itself. Instead, I roll onto my back. I stare at the ceiling, where the yellowed tent's most discolored, stained by a hundred storms. Slowly, I force the words out. "Sometimes I can't sleep. I see things. Every time I think about . . ."

I start to shut down again, but Mary takes my hand. The gentle squeeze in her grip wrings out an answer.

I struggle to meet her eyes. Asking for help seems the hardest thing of all. "Tell me how . . ." I say at last. "Tell me how to make it stop."

Mary has lots of ideas about my recovery, but none of them look so good in daylight.

I stand in the doorway of a small, concrete-walled room. It's just an attached storage hold behind the prep area of the mess hall. I suppose it makes sense to meet in the middle of the day, when hardly anyone else is around. Better to come here, where there's privacy. We can have our own safe space, beyond the dishwashers and bubbling pots.

The sliding metal door is cracked, and I linger behind it, rooted in a cloud of filmy steam. Looks plenty cool and dry in the hold, but I'm not prepared to walk in.

Inside, there's quiet talk. By the sound of it, they've already started. There's a ring of flimsy chairs, and most are occupied. I recognize a few of these guys: Belach, our quartermaster. One of the guys who works here in the mess, and one of Nandan's lieutenants. And then there's Mary, sitting next to another officer, an elderly Biseran woman, who I've heard used to serve in a far-flung monastery.

My hand hovers at the door, but I can't bring myself to push it wide open. To sit there and talk about what I've been through in front of them is not going to help. Just standing here, on the edge, is already pushing my brain into that blinding space where my pulse wakes up.

I take a step back, but I'm not quiet enough. Mary's eyes shift to the doorway, and it's too late.

"Phee," she says. Her eyes command me to come in and sit.

I slip into the empty chair.

Mary nods, and gestures for the session to resume.

We're asked to give our names, and share what brings us here. Deni, the cook, goes first. His village was bombed four years ago. He lost his wife and two sons, but these days, he's actually sleeping at night. The grief never goes, he insists, but the nightmares don't come as often. Then it's Belach's turn.

I know Belach well enough. He is older than Hal and Nandan, maybe older than dirt. Grew up in the shadow of the fuel mines in the Gap, then lived through war with Cyan and the aftermath. Here's a man who's seen it first-hand: Benroyal's brand of jack-booted peace, with IP troops sweeping in to take what they wanted. But thirty seconds into his confession, my stomach begins to drop.

IP Attack. Heavy Casualties. Capture. Interrogation.

The room is so still. It's as if there's no more air, just the stench of vinegar and leftover stew and bleach, and all I can do is clench my teeth against it.

"They picked me off in Barbouros, east of the Gap,"

Belach says. "We weren't well organized then. We weren't rebels or even guerillas yet, just kids jumping into a fire-fight."

His eyes are sunken, and his voice is hoarse and burred by hard memory. "The IP pushed back. We were on the retreat, but I couldn't keep up."

Suddenly, I look down and my hands are digging into my lap. My breath's shallowing up, and I'm squeezing the sides of my legs.

Belach keeps going, though each word seems to cost more than the last. He points to the scars on his temples, his wrists, and his neck. "They . . . they used stim wire to torture us. Live current. One hour of sleep, then they'd wake us. Seven months they had me, and I still remember . . ."

I look down at my hands. What Belach endured . . . I've got no business being here. To sit in this chair and say I'm afraid. I don't have the right to be this broken.

When he is finished, they all look at me.

"Excuse me," I whisper, standing up. "Excuse me. I'm sorry." I can't stop saying it, even walking out the door.

I hear the scrape of Mary's chair as I hustle through the kitchen. I'm past the cooks and halfway through the empty dining hall when she catches up.

"Phee . . ." she soothes. "Don't."

My pulse jumps as her hand catches my wrist. It takes

everything I have not to pull away from her. To give in to the irrational scream crouched in my throat.

"You said you'd give me something." I say. "A treatment."

"I know," she says calmly. "But if we don't get to the root—"

"I don't have anything to share. It's not like that. I wasn't tortured. I wasn't left for dead."

"But you *were* hurt, Phee. As surely as anyone else in that room. Just because we can't see the scars, it doesn't mean they're not there."

"I don't need to talk about it. Not in front of them. This isn't what you said. You said—"

"I said we'd try a new program. And I *am* working on a treatment for you, but you have to be realistic, Phee. No regimen on the planet is going to work without counseling too."

I take a breath, tilting away.

"This is a first step," Mary adds. "You need to do this."

Her voice is warm and steady, but I can't give in to it. At least not yet.

"Come back with me," Mary says.

"I will," I tell her, but I'm already walking away. "After Manjor."

CHAPTER NINE

I LEAVE WITH MIYU.

We won't be flying directly into Manjor. Instead, at her suggestion, we make for the coast, where we jump aboard a flat-decked hydrift ship, one that's nimble enough to cut through the waves, yet powerful enough to rise and hover over the shoreline. The *Andalan,* Larken swears, is the perfect smuggler's vessel. Looks like hell, he says, but runs like it too. I know sap about seacraft, but I do like the sound of that.

Now I stand on its bridge as it races toward our destination.

Mary begged me to put off this trip, but I wouldn't back down. So we talked about coping strategies. Deep-breathing techniques and ways to anchor myself in the present. For now, practicing those routines should help to keep the flashbacks at bay. I promised to report in for therapy the second I returned, but it wasn't enough for her. She fears I'm not yet strong enough to make this journey, and that I need at least a few months to sort things out in my head. Maybe she's right, but it doesn't matter. I have to do this.

At least I'm not going alone.

Larken and his personal guard are making the voyage too. With an undercover escort watching our backs, I should feel a little less uneasy. Yet when we left, and Hank closed in for an awkward good-bye embrace, my heart jumped like a baby groat in a sack. Now I'm traveling with two people I've known for less than a week. Everyone else? Total strangers.

Unlike Hank, Bear didn't see us off. When I looked for him in our final hour at base, he was nowhere to be found. Not in the barracks, in the infirmary, or at the launch yard. When I asked Mary about it, she sighed through her teeth and wrung her hands before putting them over mine. "On patrol. Double shift. I'm sorry, Phee."

We are all sorry. Benroyal's turned us into walking apologies. But I said nothing to Mary. Bear and I, we had our good-bye.

Aboard the *Andalan,* Miyu and I have berths alongside

the crew. Among thieves and rebels and drifters, we hug the Manjoran Gulf, slinking along an outlaw route. It's safer to put on rust-colored robes and pretend to be smugglers pretending to be monks. Even Miyu's vac wears its own disguise. On deck, I spy it near the prow of the ship. It's parked and covered in sap-stained cloth, hiding among cases of poppied hooch and a hundred other crates of bootleg export.

Now, after two days and two nights of seasick progress, we're almost there, cloaked in the kind of mist that kisses your skin but never quite turns into rain. A flight in Miyu's vac would've been so much faster, but an unmarked aircraft roaring in from the Strand? Too suspicious. Benroyal's Interstellar Patrol watches every bit of inland sky. No, with the billion-credit bounty on my head, the crooked harbor is our best bet.

From the bridge, I watch the harbor's mouth grow wider and wider. I'm pretty sure we'd make a fine meal for this sharp-toothed city. Bear tried to talk me out of this, and now his words ring like good sense. I sigh. Too late to turn back now.

Miyu approaches, her monk's hood pulled low. She sweeps it back, and I get a good look at her face, which is coated with paint. The streaks of orange and black and white are startling, and they make it seem like she's wearing an elaborately patterned mask. Her hair's neatly braided into thin monk's ropes.

"You. Look. Ridiculous," I say. The sight of her is so rusting absurd, I can't help but bust up. I have to brace myself against the railing to catch a breath. "For sun's sake, whoever held you down and painted you up, I hope you punched them in the face."

Prim as ever, Miyu barely reacts. She flashes the same unreadable half smile she always does. "I look convincing. I look like a Biseran monk in proper mourning makeup, who's come to pray for the dead. You, however . . ." She pauses, giving me the once-over, as if *I'm* the one who's out of place. ". . . Look like yourself. Which at the moment is dangerous."

"I'll keep my hood on."

"I suspect that's not going to be enough."

I slump, resigned.

"Are you always this impractical?" she asks, matter-of-factly.

"Well . . ."

"I take that as a yes," she says, still unfazed. "And I suppose everyone else lets you get away with it?"

I twitch like a bluefin on a hook. There's something about Miyu that disarms me. This girl's right up there with Mary in the shut-your-exhaust department.

When I don't answer, Miyu goes on. "You *are* impractical, I think," she says. Her half smile cracks, turning up ever so slightly. "But it suits you."

I let Miyu brush gloppy, thick stain all over my face before we meet on the deck. At least the paint dries quickly, and it doesn't smell too bad. I suspect there's balm leaf in it; I catch the faint whiff of it every time I inhale. The scent reminds me of Cash. And it's a weird thing to look like the wrong end of a brush monkey while remembering him. If he were here, I think he'd laugh.

The thought makes my eyes well up.

Gently, Miyu fusses. "Stop, or the colors will run."

"It is a mourning mask," I say. "Just striving for authenticity here."

Larken slips beside me. No monk's robes for him, since he's staying on the ship. He could almost blend in with the crew, as scruffy as his borrowed clothes are. But as Miyu would say, it's just as well. Scruffy suits him.

He stretches his hand toward the approaching shore. Almost there now. I hear the hover engine begin to power up. "Take a good look," Larken says.

I scan the shallows of Manjor, then the horizon. In the distance, high-rises and turreted temples pierce the skyline. Vessels of all sizes and shapes crowd the shore, some rooted in the surf, some hovering just above the sand-silky tide line. As we get closer, the Manjorans on the docks look less like scurrying insects and more like workaday grunts.

We grab hold of the railing as the second hull siren blares. It's a warning to hold fast as our ship roars into hover mode. And roar it does. I resist the urge to cover my ears as we rise, displacing sea water in high-pressure blasts. The thrust's twice as loud as a dozen circuit rigs in a race day lineup, and that's really saying something.

Another hydrift pulls in beside us. I sneak a look at its prow and spy the name etched on the hull. And when I glance around the harbor again, I see a handful of other vessels share this same script. There are other ringers too. Three *Kukiri Malandars*. Two *Farkourrens*. Five . . . no, wait . . . six *Gabban Gallas*.

"They all have the same names," I shout over the roar.

When the hover engines soften into a stabilized hum, Larken answers, "It's a smuggler's trick. Sort of a joke, really. It's designed to frustrate local authorities. For example, say a black-market merchant's caught by a squad of IP, or the city guard. They ask him which vessel's running his bootleg goods, and he answers—"

Even I can appreciate the brilliance in this simple ploy. "'Why, the *Andalan*, of course.'"

Larken nods.

"Six decades of Castran occupation," Miyu adds. "And the Biseran manage to fend off the conquerors—resisting a well-armed Interstellar Patrol—with nothing more than dishonest ingenuity. Well done."

"And the ruse doesn't end there," Larken replies. "All these names? Like many Biseran words, they have many meanings, depending on how they're pronounced. For example, emphasize the first syllable of *An*dalan—and you speak of a precious jewel. Pause on the second—An*da*lan —and you're talking about a bottomless well. Accent the third—Anda*lan*—and you've just insulted a woman, calling her a faithless wife."

"If you're a native of this planet, you'd catch on," Miyu interjects. "But if you're an IP, or an occupying soldier, you'd need a lot of patience and a very sharp ear to make an arrest."

I picture the IP—Benroyal's corporate mercenaries— running from boat to boat, chasing false leads. Miyu's right. The Manjorans are resourceful, and I'm sure Cash— Crowned Biseran Prince, Duke of Manjor—would've approved. His brother, firstborn Dak, gets to claim Bisera's capital, Belaram. But *this* city was always meant to be his, a clever seat for a second-born son.

Now I am here to find myself and carry on the work he left behind. Somehow, I have to claim whatever fortune my uncle might have saved for me. If I can, I'll use every last credit to take down Benroyal, end the Sixers' rule, and bring Cash home.

I look up. Larken and Miyu are talking. I've drifted off, and this is no time to lose a second of focus.

"You must take care," Larken says. "This city is built on false fronts and misdirection. It's the Manjoran way, and the city's survived for over a millennia because of it. It's still the last great stronghold of Bisera. No invading army or conqueror has ever been able to take this port and hold it. The IP might have a presence here, but they've never been able to subdue it."

"Grace says that you don't leave your mark on Manjor; it leaves it's mark on you," Miyu adds.

"True enough," Larken says. "But if all goes according to plan, you won't be there long enough to find out. Are you ready?"

I take a deep breath. "I hope so."

Larken puts a hand on my shoulder. "We'll watch IP movement and keep track of what's going on in the city. You and Miyu slip in quietly, and I'll keep an eye out. Don't worry. Miyu knows where to go and what to do."

Miyu looks at me, straight-faced and calm underneath her mourning mask. "We can do this. The two of us; it's perfect. They won't be expecting a couple of scrawny monks."

I nod. Pretend I'm prepared, steely-eyed and certain.

"Get in. Get what you came for. Get out." Larken adds. "Check in often. If you run into trouble, flex or call, and I'll send an extraction team. And if you don't check in, you better believe I'm sending one."

"You're putting a whole lot of faith into this plan."

After a second or two, Larken laughs, then finally looks back at me. "It's not the plan I've put my faith in. I've put it in you, Phee. After all, who better than public enemy number one?"

CHAPTER TEN

THE RICKETY SHIP-TO-SHORE BRIDGE EXTENDS LIKE A DIRTY needle, injecting Miyu and me into the city like an experimental serum. Soon after we step off, the market day bustle of the dockside street unexpectedly mutates. A procession of black armored rigs turns onto the busy street. A diplomatic motorcade, by the look of it. I spy Bisera's Evening Star on the flags they're flying.

And I'm not the only one who's noticed. A second later, the hum of the market crowd becomes a riot-shaped roar, and half the people surge, determined to follow the rigs. I stumble back, but Miyu grabs my arm and we're swept down a footpath in a chaotic tangle of push and shove. Even growing up on the lawless end of Capitoline is no preparation for this.

We keep moving. The air is a thick, eye-watering cloud of sweat and sea mist and smoke. I cough, taking an elbow to the ribs, and the next breath burns. There are many languages spoken, murmurs and music and shouts, and in the bright howl, I strain to catch a few phrases.

"Manjor arrast! Bisera arrast!"

"Berren set an kalangkiver. Set sef?"

"Carda! Carda! Carda Kaleed Dakesh!"

I freeze at the name *Dakesh.* Miyu collides with me as I dig in my heels. The crowd forks around us, bodies bruising our shoulders as they pass. Going against the flow, I manhandle her, quickly dragging us both into an empty alleyway.

Miyu shakes loose, and catches her breath. Wide-eyed, we stare at each other. I have no idea who might be watching unseen, so I whisper in her paint-smudged ear. "That was—"

She cuts me off with a nod. Dakesh. Benroyal's puppet ruler and Cash's older brother. For her, the shock's already wearing off. But the calculating calm in her eyes does little to ease my mind. I struggle to dial down the panic, but it's a losing battle.

"If he's here, and we're spotted, we're dead," I whisper. "Worse than dead. Ambushed, interrogated, gift-wrapped, and delivered to Benroyal. We've got to get out of here."

"You're not thinking rationally. If you would simply take a moment to—"

"I don't do rational."

"Then it's a good thing I'm here."

Yeah, it really is. I take a breath and will my brain to actually, maybe just for once, spit out a coherent thought.

Miyu's already one step ahead. "None of our intel indicated there would be a royal visit. But this may actually be in our favor." Even in her ridiculous disguise, I can see the gears turn behind her eyes. "We could easily slip through a crowd in such disorder. You up for a little chaos?"

"That I can handle."

She looks me up and down, as if making her own assessment. She adjusts the hood of my robe, pulling it forward.

"There," she says. "Much better. I can't see the terror in your eyes now."

I start to take the bait and mouth off, but then it hits me. I'm not afraid anymore.

It takes most of the afternoon to wind our way through the heart of Manjor. We slip through the crowded market district, avoiding IP stations all along the way. Beyond the storefronts and alleyways, the roads narrow, and we walk in shadow, between the run-down high-rises and crumbling villas of the slums.

By noon, we are hot and tired. Children rush onto the street, ready to scavenge a midday meal or pick up a job. Some of them are wiry and quick enough to put me on alert. I keep my hands in my pockets as they pass. Others jostle and shove each other, trading trash talk and laughter. So many of them wear a smile like Cash's, a grin that crackles with clever defiance.

A handful of them beg or offer small wares, a handmade bracelet or some other trinket. I don't speak the language, but it's easy to figure out just about everything's negotiable, and all for a "bargain" price. Rapidly, Miyu deals with them. Most, she chases off with a stream of Biseran words. A lucky few get a handful of credits.

They shout back at us, hand over heart, before running off.

"We need to keep moving," Miyu warns.

So we walk.

Finally, after another half-hour march, we reach the oldest abbey in the city. Here, we're to meet Miyu's contact, who's supposed to take us to my uncle's vault. Sweat-soaked and bone-tired, we walk up the wide steps through the high stone archway. Through clouds of spice into a vast, dimly lit church.

"Watch your step," Miyu warns.

I look down just in time. I nearly stumbled over a curb.

No, not a curb exactly, but a low ring of brick, bordering a small fountain. A ripple of light draws my eye to the water inside. The pool's a black mirror, reflecting candlelight, and the whole chapel's filled with them. I count at least a dozen little wells, each a few feet in diameter, spread out with pathways between.

The air is thick with the scent of poppied incense and the hum of whispered prayer. There are many other mourners here. Murmuring, they kneel and light candles. They wash away their mourning masks and leave offerings at the wells. My eyes slide away from their earnest faces. Ours is a false pilgrimage; I've got no right to stare.

Miyu stops in the middle of the room, near the most central pool. I drop beside her. Wary, I touch her wrist, but she shakes her head. "We're safe here," she whispers. "It's dark enough, and we need to blend in."

I scan the room. I see mourners focused on their own prayers. Here, in the shelter of the dim, everyone's washing away the masks.

"The water," I whisper. "What is it for?"

"The current of souls."

"What?"

"Most Biseran believe that the soul—sibat—is immortal, a current that can never be destroyed. They say that all life is connected in that current, and that all wells . . ." She skims her hand over the surface, sending ripples through it. "All worlds, past and present, are also connected, because the current of sibat runs through each."

There's a pile of fresh linen beside the well. After pulling one of the towels into her lap, Miyu leans in and begins to wash away her own mask, splashing her face until it's hers again. The paint bleeds in rivulets, spilling through her cupped hands. In the water, the tendrils of color curl out and dissolve, unfurling like dying blooms.

"So when you die, your soul is carried from one well to another," I say when she's done.

She nods.

Cautious, I test the rushing water, letting it slip through my own fingers. It's fragrant and cool. So I wash up too. Less gracefully, of course. I scrub and scrub and scrub away the sticky mourning mask. My face comes clean, but I end up drowning the sleeves of my robe. Miyu hands me a towel. I mop myself up as best as I can.

She presses her face into another, then puts it aside. I see her now, raw and unguarded. She's looking exhausted, and I can't really blame her. And yet the prim satisfaction remains. When it breaks, turning up the corners of her mouth, I read the truth. Miyu likes saving the day. She's good at it. And with all the stupid people in the world, she knows she'll always have to.

We both glance around the church again.

"Why do they pray?" I ask. "Why do they come here at all, if there's no true death?"

"They mourn a soul's passage," she says thoughtfully. "They pray for its return, or for reunion in another life, in another world. And they ask for balance, that if they have lost a loved one, that this world receive his or her equal. *An sibat sibat.* Soul for soul."

"An sibat sibat," I repeat.

"*Emam arras amam.* In this life or the next."

"In this life." I close my eyes and think of Cash. Silent, I bargain with the current. *Please. Let it be this life.*

A swish of movement catches me off guard. I open my eyes and spy the dark robe, its mud-spattered hem skimming the floor. Someone looms over us, hood pulled low. The head-to-toe black of the outfit is startling. Instinctively, I shiver, as if death itself has dropped in.

Miyu stands, speaking to him in Biseran.

When he shifts to listen, I catch a better glimpse of his face. There are two *x*'s scarred into his cheeks. One under each eye, surely made by knifepoint. When I stare at him, he says something in Biseran, then walks away. After I stumble to my feet, Miyu and I follow him to the back of the church.

There, he pulls back a curtain and we step into a dark

alcove. No more candles, and I can just make out the first few steps, twisting below. The man in black starts to descend, then stops. At Miyu's shoulder, I look down the turn, where the stairwell's pitch-toothed mouth eats the last shadows.

"Come on," she says.

I hesitate. Up until recently, I've always trusted my instincts. I get a knot in my gut before a hard right? I go left. Trouble is, I look at this man and I see a blind turn. He may be our guide, but he's not working for us.

"We don't know this guy. We don't know where he's leading us," I say quietly. "We can't even see."

"It's an acceptable risk," Miyu counters, irritated that we've stopped. "I'm told we can trust him."

"Trust him? How do we know our real guide isn't dead or whatnot because this guy—who's dressed like death incarnate, by the way—choked him out and is just taking us down here so he can push us down the steps or drop us into IP hands? Shouldn't we be using some kind of signal or code word or something?"

It's too dark to see, but I can practically feel the roll of her eyes. "For sun's sake, I've already used the signal. And the robes are perfectly suitable for our point of contact."

The guy's just standing there, waiting on us while we bicker like some old married couple. When she and I sigh at the same time, it might as well be a signal of our own.

The man clears his throat. Looks at us like he's got better things to do.

So we stop arguing and do the sensible thing: We start inching our way toward possible death.

CHAPTER ELEVEN

FOLLOWING OUR GUIDE, WE EASE DOWN THE SPIRAL. TWENTY
steps, and we lose all light. Forty, and the dank air puts a rasp
in my breath. Pressed against the wall, my fingertips sense
the rush of water behind rock. It whistles through my bones.
Soon, I stop counting steps. The darkness has teeth, clamp-
ing down on us in a cold, blood-shiver bite. The farther we
sink, the more tense and uneasy I get. Despite Miyu's reas-
surances, bugging out seems like a reasonable option.

When we finally come to a stop, I'm sure we must be
near the source of the wells. I can feel the spray in the air.

At the bottom of the stairwell, our guide fumbles around
in the dark. A door swings out, squealing on rusty hinges
and slicing through the pitch.

At first, the brightness blinds me, and I focus on the electrical hum. Then my eyes adjust to the eye-level glow of emergency lights, racing down a narrow walkway. At my left, a rippling canal. On my right, stone and shadow and hard-packed earth. The path before us stretches out farther than I can see.

I hear voices. Not echoes from the church above, but conversations bubbling over the splash of the canal. Instinctively, I press my back against the wall, ready to scrap it out with whatever springs from the dark.

A boat drifts by, then another. The first holds a few passengers. It's their voices I hear. And the second vessel isn't a boat after all. It's a small hydrift platform, gliding over the water. Loaded with cargo, it trails behind; a lone woman steers it. When both vessels pass us by, the fight-or-flight hammer of my pulse simmers down a notch.

"Smugglers?" I ask.

Our guide nods. "The aquifer runs the length of the city, all the way to the shore."

His Castran is near flawless, and I try not to think about how much he's already heard. I'm terrible at stealth.

"And the tunnel?" Miyu presses.

"Tunnels," he corrects. "Miles of tunnels."

"And every one of them a bootlegger's best friend. That about right?" I ask.

"Something like that." His scarred face splits in a surprisingly honest smile. A third boat drifts by. Another platform, but this one's less laden with cargo. Our guide hails its pilot, who answers by bringing the vessel to a stop beside us. Both men speak in rapid-fire Biseran, a blur of unfamiliar words. I look to Miyu. At least she knows what they're talking about.

She reads my mind, whispering, "The pilot called you a little gan-gan."

"What's a gan-gan?"

"It's an insect." She pauses. "Kind of like a sand flea."

"Great. Now I'm a blood-sucking little—"

"Not exactly," Miyu interrupts. "*Ganganarem,* as they are more properly known, live on the backs of brush monkeys. But they don't draw blood. They digest the feces of their host and—"

"Stop. Just stop, okay? Why would you think I'd ever want to know that?"

"Well," she replies. "You did ask."

She's stone-cold serious. At least I think she is, by the look on her face. I'm not even sure whether to cuss her out or bust up laughing. But I don't get the chance to decide. Our guide interrupts.

He motions for us to climb aboard the platform. When I don't get a move on, the pilot, a leathery old man, mumbles in Biseran.

"What'd the pilot say?" I ask Miyu.

"He said 'let's go,'" our guide answers.

Miyu's eyes narrow. "Actually, it sounded like he said—"

He silences her with a look. "He said he hasn't got all day. He said let's go."

We climb aboard, even though I'm certain the pilot's words put Miyu on alert. But now we're drifting in fog and mist and shadow, so it's too late to ask what or why. All we can do is keep near the edge—our eyes on the men, our backs to the current.

As we drift along, I start to notice things along the route. The guide wasn't kidding about miles of tunnels, but we keep a straight course. Dockside, along the walkway, recessed thresholds line the canal. And the farther we go, the more people I see.

Sure, I spy a few nasty-looking toughs like our guide, but there's an odd assortment of seemingly ordinary folk too. Dock workers haul dry goods off boats, couriers scurry from one spot to another, would-be merchants watch as buyers appraise their everyday wares.

This isn't just some scummy black-market hive, like you'd find in a Castran city. In Capitoline, the facades are as pristine as a Sixer gown. But turn up the hem, and you get the crooked seam, woven by dealers and thieves. But here in Manjor, only the surface is chaos. Underneath, there's order and common trade. Splash a little sunlight on this place, and you'd have your own little riverside borough. It's as if I've fallen into some weirdly stitched alternate universe.

Our guide mistakes my gaping for fear. "You're safe enough for now, if you do as I tell you," he says. "Down here, we steer clear of IP business."

Easy for him to say. He's not the one with the bounty on his head.

"It's just not what I expected," I say aloud. "I expected—"

"A festering sap-hole?" the pilot cuts in.

So they both speak flawless Castran. Larken was right. Here, nothing is quite what it seems.

The old pilot stares at the roof of the canal. "The real heart of Manjor is all underground. We know how to keep to our own business. And how to keep the wrong sort out."

"And who exactly is that?" Miyu asks, raising an eyebrow.

"Anyone who doesn't pay a full fare," he grumbles. When he says something else in Biseran, Miyu's eyes sharpen. I scrawl a mental note to self: If we make it back to the Strand in one piece, I'm studying Cash's language like my life depends on it.

Maybe it does.

Miyu lets it go, and after the old man stops grousing, our guide pulls off his monk's robes. Underneath, he's dressed neatly enough, in a crisp shirt and pants, polished belt and boots. And there's something about his manner—the straight-backed way that he stands, the command in his voice—that betrays him. He's not just another thug for hire. Surely there's more to him than that.

Either way, I can't blame him for ditching the robes. Even down here, in the chill, the weight of them's oppressive. But when I start to shrug out of mine too, he stops me.

"You said we were safe down here," I protest.

"I said you were safe, if you do as you're told. I didn't say you should draw attention to yourself. I have no need to hide down here, but you must. Keep the robes. At least until we make the drop. There, you can burn them, for all I care."

"Are we close?"

"Very."

"Will you be bringing us back?"

His smile turns up like a cutthroat slash. "No, but I'm certain our paths will cross again."

"What's your name? What do we call you?"

The old man's eyes dart our way. He gives his friend a warning look, but our guide still answers. "Call me what you will," he says. "But most would say 'Fahrat.'"

The pilot laughs. "Fahrat, indeed."

His cackle reeks of disrespect. Even Miyu flinches. But I ignore the old man. "Thank you, Fahrat. For safe passage."

He nods.

The pilot brings us dockside. "All ashore."

We climb out and follow Fahrat, who leads us into a section of canal so shadowed and quiet, I hesitate, even as Miyu follows. Without missing a step, our guide coaxes me on.

"If I wanted the bounty, I'd be spending it now. If I wanted you dead, you'd already be facedown, floating into the sea," Fahrat says, all too matter-of-factly. His back is still turned, and he curses softly in the dark. His right hand searches the rock face of the cavern wall. "Come along or turn back. Choose, and stop wasting my time."

A few more feet, and Fahrat grapples with one of the small outcroppings in the rock. I startle at the sudden, grinding scrape as it comes loose. After putting it aside, Fahrat reaches into the pocket of rock behind it, fussing and cursing some more. It's as if he's found some kind of invisible, secret switch, but . . . no. Nothing happens.

He snaps, jerking his chin at me. "You. Put your hand in."

I open my mouth to argue, but he's having none of it. "I have no business here. You must come and open the door."

"What? What door?"

"This sensor . . . it is not programmed to open for me. It is not my appointment."

Quickly, Miyu nods and I move beside Fahrat. I'm sure as sap not slipping my hand into a blind hole, so I lean in to get a better look. Squinting, I detect a tiny glimmer of . . . something metallic?

"Please," Fahrat says after a moment, clipping each word. "Take your time, while we stand here exposed outside this secret entrance. I would like it very much if someone else drifted by, so we could compromise it."

I mutter a curse, then put my hand inside the small, shadowy pocket of stone. This *is* metal, smooth and unmarked. A second later, I jump back at the quiet click and whir that begins the moment my palm makes contact. At my right, an entire section of wall begins to move. It opens, revealing a sleek Pallurium door, as polished as any elevator entrance in the Spire.

My pulse starts to gallop. A Sixer-built, blast-proof hatch? Down here, it doesn't belong.

I glance at my reflection in the gleam-gray surface. I'm fuzzy and faceless. Above, the red eye of a security camera blinks at us.

Too quickly, the reflection slides away. I flinch as it disappears. The door's opening.

And someone is waiting for us.

CHAPTER TWELVE

AT THE THRESHOLD, WE FACE A YOUNG MAN IN A VERY SHARP, very dark, very expensive-looking suit. Without a word, Fahrat nudges us forward, then takes a step back. Just as quickly as it opened, the door closes behind us. *Between us.* Our guide is gone.

"Good afternoon, Ms. Van Zant." The man in the suit bows politely. "Ms. Yamada."

Miyu returns the gesture, but I don't answer. I'm still in shock, staring at the world behind him. This isn't some shabby underground blast shelter or a clandestine little vault. My eyes sweep over the flex walls, the grand statues, the crystal chandeliers. I breathe in the scent of fresh-cut limonfleur and fine leather shoes and freshly polished floors. It reeks like the Spire, and that doesn't exactly put me at ease. Only difference is, there are no security guards. Beyond our host, we are very much alone.

He must read my alarm. Smiling, he leans forward slightly as his hand sweeps out in invitation.

"My apologies," he says. "Allow me to introduce myself. My name is Sindal, and I'm here to assist you. Welcome to the First Interstellar Bank of Manjor."

"Well, rust me . . ." I mutter under my breath.

Miyu raises an eyebrow, but Sindal doesn't even blink. "Yes, Ms. Van Zant. We are the largest financial institution on the planet, thanks to the prudent investment of—"

"Mother," Miyu interrupts. The word slips out like something foreign at best. "This place is one of her holdings."

"Oh, a secret underground bank?" I half whisper to her. "Yeah, that's not something you might have mentioned before."

Miyu dodges the sarcasm. "Well, I've never been here. Grace told me we'd be escorted to James's vault, but I've never been *allowed* down here before."

Grace. Not "Mother." No, that was a one-time slip.

I look back at Sindal. "There's no one else here."

"Of course. We operate by appointment only," he answers. "This is a *special* branch. Here, we serve the more sensitive needs of our interstellar clients. The highest level of security and discretion are guaranteed."

And that's when things click into place. Bet Miyu would never admit it, but Sindal probably knows more than she does. It must sting to work for your own mother strictly on a need-to-know basis. I glance at Miyu's face. For the first time, I see beyond the half smile. I read a trace of embarrassment.

"Well, I guess you're allowed now." I shrug out of my robes and chuck them at Sindal. "Not too shabby. But what's a girl gotta do to slip into her own super-secret vault already?"

The sass pins the confidence back on Miyu's face. She tosses her own disguise at him, and it's a small victory. Mr. Preening Branch Manager—I'm sure he's less than thrilled to carry our dirty clothes.

"Yes, Ms. Van Zant," he answers, a shade more meekly. "Right this way."

We finish crossing the lobby, then turn into a long corridor. At the end, there's an elevator. A stone-faced guard waits inside. I'm not prepared for the light show that starts the moment we step into the elevator. The lasers sweep over us, just as they did in the armory, at my hearing.

"Authenticating," a female AI voice purrs. The security guard stands with his hands clasped behind his back. Stock-still, he hardly looks at us.

The lights sweep over me once more. "Identification complete," the voice finally declares; then the doors close and the elevator begins to descend.

"Rest assured," Sindal explains during the drop, "at First Bank, you'll enjoy an unparalleled level of security. Every inch of our premises is monitored, and our authentication protocol is failsafe. In a matter of seconds, we're able to rule out anomalies."

"Anomalies?" I ask.

"They're making sure you're not an impostor," Miyu answers. "The system's equipped to verify your identity. The scanners detect heat signatures, check retinal patterns, read fingerprints, etc. Although, these are probably due for an upgrade . . ."

I really, really want to roll my eyes. Instead, I just let her keep going. And she obliges. Because apparently Miyu is a fully functional, completely fascinating wind-up genius. "Honestly," she says. "Do you have any idea what a headache bio-index interfacing is with these old things? There's a point-six-second lag with this hardware, but none with the latest models. But then again, system updates are such a pain in the exhaust."

"Oh yeah?" I'm not *exactly* sure what's she talking about, but I appreciate her breaking it down for me. Sindal's not as impressed. He inspects his fingernails. The security guard barely blinks. "So," I say to Miyu. "You're a crack pilot *and* a tech expert?"

"Not at all. My girlfriend's an intern at AltaGen. Research and development," she says. "That's her day job, at least."

"What else does she do?"

Miyu smiles. "Let's just say she takes on a lot of free-lance work."

I don't have the chance to pry any deeper. The elevator stops and the doors open.

"Here we are," Sindal says. He steps out, and we follow.

There it is. What we've come for. Right in front of me: a massive armored entrance.

Immediately, we're scanned again, baptized in another grid of red laser light. A second later, there's a pressurized gasp, the metallic snap of bolt after bolt after bolt, and the motorized buzz of a yawning hinge. It hums through me like a signal, a hundred-decibel warning that my future's about to be irrevocably altered. I take a deep breath.

The vault opens.

Sindal and the security guard lead us inside the vault. Each part of the room seems to tell a different story. According to a large panel of gray-faced, closed safety-deposit draw-ers, this is just another part of the bank. But the luxe rugs on the floor, the table and chairs—they whisper comfort and living space. Through an open doorway, I see a bedroom, and I'm pretty sure we've stumbled into the planet's swankiest subterranean apartment.

But it's the desk that draws my eye. I have seen this flex-topped monster of a table before, or at least one like it, in another place, on another planet, not more than four months ago. The high-backed chair behind it swivels our way.

For a second, I'm not sure if my legs are going to give out. But the panic attack doesn't come. Instead, a different shot of jarring anxiety hits. Relief. Rage. Joy. Grief. It's as if all my emotions have been dumped into one combustible fuel cell, then locked, loaded, and fired.

My uncle James stands up.

"It's good to see you too, Phee." He doesn't smile. No, he doesn't dare. But he'd like to, I can rusting well tell. Which makes me want to crack his skull. I thought he was dead. They said he was . . .

"Son of a . . ." I say, my voice already tightening into a croak. "You mother-rusting son of a bitch."

I lunge toward the table, but Sindal drops our bundle of robes and reaches out to stop me. Lucky for him, the security guard catches me first. The guy gets an arm around my waist, and I can't quite slip out of his hold. I'm about two seconds from elbowing him exactly where it hurts when James starts in.

"Phee, calm down," he says, inching closer. He approaches like a wild-animal handler.

"They said you were dead." I'm losing it, squeaking out the words.

"Before you climb over the desk and punch me in the face . . . you need to understand that everything I've done has been for your own good."

"I didn't know where you were, or if you were alive . . . and I thought . . . You should've . . ." I say, half breathless. Then I twist and growl at the guard. "Get off of me!"

"Let her go," James orders. "For sun's sake, just let her go and be done with it."

When the bodyguard complies, I nearly tumble to the floor. Miyu reaches out just in time, and I cling to her arm, catching my balance. "For the record, I think you're allowed to punch him in the face," she murmurs as I recover.

I let go. I rush James until we're nose to nose. Or nose to sternum, as it were. I look up and pretend I'm taller.

"Phee, do we have to do this? I'd rather skip this bit." He takes off his glasses and pinches the bridge of his nose.

I stare at him, but the fury's already dead and gone. He closes in for an embrace, and I find myself reaching back. When the corners of my lips start turning up, I don't even try to resist the pull.

"I was so worried about you," James says, still squeezing the life out of me.

For a moment, I freeze. Care and concern? This is a first for us. A few months ago, I didn't even know my uncle existed. Then he became the architect of my escape. But a part of me always kept him at arm's length. I still haven't gotten used to the idea that we're actually family.

"I *am* so worried about you," he says again.

I pull back. "It's okay. I'm fine."

He appraises me. "I don't think you are, Phee."

I shake him off. I turn away and slump into the seat at the far end of the table.

"We need to talk," he says.

He looks at our audience. I'd almost forgotten that Sindal and Miyu and the guard were still here. "Would you three mind excusing us for a bit?" James asks. "My niece and I have some catching up to do."

They all turn to leave, but I look at Miyu. After all the trouble she's gone through to get me here, I won't let James dismiss her. "She stays," I tell him. "Whatever you've got to say, you can say it in front of her."

"Very well," he says. He gestures at a seat between us. "Please join us, Ms. Yamada."

Miyu nods, and she makes her way to the desk. After she

sits, Sindal and the guard slip away without another word, leaving us alone in the vault.

"First things first," James says. "We need to talk about your—"

I cut him off. "No. First, you've got some explaining to do. Where have you been, why did you keep this from me, and what happened to Cash?"

All the light in James's eyes dies when I ask him about Cash. And then I know: There won't be a surprise ending or happy reunion. He's not summoning his bodyguard to fetch a lost prince from another room.

"What happened?" I press.

"I went into hiding as soon as the rally started."

I remember that day. Every second of it. Including the last time I saw James. Before my last race, he told me not to worry, and swore he had a hundred places to hide, should our escape plans fall apart. I guess I should've taken him at his word.

"Benroyal searched your vac," I say. "It was waiting, but you weren't there."

"I'm not stupid. I left it there to throw Benroyal off. He never had me, and he never will."

"But Hank said—"

"Hank knew nothing. This was my emergency contingency, and I couldn't risk him or you or anyone else getting interrogated. Outside these walls, Grace Yamada is the only other person who knows I'm here. She can be trusted."

Miyu shrugs, as if she knows just as little as I do.

"You should've prepared me," I say to him.

"I did what I had to."

And there it is, the default answer for everything. *I had to. I was protecting you. Just follow along and do as I say. It's for your own good.* But I don't say any of this out loud, because I'm tired of our little dance. He keeps secrets and I keep fighting to pry them loose. "You haven't answered me. What happened to Cash?"

"Honestly?" He sighs, then splays his fingers over the tabletop. "I don't know."

I don't have any sarcasm left. I have to swallow hard, just to get anything out. "Someone has to know, James."

"I've used every resource I have, but none of my contacts have been able to dig up any leads. After the ambush . . ."

He stops, and I wonder if it's because he knows. Just the word waylays me. It's the trapdoor that swings beneath my feet. I put my elbows on the table and rest my head in my hands. When my hair falls in my face, I rake my fingers through it to mask the shakes.

"After the ambush," he says again. "Hank sent two squads to find Cash. There was no trace of him left at the old rebel base, and no one's seen him since the day of the attack. Even my eyes in Interstellar Patrol have uncovered nothing."

"We have allies in the IP?" Miyu asks.

"Of course we do." He glances at her, then me. "Not many, but enough to know Cash isn't being held in any of the usual prisons or interrogation holes. He's not here or on Castra. If he were, I would've heard about it. I know you don't want to hear this, Phee, but maybe it's time to accept the reality of the situation."

I raise my head. "I can't accept it. You don't know. Even the newsfeeds admit there was no body. And the clip they keep showing isn't real. Maybe he's still alive."

"The newsfeeds say what Benroyal wants them to say. You know that. All signs point to execution. Benroyal would've done it quickly and quietly. He wouldn't leave things to chance. Cash was a liability, and he wouldn't have been allowed to survive."

I pull my hands under the table, where they can tremble out of sight. I don't beg James to let me have this hope. I don't tell him that my days are just something to survive, and that cold sweat is my new default, and that since I've been blown apart, dreams of Cash are the only things still holding me together. Instead, I let something else stitch its way through. I let the anger fuel me.

"Don't talk that way," I snap. "Don't use words like *liability* to describe Cash. I hate it when you talk like this. You sound like a Sixer."

"I'm a realist," he protests.

"Well, good for you." I inhale sharply as the memory floats up. Cash and I, bickering outside racing HQ. *I have to believe in impossible things,* he'd said. I was the cynic then. Now I strain so hard to cling to that open-hearted faith. "I'd rather fight."

"You misunderstand me," he says. "No one's giving up. I just think it's time to move forward."

"I am moving forward."

He starts to argue, but Miyu interrupts. "At this juncture, does it matter if he's alive or dead?"

We both answer at the same time. "It matters."

"In the long run, yes," she says. "But for now, perhaps you should both consider him missing in action. Keep your eyes open, in case he's alive. Fight in his stead, as if he'll never return."

My uncle stares at her.

I nod. "All right, I follow. Missing in action."

"Good. Then why speak as if you're at cross-purposes? You aren't. You both support Prince Dradha's rebellion. You both have a common enemy. Phee, you're a fugitive of great import, and Mr. Anderssen, you're an invisible player with incredible resources at your disposal. You can work together. It's not so complicated."

"Miyu Yamada." My uncle laughs, bitterly amused. "So pragmatic. You sound like your mother."

He'd meant it as a compliment, but I swear, she almost winces. This time, I rescue her.

"She's right. We're not here to argue. Maybe you'd like to talk about what I *am* here for," I say. The gut-sick wave begins to pass. I pull my hands from my lap and rest them on the table. "Let's get down to business."

With a swipe of his hand and a few taps on the flex glass, James pulls up a dozen screens. He reaches out and brings one document to the forefront. He enlarges it, until the tabletop's a sea of white space and dense, black text.

"What is this?" I look at him, but he doesn't answer.

Miyu swipes through the document. Her eyes scan so quickly; I watch her take it all in. "Grace's handiwork?" she asks him.

"I made certain every clause is in order and she made sure every credit's clean." James nods, and rust if they aren't trading the same self-satisfied looks. "We deposited them into a hundred different numbered accounts. Untraceable."

"Would anyone like to tell me what's going on?" I ask. "Is this about Locus?"

Miyu's gaze flicks between James and me.

"Locus is dead now," he says. "I stole every bit of its liquid capital. More than seventy billion credits."

The sum takes my breath, but Miyu's unfazed.

"Technically, you can't steal from yourself," she corrects.

"Drained it, then. Repurposed it." He stares at me. "Take a look, Phee."

He pulls up the last page of the document and taps at the signature lines. His name is listed, and so is mine—it's the only blank left; he's already signed.

My eyes sweep the screen.

I hereby relinquish all my . . .

The realization dawns on me, and for a moment, my brain stutters. Sure, maybe I'd seen this coming. Maybe I'd entertained illusions about safety-deposit boxes stuffed with gold and Pallurium and stocks, and I'd fantasized about handing it all over to the rebellion. *Here, take this. Fix everything. Build a resistance.* But now that we're here, I see how childish those delusions truly are. I look down at the table again. This is real. My future's staring me in the face, and I'm not prepared.

Stunned, I blink at James. I brace for a familiar reaction—one of his irritated sighs or patronizing looks. But his expression's quiet and unguarded. "The Anderssen fortune. Everything I have left . . ." he says. "I'm giving it to you."

"But you're still alive." I pause. When I breathe out the next words, I'm not even sure if it's a question or not. "You're serious . . ."

"I am," he says.

"Why?"

"Because I owe you much more."

"You don't owe me anything."

"Because if Joanna were in her right mind, she would want me to," he adds. I'm shaking my head, but he'll have none of it. "Because I don't know what will happen to me, or to you, or any of us, tomorrow. Because it's time."

"You want me to take all this money and . . ."

Again he nods. "Do with it as you see fit. All you have to do is sign."

Hesitating, I look back at the screen. I faced another document, every bit as intimidating as this one, not so long ago. I sat in a conference room, in a space just as luxe, and took Benroyal's circuit deal. Once, I signed my life away. At the time, I was so perfect for the job. Who better than a spitfire girl who rages in circles? What better than a blaze that roars—all crackle and curl and blinding smoke—but never really burns?

But I am not that girl anymore. Today I won't be signing myself away. This time I aim to start a real fire, with a great big pile of kindling. *Seventy billion credits*. Even now the sum's big enough to make me gasp. How much would it take to win back my name and finish Cash's work? How much to buy back all our lives?

My hand hovers over the signature line. I take a deep breath . . . and it's done. A second later, James and I are frozen in awkward silence.

"Well then," Miyu says, breaking it. "I'm assuming someone has a plan? Seventy billion is nothing to gamble. What's the play here?"

Expectant, we both turn to James. He leans over the table. "The plan? We need to regroup. For now, the play is survival."

I sit on my hands and sink deeper into my chair. I could probably stay this way for a long, long time. Secure enough. Hidden away. Surviving. But Larken warned me: The wisest victors don't wait for the enemy's next move. They strike, rather than defend. He's right. I can't bide my time. I have an objective. There must be a plan.

"Survival isn't good enough," I say at last. "We have to find out what happened to Cash and rescue my mother. We have to stop Benroyal."

Slowly, James sits up. "We can try."

"You said no one's giving up," I press. "Try harder."

"We can't just buy more weapons," James replies. "Ben-royal will always find a way to outspend and outgun us.

And we can't fight him on the stock exchange anymore."

"We're past that now," I say. "We can't just fight on the ground. We need hearts and minds. A real revolution, both here and on Castra."

Miyu's listening, but my uncle's unmoved. He shakes his head. "You'll never sway Castra, not as long as Benroyal's propaganda machine—"

"That's why we've got to shut it down." I close my eyes and reach for Cash, for all his impossible dreams. Straightening, I try again. "We need the people on our side. They can't see through Benroyal's lies. Somehow, we've got to rewrite the headlines and win them back. And we're not going to do that unless we expose him."

"She's right," Miyu says. "We have to control the message. It's Benroyal's favorite strategy."

"And maybe it's time we learned from that strategy," I say. "We cut off his public support. We go for the throat."

"How, exactly?" An old spark flares, and James is almost himself again. "I told you Locus is gone. You think I still have access to every feed? That I can just snap my fingers and broadcast something across every network?"

I sigh. "I didn't say that."

While we argue, Miyu cradles her jaw. Thumb to chin, forefinger to temple. "You're still thinking like a suit, Mr. Anderssen," she says. "You don't need Locus anymore, for access or for anything else. You need . . . flex hackers." I read it all over Miyu's face—the gears are really turning now.

"Flex hackers?" James says. There's so much contempt in his tone, it's not even really a question.

Deadpan, Miyu stares back, and I imagine her asking, *Did I stutter?* But her real reply is far more diplomatic.

"What have you got to lose?" she says. "You're already enemies of the state. There are plenty of hackers out there, and most of them already hate Benroyal. It's not as if it'd take much convincing to rally them to your cause. Why not listen to Phee, and fight back on the feeds?"

I don't give James the chance to answer. "Benroyal stole my true identity, and we can use every credit we've got to expose his, in the biggest possible way. We show the people what he's done. This time, we take the offensive."

"If you . . ." James pauses. "If *we* do this, there will be no more hiding. Not here. Not in the Strand. You go after him publicly, and he'll fight back with everything he's got."

I nod. "I accept that. I refuse to hide out any longer."

He leans in. "If we fail, I won't be able to protect you. You'll pay with your life."

"We can't live like this." I reach out. I touch his arm. "We have to try."

When he looks down, I swear, a lifetime's worth of regret

and unshed tears haunt the smoke-signal gray of his eyes. Seconds tick by. Suddenly, he straightens; his gaze turns steely. I don't know what's hardened his heart: resignation or resolve. I wonder if it matters.

"Ms. Yamada, Phee, settle in," he says, raising his head. He swipes the table clear. "This battle of yours, for hearts and minds . . . it's not going to engineer itself onto the feeds. We've got a revolution to plan."

CHAPTER THIRTEEN

WE SPEND THE NIGHT IN THE VAULT. THIS MORNING THERE are the same number of steps between the canal and the abbey as there were yesterday. But the climb takes so much less from me. Miyu leads the way, steady as usual. I'm at ease because under my robes, tucked inside my pocket, is a double-blind, encrypted flex card loaded with seventy billion credits. And, of course, a blueprint for an uprising. A last-chance campaign, waged with images and words. A battle for the truth.

All I have to do is get back to the Strand and share the plan.

I flex Larken again, and tell him we're fine.

PV: BE READY. SOON.

"Almost there," Miyu whispers. "Careful. It'll be bright."

Finally, we reach the little alcove and we're back in the abbey. And Miyu's right. At first, even the light filtered through the curtain nearly blinds me. I blink, then realize too late we are not alone.

Three hooded toughs. They were waiting for us. Probably all along.

Betrayed. The word hums through my body.

We're no match for our attackers. Miyu gets one solid hit in, a perfectly executed right hook, but it's no good. Half a breath, half a stumble, and he's already recovering. The second lunges at me. Both fists closed, I jab once, then twice, but I'm bugging out, sloppy and out of control. My enemy's ready for it, dodging the second punch.

He turns away from me and in one elegant twist, he's got Miyu. He pulls her into a sleeper hold. She stabs the air, gesturing wildly, but the second goon assists, batting her hands away. Her wide eyes scream at me. *Behind you.*

Too late. A sting at the back of my neck. The needle sinks deep near the edge of my old scar.

For a moment, the needle's venom electrifies me. Roaring, I twist to catch a better glimpse of the third man. I take a wild swing, but my adrenaline fails and I'm fading out. My fist connects with the air, then falls heavy at my side. One quick glimpse under the hood is all I get before the black bag's pulled over my head. But I know who sold us out.

"My apologies," he says.

Rasping, I spit out his name. It's the last thing I say before the drop.

Fahrat.

For me, there is no dull sense of waking up. Instead, my chin jerks, my eyelids snap open, and my heart explodes. I rasp and cough. Everything is too bright and I'm lead weight in a straight-backed seat. There's a gloved hand near my mouth. The hand holds a damp square of cloth against my nose.

My eyes water and sting. I can't see through the pungent veil of balm leaf and . . . something else, chemical and bitter. I try holding my breath to shut it out.

"Take a breath," Fahrat says.

I blink and strain, but I'm still seeing stars, little more than blurred streaks of light. I try to stand up, but I can't. Pain rips through my shoulders. A sawtooth ache blooms around my wrists and ankles. I'm strapped, arms behind my back, tied down to the mother-rusting chair.

For a second, my whole body kindles in expectation. This is it. Interrogation by Benroyal's men, then execution. I brace for the sting of another needle or the slide-click sound of a gun. When it doesn't come, I strain and jerk and squirm hard enough to teeter the chair. I'm about to topple over, but Fahrat holds tight. He steadies me, his hand still holding the cloth under my nose.

My brain cries out for oxygen, and I'm forced to rake in a breath.

"Easy," Fahrat says. "That's it. Don't fight it. It's not poison."

I struggle again, and he tries to talk me down. "It's balm leaf and anti-gel. It'll clear your head."

"Look at me," a woman says.

I don't recognize the voice. Stubbornly, I refuse, my only answer a half growl, half groan through the cloth.

"Impossible girl," the woman complains, then mutters something in Biseran. I sense the swish of movement as she steps closer. "Forget the remedy. Captain, let her go before she hyperventilates."

His hand drops and I look up. As my vision clears, my eyes sweep from her jeweled flats to her delicate crown. But it's her gaze that paralyzes me. The gold-rimmed irises, the black-hole sparkle of oh-so-familiar eyes.

Queen Napoor. Cash's mother.

"Your Majesty?" I gape.

She nods. "Welcome to the Summer Palace."

I look around. Elaborate mosaic floors. Carved-stone walls with no windows. A bone-bare fireplace big enough to hold court in. One door, heavily barred. I have no idea if it's day or night or how long I've been here. The wall sconces cast enough artificial light, but with all the drop cloths on the tile and the dusty sheeting covering just about every other surface, it looks more like we're in a forgotten corner of a very creepy, very deserted wing.

The queen watches me scan the room. "Dakesh has insisted we bring the palace into the twenty-third century, but renovations of my quarters have come to a temporary—and deliberate—halt," she says. "We are safest here."

"Really? Because I don't feel very safe," I say, testing the rope binding my wrists.

"I apologize for the unusual introduction," Fahrat replies for her. "Precautions were necessary. No one can know you're here."

After the shock wears off, a couple of curse words ping around in my head, but I manage a little control. "Precautions? You mean the black bag over my head? The way you kidnapped . . . Hey, where's Miyu? What have you done with her?!"

The queen waves me off. "In due time. We have business first."

"I want to see Miyu right now."

"I can assure you," she says, "she is safe. You will see her when we are finished here."

I don't answer. Honestly, I'm not sure what else I *should* say. This is Queen Napoor, Cash's own blood. I'd like to think that Mary taught me some manners.

My head clears a little. Perhaps it's the sting of the ropes. Yeah, maybe manners are better spent on people who don't have you drugged and abducted. "Cut me loose."

She laughs.

My cheeks catch fire. She's so . . . small. No bigger than I am. I'm letting this tiny woman get the best of me.

"You're a bold one." She turns to Fahrat. "Is that what he sees in her?"

When Fahrat shrugs, she shifts back to me. She leans over. Lifts my chin to get a better look at my face. When she does, I wince at the unexpected strength in her fingers. "What *does* he see in you? I have to wonder."

Like me, she won't surrender Cash. He still exists in the present tense.

"What do you want with me?" I ask.

"I was bold once too," she says. A shadow passes over her. Her hand drops from my face.

"Reckon you don't have to be bold," I snap, jerking my chin Fahrat's way. "Why should you? You can hire people for that."

Another wisp of laughter escapes her lips. I haven't rattled her at all. "Phee or Phoebe or Phoenix or whoever

130

you are . . ." she says. "When you've watched king and kingdom fall, as I have, it takes a lot more to get under your skin than a few cross words. You'll have to do much better than that."

"Let me go." I try again, more resolve and less sass. "What do you want?"

"What I want . . ." She touches the pendant at her throat. Its five points sparkle, ruby bright. She wears Cash's beloved Evening Star, the royal symbol of the House of Bisera. ". . . is to know what you're doing in Bisera."

She hovers over me, a thundercloud of suspicion, and suddenly, I am certain my life hinges on my answer. From Fahrat, she must already know about my visit to the vault. If I lie, I may never leave this room. "I came back for my inheritance."

She turns her back on me.

"Is Cash alive?" I ask. "I need to find out what happened to him."

The queen doesn't answer. Slowly, she circles my chair. I sit, mesmerized. It's like watching the planet's only four-foot-eleven apex predator. "Can she be trusted?" she asks Fahrat.

I don't give him the chance to vouch for my good character. "You want know to if *I* can be trusted?" I snort. She stops circling. I have not amused her.

Rust, my head hurts. I should've listened and taken a

few more whiffs of that cloth. Not that I'll be asking for it now. Temples aching, I match the queen's icy stare. "Funny, I'm the one tied to the chair here. Pardon me, Your Majesty, but from where I'm sitting, I'm not much inclined to pledge anyone allegiance."

She steps back and gestures at Fahrat. He pulls out a dagger. Before I have the chance to bug out, he cuts me loose. The relief is immediate. The fire in my pinioned joints simmers down and the blood rushes back where it should. I move to stand up, but Fahrat puts a warning hand on my shoulder. I drop back into my seat, and he puts the blade away.

"Thank you, Captain Fahra." She nods.

He bows. "Of course, Your Majesty."

I give him the side-eye. "I thought your name was Fahrat."

The word *Fahrat* puts a wrinkle in Queen Napoor's brow. Almost imperceptibly, her right hand twitches at her side and I get the distinct impression she'd like to slap someone or have them beheaded. Probably me. But she wheels on him instead.

"I must take the blame in this, Your Majesty." He bows again. "She asked what to call me, and I told her as much. I meant it in jest."

"It's enough that you have to tolerate such disrespect

from Dakesh. You shouldn't encourage it." Her words are stern, but there's softness behind them. "I'll not hear you called that, Captain Fahra. Not by anyone else. We owe you our lives, and—"

"Yes, Your Majesty," he says, daring to cut her off. Deeply, he bows a third time.

They share a look, both contrite, and I'm sure his interruption bore no disrespect. No, he was sparing her, somehow. The indignity of further explanation.

Now that their little argument's ended, they both come around again. Captain *Fahra* hands her a flex card, then rearranges the edges of the drop cloth on the floor, revealing a flat metal ring. A slipstream ring, just like the one at my armory hearing.

"I'd like to show you something," the queen says to me. She swipes the card and the palace disappears.

Queen Napoor and Captain Fahra move behind me as the virtual scene comes to life. I'm still in the chair, but now we're in the middle of a sterile, white-walled cell. There is little else here, except for the medical examination table, about fifteen feet away. There's a patient strapped to it, but a man in a suit blocks my view. Overhead, wires hang from the ceiling. Enough to string marionettes, but I can't see exactly where they end.

The suit's back is turned to me. The way he looms over the table makes it hard to see much. I get a glimpse of the patient's legs, a flash of his shoulder. There's something distinctly institutional in his blue-gray cotton pants.

I don't know why, but I laugh. Maybe because I'm scared. I try one of Mary's coping techniques. *Pay attention to your breathing*, she'd said. *Keep your eyes open. Focus on the present.* I glance at my surroundings, which is now only an immersive, virtual stream. If Mary were here, I'd ask her: *What about when the present's invisible? When someone pulls the rug out from under you, and there's no staying in the moment at all?*

In the background, the low, ambient buzz steals my focus. An air conditioner? A generator? I can't place it. "Is this streaming live?" I ask. "What is this place?"

Fahra shakes his head, his deep voice almost cracking. "Just watch."

But I can't watch. The suit won't get out of the way.

The suit straightens up. His back still turned, he says something inaudible to the patient, then swipes a control panel. I catch the flinch of movement. A hand, tethered at the wrist, startles. The painful knee-jerk twitch of a foot. The wires at the ceiling jump, and I realize they're the same kind Mary used in Aram's treatment the night he lay in the infirmary. In half-second glimpses, I see they're attached to the prisoner's shoulders, hands, and wrists. But I don't think they are *de*-stimulating this patient. They aren't here to turn the volume down. They are here to turn it *up*.

I'm not laughing anymore.

The suit touches the panel again. Makes an adjustment. The prisoner hisses. I'm sure it's him and I know that it's not, and I'm certain I'll break if either is true. Stretched between horror and wishful thinking, I strain to get a better look. I shudder when his hand jerks up, struggling against the cuff of his wrist restraint. His fingers stretch and he reaches out, as if to me.

I can't see his face. I need to see his face.

Shaking, I try to stand, but Fahra's hand falls on my shoulder. "Watch," he commands.

I obey, because I cannot look away now. The suit leans over the prisoner again. "Who are your contacts in Manjor?" he barks. "Give us a list, and I'll stop. One name and I'll turn down the pain."

Another breath, but still no answer. The prisoner strains to make a fist.

I'm desperate to leap forward, but I'm rooted to the chair. My mouth dries up and suddenly, I'm shaking, gasping for breath.

"Stop it," I beg, teeth clacking.

The ambient hum intensifies. The prisoner screams, breaking at last. Tears stream down my cheeks. I need this to stop as much as I need it to be true.

Behind me, the queen falters. A breath catches in her throat.

"That's enough." In the virtual stream, a voice commands the man through a speaker on the cell wall. "No more for today."

The suit complies, tapping a flex and putting it back in his pocket. Roughly, he pulls the electrodes from the prisoner's body, then, in a blur of movement, walks around the table. The prisoner's lying still, his head lolling, but his interrogator grabs a fistful of hair at his crown. He pulls hard, until we finally see the prisoner's face. "Smile at the camera, inmate four-oh-three," he says. His tone's laced with a mix of boredom and cruelty. "Smile, and say hi to Mommy."

Silent, Cash refuses.

His eyes aren't defiant. They are empty.

CHAPTER FOURTEEN

QUEEN NAPOOR SHUTS DOWN THE VIRTUAL FEED, AND WE'RE
plunged back into the present. The room spins like a side-
swiped rig, and when I move to stand, my legs fail me.
"I'm going to be sick," I manage to spit out.

Fahra reaches out, and I lean on him. He guides me into
a side room, a royal lounge complete with a water fountain, mirror, and sink. The captain won't leave, but I'm too
far gone to care. After heaving everything up, I rinse and
splash my face and stare in the mirror. The cold sweat, the
nausea, the thrum in my chest—it's all gone.

"Take me to Miyu," I say to Fahra.

He does as I ask.

Turns out I shouldn't have worried. Miyu was being
held in the next room all along. And by "being held," I

mean showing off and trading defensive moves with three royal guards who are probably supposed to be babysitting her. When we walk in, she and the soldiers are debating (and demonstrating) the virtues of open-handed versus closed-fist strikes. They see us and freeze; it's as if we've busted up a party.

"So I guess it's safe to say you're all right."

Miyu crosses the room and stares at me, as if checking for damage. Not sure I pass inspection; her look's a little uncertain. "And you?" she asks.

"I'm fine." I turn on Captain Fahra. "Despite getting black-bagged."

"My apologies," he says. "We weren't yet certain if you could be trusted."

"And now?" I say.

He bows. "I should not have doubted."

I nod, and turn on Miyu. "I saw him."

"Saw who?"

"Benroyal has him. He's ... Cash is alive." I'm too shaken to elaborate, and Miyu doesn't get much time to react.

She opens her mouth, but Fahra interrupts.

"Please follow me," he says.

We trail him to the queen's sitting room.

At Her Majesty's command, Miyu and I take a seat. I must still look pretty wrung out, because Fahra hands me the medicine-soaked cloth. This time, I'm more than happy to take it. A few deep breaths and my head starts to clear.

"I was right to bring you here. You do care for my son."

"Very much," I say.

There's a quiet beat, and as she studies my answer, I know the soft shine in her eyes is the closest thing to an apology I will ever get. But it doesn't really matter. We both know why we're here. No need to work at cross-purposes, as Miyu would say.

She takes a deep breath. "What you saw was a recording one of Benroyal's couriers delivered to me, at the palace in Belaram, three days ago. Captain Fahra tells me an analysis of the feed's . . . What did you call it?" She turns on him.

"Metadata?" Miyu volunteers.

Fahra nods.

"Yes, that's it," the queen adds. "It indicates the feed was recorded nine days ago."

My throat is thick and tight. "So he's still alive."

Her Majesty frowns. "At the very least, he was alive a week ago. It all depends on how much one relies upon Benroyal's word."

"He has Cash." I'm on the edge of my seat now. "Where is he holding him? How soon can we get there?"

"Good questions. I, Captain Fahra, and what few loyal palace guard remain, have tried in vain to answer them."

"If the feed's metadata tells you when it was taken, why not track its location as well?" Miyu asks.

"The location was scrubbed from the file before it arrived," Fahra answers.

"I see." Miyu perks up. "Benroyal wants you to know *when* the feed was shot, but not where."

"Precisely," the queen replies.

I stand up. The movement leaves me prickly-headed as the blood rushes to my brain. I speak through the fog. "There has to be a way to find him. We have to track him down, and you have to—"

"I have to watch my every move," the queen answers sharply. "My firstborn trusts no one, least of all me. I cannot so much as leave the palace without Dakesh's permission."

"But you're still the queen. That has to mean something. Don't tell me you don't have some influence left. You're not going to even try to help him?"

When the hard line of her mouth softens, it's like watching a last battalion fall. "I *am* trying to help him. Why do you suppose I brought you here? I have done everything. My spies, my servants, my guards, every lead and remaining connection . . . I have exploited them all, to no avail. And if Dakesh catches one whiff of betrayal, not only will he have my head, but he'll have Cashoman's. Why do you think Benroyal sent this to me in the first place? For sun's sake, they want me to know his life's at stake. Message received. I will not risk it."

"You stay silent and out of the way," Miyu says. "So your subjects believe all is well and continue to submit to Dakesh while Benroyal pulls the strings."

The queen pauses, bottling up a sigh. The frustration blazing in her eyes . . . She is so like Cash. "It's the bargain I've been forced to make. If my Cashoman is to have any hope at all, I cannot break my contract with Benroyal. It's the only thing protecting his life. I had no choice but to sign it."

And there it is. In one breath, she's laid it out—the thread that's drawn us together and forced us here, our backs against the wall. I know something of bargains and contracts. I've seen enough of Benroyal's to calculate the no-win exchange. "So you need my help."

She nods.

The press of unshed tears aches in my jaw. I can barely get the words out, but I force myself to straighten. "I will find him, Your Majesty. I will bring him home. I swear it."

"Whatever we can do to help," Miyu offers. "You have our word." It's an unexpected vow, and I am more than grateful for it.

But Her Majesty shakes her head, as if our promises carry no more weight than Benroyal's. "There's been no trace of him anywhere, not here or on Castra. Not even a whisper of gossip, as we'd expect from our usual sources. We can't find him at all."

"My uncle said as much," I say.

"Pardon?" The queen raises an eyebrow.

"My uncle. James Anderssen."

"I'm aware of who your uncle is. But I was under the impression that he was . . . dead."

Miyu shoots a warning glance, but I catch the mistake too late. I'm sure James is going to love that I just blew his cover. I think very hard about my next few words. "He left me plenty of intel and resources."

Her Majesty doesn't ask me to elaborate. "As you will. I have secrets of my own; I've no qualms with you keeping yours. All I ask is that you use those resources to rescue my son. And in return—"

I shake my head. "No. This isn't a bargain. I want Cash home and alive as much as you do. I'm not asking for anything from you."

"Perhaps." She wears a smile that'd rival any diplomat's. "But I think you might change your mind after a visit to my gardens. There's a rare bloom I'd like you to see. She needs a little tending."

When I don't catch on quickly enough, she adds, "Let's check in on your mother."

〜〜〜

There are the things you see, the things you're told, and the things you still can't believe. And as I stand in the prince's old nursery courtyard, my body pressed against the cool stone and vine-twisted lattice of the garden wall, my eyes squinting through the tiniest gap between leaves, all of those things collide.

What I see is a much larger garden on the other side. A rippling fountain and the gray-tiled walk and a splash of red buds against creeping green. Beside the water, a low set of chairs and tables. And a woman. Dozing in a cushioned settee, she is pale and thin, a scrap of cloth stretched too tightly against the light.

My mother. Joanna Anderssen Benroyal. She has fallen so far, so fast, in the past few months. Even from here I can see the black sap addiction's nearly pulled her under. I taste the curse words—a whole string of them crouch behind my teeth, but I don't let them out. I don't make a sound.

Her Majesty tells me Benroyal's sent her here to summer in a kinder climate than Castra's. To take comfort in the cool, moist air and breathe in pure balm leaf from the royal groves. She's here because home's hell this time of year. Because anti-gel can heal a lot of things, but it can't bring back a broken mind. Because the doctors have done all they can.

I still can't accept it. My mother is steps beyond this wall. And she is dying.

Her eyes flutter, then close again. She sighs, and the soft wince is enough to gut me. Instinctively, I back away from my hiding spot, as if I'm somehow disturbing her rest.

I should never have left her behind.

My chest tightens, but the rage doesn't come. I've cried so many tears, I'm broken. Just a shred of a girl, fragile and paper hearted. I turn away from her and slip back inside.

When everyone else follows, Fahra closes the doors behind us.

I glance around the old nursery, at faded cushions at the window seat and the tiny table and chairs. I wonder if this was once Cash's little kingdom, and if there's anything left of him here.

In the rest of the queen's wing, there are murals on the walls, each one made of millions of bits of blown glass. They shine like stolen starlight, spun into history. You can watch Bisera's rise and fall marching down the long hallways. But here, in this child-sized suite, there are no more lessons, only fables and storyfeed tales. I only recognize two. *The Barden's Song. The Legend of the Castran Sun.*

"I still don't understand," I say. "Benroyal hardly lets her out of his sight. There's no way he'd just dump her here."

"It was a surprising concession on his part," Her Majesty replies, and it's as if the real Queen Napoor—the steely-eyed predator—has returned. "But he has my son, and he still needs my silence. If I were to speak out, Benroyal knows it would spark a very messy, very costly civil war. So I've been given a hostage of my own, in exchange for Cashoman."

Of course. Forced allegiance is Benroyal's favorite game. "And if something happens?"

"He dies, she dies. It's his little show of good faith. A false one, but still. Besides, someone's got to take care of her."

The jab's good enough to stir the last ember in me. "You wouldn't kill her," I say. "He wouldn't let you."

"Perhaps Benroyal doesn't value your mother quite as much as you think he does. It wasn't hard to sell him on this end of the deal."

"My mother's not some chip to bargain with," I protest.

For a split second, Her Majesty seems to soften. "Oh, child. You must know by now . . . she always has been."

The words cut me to the heart, but the queen huffs, half annoyed, half amused. "For sun's sake, you insult my hospitality. I have no plans to execute anyone. Not today, at least. And truly, if you didn't want her leveraged as a political prisoner, why didn't you keep her at your side?"

The question stings. I don't answer. In the silence, I see

my mother's face, her image saved on my father's flex. I never had the chance to see that dazzling smile in person. Just hollow cheeks and vacant eyes. Joanna, haunted. It's the only version of her I've ever known.

"Give her to me." I turn on Her Majesty. "We have allies in Cyan. They can help me keep her safe. Let me take her."

"For now, she stays here. But find my son," Her Majesty says. "And she is yours."

CHAPTER FIFTEEN

WE'RE SMUGGLED OUT OF THE PALACE IN A DUSTY TRANSPORT
full of construction debris. Fahra gets us underground again,
and we make our way back to the abbey. Now we're right
where we started, in the dim alcove at the top of the steps.

"Here," he says, handing over what little we'd brought—
our robes and our flex cards. "These belong to you."

I pull on my baggy disguise, then shuffle through the
deck of razor-thin screens. I'm frantic until I find the one
from James. I check it, and see that it's still loaded and
secure. Then, as Miyu puts her robes back on, I scan the
rest of the cards. On mine, there are at least a dozen messages from Larken. He's panicked. We haven't checked in,
and he's threatened to storm the city if we don't reply by
nightfall. And rust if nightfall isn't creeping close.

Quickly, I text him back.

PV: WE'RE FINE. ON OUR WAY NOW.

Almost instantly, his answer blinks at me.

KL: WHERE ARE YOU

PV: LONG STORY. LATER.

KL: WHAT HAPPENED?

My thumb hovers over the screen, and I think carefully about my answer.

PV: GOT SIDETRACKED. WE'RE FINE.

KL: ETA?

PV: HOLD YOUR POSITION. SOON.

And then nothing. Miyu's standing at my shoulder, reading the exchange.

"We need to return," she says. "The longer we stay . . ."

She doesn't finish. Doesn't have to. I turn on Captain Fahra. "We need all the information you have, if we're going to help."

He holds up his own flex. "I have everything."

"Send the data my way. I've got an encrypted account. Here, I'll enter the flex number for you." I reach for his card, but he jerks it back.

"I don't need to send it," he says.

"But I've got to have your intel," I argue. "We can't pull together a mission without getting everything—"

"I'm coming with you."

Miyu raises an eyebrow "We're not just making the rendezvous, I'm flying us back to base."

"I understand," he says. "I will return with you."

"And you're just now letting us know?" I say. "No one said you were part of the bargain, Captain. We need to talk about this."

He straightens, undeterred. His expression's stoic as ever, but the scars under his eyes pink up as the blood rushes to his cheeks. "I am the captain of the Queen's Guard, servant to Her Majesty, assigned and at oath to protect His Highness Prince Cashoman Vidri Pelar Dradha, Duke of Manjor, Second Son to Her Majesty Queen Napoor. I failed to protect his father, the king—*may he return, in this life or the next*—but I will not fail to see His Highness safely recovered and crowned. There will be no more talk of parting. I have arranged transport to your ship. I will return with you."

For a second, Miyu and I gape, speechless.

"You're the pilot. Can you make it work?" I ask Miyu.

"He could squat in the cargo hold," she says. "If nowhere else."

Then she nods. Not at me, but at Fahra. "It's fine. We'll manage."

In return, he bows, as if we were as royal as his queen.

〜〜〜

I'm told a couple of decades ago, flying rigs were all the rage. Everybody wanted one, and the Sixers raced to meet the demand. Soon, both Castra and Cyan-Bisera were swarming with street-to-air skybrids.

Which, of course, spelled complete disaster. Whoever was in charge and thought that skybrids could peacefully coexist alongside regular airborne vacs and street rigs, without building stable networks or reliable infrastructure for say, oh, thousands of daily takeoffs and landings . . . they must've been a real rusting moron.

Whoever it was, you can thank them for the great vehicular apocalypse of 2376. A system overload crashes the entire network, and ten seconds later . . . skybrids colliding into vacs. Skybrids crashing down on rigs. Skybrids running headlong into each other. Never mind the massive recalls. What a nightmare.

Same year I was born, Hal always likes to point out. Thinks it's hilarious that I came into the universe at high tide for smash-ups and raining debris. So I wonder what he'd say now, if he saw the transport in front of me, the one Fahra's asking us to climb inside.

Because right here, three streets away from the abbey, parked behind the sun-forsaken, rot-stinking fish market, is a vintage Lucky Star, the fastest make of skybrid ever built in the galaxy. The day's nothing but rosy haze by now, and I have to squint to make out the details, but I can see this old monster well enough. The rig's pretty beat-up. The paint scheme's scratched and faded, but I spy traces of bright, eye-gouging orange.

On Castra, you don't run into these much anymore. You can hardly even find them on the black market. I've only seen one other Lucky Star up close, a sweet silver restoration. Benny only let me drive it once, and even then, he'd only let us take it for a quick run around the dunes. Because back home, vacs own the skies and rigs eat the pavement, and never the two shall meet. Keeps things nice and simple and safe. But this old cruiser? Looks dangerous as hell. Count me in.

"Aren't these illegal?" Miyu asks.

"On Castra," Fahra answers.

"And here?" I say.

He swipes his flex against the rig to unlock it. "In Manjor? As long as the accelerant core's disabled, no one cares. Take a look around. These people have nothing. Rigs are expensive. Better to modify one than to scrap it."

Fahra lifts the side door of the dubious skybrid and waves us into its small passenger hold. Three jump seats in the back, pilot's and copilot's in the front. Compliant, Miyu scrambles to the rear, but I slip past her, taking the pilot's seat. There's a modified steering wheel, throttle and controls. I check out the dash-screens—original design, same setup as the one in Benny's garage. Surprisingly simple. I guess it'd have to be, to allow just about anyone to gear up and fly.

"Move aside," Fahra protests. "Or sit in the back with your friend."

"No way. I'm not passing up the chance to drive one of these again," I say, hands already on the wheel. "If we're rolling, I'm driving."

"That is unacceptable, I cannot—"

"I am a former Corporate Cup racer, winner of the 2393 Sand Ridge 400." Already, the smile's tugging at my lips. "Before that, lead crew for Benny Eno in Capitoline. Best in sixty-three straight runs. So go ahead and forget any more talk of riding along. Get in. I'm driving."

I swear I nearly get Fahra to grin. He takes the copilot's seat and buckles in. Miyu climbs in the back. "I'll navigate, then."

I press the ignition. The skybrid—our Lucky Star— answers in a rhythmic, low but climbing roar. I hear systems powering up and thrusters idling, and the sound of it pierces deep, awakening something within me. Flaring into life, a long quiet itch begins to burn. Deep breath. Gut check. Hands on the wheel.

"Alrighty then. Let's blaze."

And then, of course, I punch it.

"Stay on this course," Fahra commands. He programs a route on the navigation screen, and I'm quick to follow it. I can tell he and Miyu are none too thrilled to be plastered against the backs of their seats as I zip down the crowded alley, then career onto the main road, the sputtering, raging river of traffic cutting through the center of Manjor. And I'm not even going at it that hard. There are plenty of cabs around us, speeding along far more recklessly.

Those rigs, they *want* attention. They need everyone to know they're coming through. But I'm stealth gliding, ghosting through split-second gaps wherever I can, tucking us into night's empty pockets. Slipping past every rearview mirror, I push the limits of inconspicuousness. In the dim fog of sea spray and exhaust, we're nothing more than a flash of paint and taillight.

And it's getting us where we want to go in rusting good time. We've nearly reached the top of the hill. In seconds, the twilit bay will be at our feet.

"When should I exit?" I ask Captain Fahra.

"Three more gates, then—"

We crest and he stops.

And suddenly I see it too. Shadows looming in the skyline. Officers parked at the next three exit gates. The armored rigs on the ground and the squadron of sleek black battle vacs hovering over the harbor. Guns out and searchlights on, the IP are on the move, blighting the city like flies on a spoiling feast.

"Tell me this is routine," I say to Fahra. "That the Interstellar Patrol is always out like this."

He shakes his head. "No, not this many. Something is wrong."

Miyu groans, and I see what's caught her attention. Through the windshield, I spy half the ships in the bay start to move out. All lit up, they drift like scattershot constellations. The smugglers are leaving, and that's a bad sign.

Here on the hill, traffic slows and we're almost crawling. The hovering vacs turn and begin heading our way.

Miyu's saying something, but I can't hear her. The panic bomb's gone off inside my skull, and my heart skids against the back of my throat. My flex buzzes, and I pull it out. There's another message from Larken.

KL: PULLING UP ANCHOR. HIDE WHEREVER YOU CAN. THEY'RE LOOKING FOR YOU.

"Yeah," I mumble. "Tell me something I don't know."

Before I can reply, he flexes again.

KL: HOLD TIGHT. STAY IN THE CITY. WORKING ON AN EXTRACTION PLAN.

"What is it?" Fahra asks.

I toss the card at him. "Answer for me. Tell Larken we're coming. Right now."

For a second, the captain's frozen. Miyu blurts out what his eyes are asking. "Phee, are you crazy? We'll never make it to the docks." She leans forward once more, until she's at my shoulder. "Look down there. They're already pulling over rigs right and left, and we've got no way to reach the *Andalan*. You need to slide over, jump the curb, and turn around. We need to get underground until this blows over. It's our only option."

In my head, the last rational shreds tell me to listen to her. The words flap and squawk, white flags snapping in the wind. Slow down. Turn back. Lay low. But there's another voice too. The girl I used to be. The girl who wasn't afraid of wrecking her rig or getting arrested. She whispers something else.

If you go underground, you won't leave this city alive.

The IP are swarming. I have to get us all out of here. Right now or never.

Traffic grinds to a stop. I stare at the dash, the navigation screens and dual controls. There's only one way to get out over that harbor . . .

"Tell Larken to get Miyu's vac ready for takeoff," I say to Fahra. When he opens his mouth to protest, I shut him down. "Do it. Now. Tell him we're coming in hot, and to clear the aft end of the deck."

Fahra takes the card, flexing furiously as I give orders. "Tell him to empty Miyu's cargo hold. Get rid of everything but enough fuel to make it to the Strand. And tell him he sure as sap better be ready to fly."

Fahra obeys, but Miyu's still jaw-jacking at my ear. "Phee, I know what you're thinking, but—"

"I thinking you'd better reach back there and fire up the accelerant core."

"What? The core's disabled. There's no getting this thing off the ground. I thought Fahra was pretty clear on that." She looks at him for confirmation. He nods.

"So *un*-disable it." When she doesn't catch on, I walk her through, step by step. "Just look down, on the left by your seat, there'll be a small panel. All you have to do is open it. There will be four switches, two for the accelerant boosters and two for flight control. Probably blue. Yeah, they're usually blue. Flip them up. All of them. Easy as—"

"The panel. It's bolted shut," she growls.

Ahead, the line of rigs starts moving again. At each exit gate, IP soldiers are pulling over vehicles, tagging cargo and scanning drivers.

"What's our plan B?" Miyu asks.

My eyes flick to the blade at Fahra's hip. "Dagger," I snap, jerking my chin.

Quickly, he hands it to Miyu.

"There is no plan B," I tell her. "Pop that hatch."

A second later, she wedges the knifepoint into a gap at the top of the panel. At first, she tries inching the blade in, moving it back and forth. The panel groans, but won't quite give.

I feel the roar of the approaching vacs. There's not much sky between us now. "Miyu, I need those boosters . . ."

Frantically, Miyu redoubles her efforts. Fahra slips out of his restraint, as if to help, but she's already on it. Crouching, she levers herself over the panel, then gasps and kicks and curses, driving the blade in with her boot.

Thwack!

The panel snaps and flies off, hitting the back of my seat. Miyu dives for the switches.

A second later, the flight console answers. *"Core activated."*

Miyu whoops, victorious.

For a second, the skybrid holds its breath, then shivers as the core powers up.

Instantly, we're blinded by a dozen searchlights. A ring of vacs hovers over us now, their engines screaming, sirens blaring, sounding the alarm. Moving in, they tighten the noose.

I feel the panic closing in, a living, breathing monster, its jaws at my throat. Against the glare, I blink and thumb the sweat out of my eyes. Flight options flicker on my screens. I tune everything else out and focus on the words *rapid ascent* and *vertical takeoff*. The text flashes from red to green.

I hesitate. The ghost in me whispers, *wheels up. Now.*

"Better buckle back in," I shout. "Hold tight. Things are about to get ugly."

I swipe both options, and the Lucky Star answers. We lurch into a deafening roar.

CHAPTER SIXTEEN

I CAN PINPOINT THE CREST OF THE PANIC. AT MY COMMAND, the beat-up skybrid rockets up like a blazing, angry sun. Angling under an enemy vac, we reach the ceiling of our ascent and my body jerks against the restraints. Normally, the chin-snapping jolt would push the sweetest adrenaline high. But this time, I'm white-knuckling the most dangerous ride of my life.

I tighten my hold on the flight control, the modified wheel that hums and quakes in my grip. The yoke's a living, struggling thing. Too much pressure, and we'll veer off course. Too little, and we're out of control. The skybrid's nose jumps, hiccupping against the air, and we're slammed again. I strain for more altitude. Sliding past another vac, we level up, and my eyelids snap wide open to duskpurpled clouds. It's the clouds that chase away the fear.

We are really flying.

Another blink. Two enemy vacs in our path and three more on our exhaust. I pull up, and we slip between the behemoths at twelve o'clock. They have power, but we have speed. Too slowly, the larger IP ships adjust course, roaring after us.

"Captain Fahra," Miyu shouts. "Put Larken on the com."

We plunge right, and Fahra swipes my flex card against the com screen. Larken immediately answers.

"WHAT PART OF 'HOLD TIGHT' DID YOU NOT UNDERSTAND, PHEE?" Larken shouts.

"No time to argue," I answer. "Just get ready for—"

"Phee!" Miyu warns. "Watch out!"

I lever the controls again, ducking under a line of pulse fire. No, not pulse fire. Disruptor flare. I can tell by the sound—a low, throbbing, shockwave-rumbling noise that grinds in my bones—and the weird, ozone-y aftertaste in my mouth. Flare is the worst. Doesn't just jack up networked systems, but leaves you feeling like your insides are turned out. As I swing up to dodge another hit, it occurs to me: The IP aren't aiming to blow us to bits. They're trying to force us out of the air.

One-billion-credit bounty. They aim to take me alive.

Larken's still squawking on the com, and everything's coming at me at once. "Hang on Larken, we're coming your way," I tell him, then turn on Fahra. "This thing got any weapons? Sub-orbital shields? If this bird's got any super-secret special modifications, now would be a great time to let me know."

"Are you joking?" He looks back at Miyu. "She is joking, correct?"

Instead of answering, Miyu leans forward and shouts into the com. "Larken, I think Phee's going to try to land—"

"I *am* going to land. On the *Andalan*. And then we are getting the rust out of here." A hard-climbing, gut-churning left to avoid the latest burst of disruptor flare, but we catch the rim of it, and our screens stutter. Thank the stars, it's only a split-second glitch.

"Watch it," Miyu says. "We won't survive a hard systems reboot."

"Look . . ." I pause. I'm about to argue, but then I remember we don't have time to fight while three . . . no, four full-sized battle vacs are gunning for us. I course correct, and we swoop below the largest IP beast. I swipe the accelerant controls and beg the system to give me everything it's got. We lurch forward, jetting toward the freshly scuttled harbor. There are so few ships in bay now. Ours hovers at the edge.

Just when I think we're going to get over the water free and clear, more vacs drop from the clouds. It's like the skies are bleeding Benroyal stooges. I've got nowhere to go but . . . over, up, down, knife-twist up again. "Hang on!" I say as I manhandle the stubborn yoke. The *Andalan*'s directly in our sights now. It's hovering over the waves, bailing fast.

"Larken," Miyu barks again. "Working on final approach. Feed us a systems beacon for landing."

"Affirmative," he answers. "Lock in on six-seven-six-three."

Instantly, Fahra responds at the controls, and we pick up the beacon. The nav screens blink with new data, and guidelines—a narrow flashing green track and instrumentation readings—appear on our windshield.

The emerald flash distracts me from the fighter vac at seven o'clock. The one who's belching a steady rain of flare. I angle sideways, but it's too late. We stutter again, and the screens blank out. We hold our breath for one . . . two . . . three . . . four . . . five . . . six . . .

"Booster guidance is gone. Losing altitude," Miyu warns. "Think we're going to—"

"Come on . . ." I growl at the skybrid. "Come on, you battered old piece of—"

WHOOSH.

The boosters stir and our Lucky Star twitches back to life, screens winking bright.

"Core systems back," Fahra says, recovering the route. "Beacon's still a go."

No time for victory shouts. I glance at the returning guidelines. We are way off course. So far under our target trajectory, I'm surprised we're not under the waves and feeling the spray. I maneuver, straining to force us high enough. For a second, we bounce back between the guidelines. The hair on the back of my neck prickles, and intuition tells me to slide right. We move and sink beneath another barrage of disruptor flare. Recovering, I pull up, desperate to get us back on track.

The *Andalan*'s dead ahead. We are still too low and coming in too hot. Right now, if I try to land, the laws of physics will tear us apart. I ease down the accelerant and milk the controls for more altitude. Still, I fail.

The beacon alarm sounds, stealing my focus and pulling me out of consciousness. Every pulse of the Klaxon strikes like a fist at my temple until I'm limp, darkness hovering at the edge of my vision. I'm . . . going to . . . black . . .

Scuffling by my seat. A hard slap to the cheek.

"Don't you dare pass out," Miyu barks at me. Hands lunge over mine, reaching for the wheel. Captain Fahra. "Stay with me," Miyu demands. "Breathe through your belly. Ease it out. Exhale."

She thumps my hip as I come back around. "Clench up, Van Zant. Tighten your legs."

Her voice comes at me like a fuzzed-out, otherworldly signal, but I do it. Every command's a lifeline, pulling me out of the tunneling dark.

"That's it," she coaches. "Squeeze 'til it hurts."

I obey. The blood rushes back to my head. Still shaky, but rust it all, I'm back. I get a better grip on the wheel. "I'm okay," I say to Fahra.

He eases his hold. Slowly, he pulls back.

Miyu's still at my ear. "I've got this," I rasp.

"*We've* got this," she clarifies.

I nod, eyes on the horizon, thankful for Miyu. We're bouncing in and out of the guidelines, closing in on the *Andalan's* deck. On the screen, instrument readings flash. The nav system drones, "Warning. Warning. Reduce rate of descent. Adjust angle of approach. Engage landing sequence."

I start to bug out again, but Miyu talks over the voice. "You don't have to be a pilot to land this. The beacon's going to do most of the work. All you have to do is chase the right number. Use the wheel. See that ten thousand reading? Bring it way down."

I obey. The skybrid whines as we decelerate. Eight thousand. Five thousand. Two thousand. Fahra works the flight screen. Wheels down for landing.

IP vacs crisscross the sky, and I can't believe we're still in the air.

"Ease up. Keep pulling that speed down," Fahra says. "That's it. Adjust the angle."

I'm still shaking. The yoke jerks in my grip and we bounce, in and out, in and out of the guidelines. A roar shatters the sky. The rumble of disruptor flare at our tail. I can taste it, as sharp and electric as barreling death.

Almost there. The *Andalan* cargo's been pushed to the edges of the deck. A narrow channel runs through the center, a string of deck lights leading straight to Miyu's vac, the freighter's bay doors open and waiting. Again and again, system warnings trail the blaring alarms. *Decelerate. Decelerate.* We're coming in all wrong. Miyu scrambles back to her jump seat and buckles in. "Get under five hundred. Now. Now!" she barks.

I battle the yoke, gripping until there is nothing left of me but burning hands. The numbers on the screen roll back. One thousand. Eight hundred. Six hundred. Five fifty.

The deck. We crash down in a seismic hammer fall of speed on metal.

Skid. Crack. Bump. Groan.

We roll down the ramshackle landing strip like we're on fire. *Are we on fire?* I choke on smoky haze. The friction's boiling our wheels.

We cut through the gray plumes, and I see the end of the

line. We're still going too fast, and if we don't slow down a notch or ten, we'll slam into Miyu's vac, or worse, veer off, tumbling over the far edge of the deck.

"How do I brake this thing?!" I pump the foot pedal to no avail. "These only work in drive mode!"

"Landing brakes!" Miyu shouts.

Fahra lunges for the stick just right of the yoke. Gasping, he struggles to get it moving, but it's lock-jam stuck. Miyu fumbles to unfasten her restraint, but I scream at her. "Stay buckled or you're dead!"

And if I let go of the yoke, we'll all be.

Fahra pulls, straining at the brake until sweat runs into his eyes and his arms look ready to rip out of their sockets. One last growling effort and . . .

The metallic whine of brakes taking hold slices through the air. Triumphant, Fahra lets go and collapses against his seat. We hurtle down the runway like a dying meteor, grinding hard after meeting atmosphere. Two tons of flaming tin can tossed at a twenty-ton space freighter, its rear doors an open mouth.

Here it comes, my brain screams, *here it comes.* We roll on. The ramp. The loading rim. The empty hold. I hold my breath as we skid to a wheel-smoking, gear-grinding, teeth-rattling stop, coming at last to a violent rest.

"Destination alert," the system chirps. "You have arrived."

CHAPTER SEVENTEEN

WE'VE ARRIVED, ALL RIGHT, JUST A WHISPER FROM THE BACK
wall. Couldn't squeeze even a runt like me between it and
this rig. All three of us? We let out a breath.

But no time to thank our Lucky Star or jump out to kiss
the ground. The first thing I hear is the freighter's boosters
firing up. As the cargo bay doors close behind us, the sound
quakes through every surface, and we're shaken so hard I
fear we'll fall apart, leaving so many bags of bones on the
bolt-bitten floor. Only when the doors finally seal is the roar
less than paralyzing.

We stumble out of the skybrid, crippled by the gut-
swoop lift of vertical takeoff. Hands reach out to help, and
it's only then I realize that Larken's guards are gathered in
the hold of Miyu's vac. They get us on our feet and start

hustling us toward the aft end of her tough little freighter. On the stairs, at the cockpit door, I notice how the guards flank Fahra. They've pinioned his arms, their eyes alert and suspicious.

"Hold on," I tell them. "He's with me."

They don't back off, but they let his arms fall to his sides before escorting us into the roomy cockpit. Miyu's vac's got more screens than most pilots would know what to do with, and every bit of loose gear is still perfectly racked, labeled, and stowed. Girl runs a tight ship. I swear, she'd make an excellent crew chief. Forget my old boss, Benny Eno. Give Miyu a garage.

The pilot's chair swivels our way as Larken greets us. "Glad you could make it."

"Yeah. Me too." I scan the wide windows, then the defensive grid. A small army's still on our exhaust.

"Strap in," Miyu orders. "Get ready to blast." There's a long row of jump seats behind the pilot's platform. While the guards stand by, Fahra and I take our places there.

"I'm guessing you'd like your spot back," Larken says to Miyu.

"Yes, but I could use an experienced hand by the com."

He takes the hint, rising to claim the copilot's chair at her side, and Miyu sinks into her own throne. Reflexively, she guides the controls, smoothly shifting us out of auto-ascend. We pick up a hair-raising burst of speed as she shoots us into an evasive bullet arc.

We all watch the grid, bracing for a last-ditch barrage of IP fire. But it doesn't come. Instead, the enemy vacs fall back, one by one, tucking tail and turning toward the harbor. The sight should wash over me like relief, but now I'm even more uneasy.

I gape. "They're all . . ."

"Not *all*." Miyu points at the grid. "Look there. Three LF-35s at four o'clock. They're still following. Steady position. They're keeping their distance."

"They're tracking us," I say.

Miyu nods.

"Got any weapons?" I pause, prepared to stretch the truth. "I'm a half-decent gunner."

"Yes and no. I'm running a light freighter here, not a battle vac," she says. "I've modified the system and racked two barrels for pulse fire, but a lot of good that's going to do us now."

Larken answers her thoughtful frown. "I'm guessing you've diverted all power to the accelerant, just to keep up this pace. So pulse fire's out. Not enough juice for that."

Miyu sighs. "I can give you firepower or I can give you speed, but I cannot give you both."

"We're no match for those fighters," I say. "Are we?"

"Nope," she says, as if putting a lid on any wild ideas I might have had. "Lucky for us, they aren't firing."

"But we can't go back to base like this. We can't just lead them there."

"That's exactly what we *must* do," Larken says. "There is nowhere else for us to run. Besides, it's not as if your friends aren't prepared. Captain Nandan can deal with a few rogue fighters."

"I won't compromise the rebellion again," I say.

"The commmander is correct. Pray they follow us," Captain Fahra offers. "Better they follow than shoot us down on the way."

"How can you say that when it will betray our position? Benroyal will know exactly where we're hiding in the Strand."

"I guarantee he already knows," Fahra says. "And these fighters are likely ordered to merely follow and scout. They will not engage at the border. The Strand is too sacred. Attacking there would mean war."

"But you don't understand," I counter. "Benroyal would cross any line. He'd do anything to get what he wants."

"With respect," Fahra interrupts. "Perhaps it is you who does not understand. I do not mean such an attack would bring the usual conflict—skirmishes in the Gap or common riots. I mean it would beget *real* war, rivers of blood shed across two planets, such as your people have never seen or would ever see again. That is what burning the Strand would bring to Benroyal's door."

"That's enough," Larken says icily. Blue eyes lit, he glares at Fahra, then turns his back. He sighs, glancing at me. "What kind of trouble's followed you, Phee? Why did you bring this—"

Fahra straightens, unafraid. "I am Fahra, captain of the Queen's Guard, servant to Her Majesty, assigned and at oath to protect—"

"I know who you are, Captain," Larken says, freezing out the familiar litany. "I'm just wondering what you're doing here."

"About that . . ." I interject, anxious to dial back the tension.

"Guards, please escort our unexpected guest to the hold," Larken commands his guards, then casts us the side-eye. "If you'd be so kind as to excuse us, Captain. Phee owes me a mission debriefing."

"As you say, Commander," Fahra replies. Silent, he allows Larken's men to lead him away.

The moment the cockpit door closes behind them, Larken starts in. "You'd better have a stellar explanation, my friend. Why is Queen Napoor's personal bodyguard on this vac?"

CHAPTER EIGHTEEN

WITH MIYU'S HELP, I TELL LARKEN EVERYTHING. ABOUT JAMES and Cash and the queen's bargain. When we're done, he's quiet. No fussing at me for getting myself into trouble, no warnings or advice. Nothing.

"Aren't you going to yell at me or something?" I ask him.

"Why would I yell at you?"

"Because that's what old people do when you pull something stupid."

At first, he's taken aback. Then, thoughtful, he sighs. "You are not a child to be scolded. And I am not so old, Miss Van Zant."

We laugh, but only for a bitter second.

"Even if you're not going to scold me," I say to him, "I want your advice."

He takes a breath, and as always, mulls over his response. "Do what you have to," he says at last. "Plan your rescue. Take this bargain, but . . . as you'd likely put it, you should also—"

"Watch your exhaust," Miyu finishes for him.

Larken nods. "Queen Napoor is smart, and it seems her most exceptional talent lies in always landing on her feet. So I would not put it past her to leverage Prince Cashoman in some way."

"I know she's calculating. But . . . I think she's afraid. As afraid as I am. She's desperate to see Cash safe and alive."

"You say this after she had you kidnapped. And what of Fahra?"

"What of him?" Miyu asks, still focused on the controls.

Larken swivels her way. "Captain Fahra. His own people cut those marks into his face, and now call him Fahrat. You know the word? The meaning of the nickname?"

She thinks for a moment. "*Fah*-rat, the Biseran word for an animal. Small and agile, the black-eared predator. Oh. Wait . . . Fah-*rat*—accent on the second syllable," she says, her gaze finally drawn from the screen. "I see."

Larken nods.

"What?" I ask. "What does it mean?"

Larken shifts in his seat, then tilts his gaze to me. "He was there the night Cash's father was slaughtered, the very one who allowed assassins to slip into the royal chamber. Fah*rat* means 'dishonor.'"

I'm quiet for a long time.

"You've lived in that kind of shadow," I say to him at last. "You know what it's like to be branded a traitor and written off, Larken. There's more to your story than gossip and talk, so maybe there's more to his. Besides, the queen trusts him. Please trust me to give him a chance."

Larken doesn't answer at all. Instead, he looks me straight in the eye. Right fist over his heart, he makes the rebel's salute.

It happens in the last hour of flight. At dawn. Less than a thousand miles from base.

Miyu looks up from the controls. "We've lost contact with Hank at HQ," she says. "I got through an hour ago, but I just tried sending an updated transmission, and the feed blacked out. There's nothing, not even a static beacon."

Larken reaches for a diagnostic screen, but Miyu shakes her head. "I already checked. It's not a glitch in our system. We're transmitting fine. There's just nowhere for the feed to go. The channel no longer exists. It's just . . . gone."

Even as I tense up, she speaks what I'm thinking. "Something's wrong."

"Keep trying," Larken orders. "But keep one eye on the grid. We might need that pulse fire after all."

"Already on it," Miyu replies. "Guns out at a second's notice."

I watch the defensive grid, the backlit web of airspace and enemy movement. The three fighters on our heels haven't advanced. They still trail, distant but locked into battle formation, a drawn arrow, aimed in the sky.

Until we're just shy of the Strand.

They break apart. Near the border's edge, over the first sweep of high-climbing blooms, they swarm us, surrounding us at the fore.

Miyu cranks down our speed, and the clank of locking cannons echoes like a one-two punch against the hull. We drop beneath the fighters, easing back, but they're too quick on the jump. Wheeling, they break. A breath later, they're behind us again. A proximity alarm blasts through the cockpit as they move in, closer than ever before.

Still, no enemy fire.

"I can't shake them," Miyu yells over the blare. "Even if I swivel barrels, they're too close. If I shoot at this range, it'd knock us all out of the air."

Captain Fahra and the guards burst into the cockpit, quick to buckle in beside me.

Fahra turns to me. He's eerily calm.

Larken runs a defensive check. "No weapons signature. No heat in their barrels or any sign of target lock; they aren't even trying to fire. What are they playing at?"

On the grid, the outlines of the fighters overlap with our ship, and it's like watching a parasitic attack. They've become an extension of us, a cloak, a . . . "They're a shield," I spit. "They're herding us all the way to the border."

"That makes no sense," Miyu answers, frantic. "Why would they—oh my god."

I look up, at the horizon, to see what's drained the color from her face.

Ahead, the highest ridge. We've reached the Pearl Strand.

Behind it, the first hint of black sky. A hundred columns of rising smoke.

The poppy fields are burning.

CHAPTER NINETEEN

THE GRID LIGHTS UP, BUT I DON'T HAVE TO SEE THE ICONS to know there's an armada of vacs ahead. Blue and black ships, locked in combat. I flinch at the magma sizzle of whistling torpedoes. *BOOM . . . BOOM . . . BOOM.*

In and out, in and out come the shallow breaths, until I'm strangled, betrayed by my own lungs. I bite down on a sharp gulp of air, too big to swallow. No, no, no. It's happening. It's happening again.

Behind us, Benroyal's fighters stick to our tail. Before us, dozens of rebel and Cyanese and IP vacs crisscross the sky, wheeling and falling and turning in endless, interlocking loops.

Like a hapless bird, a rebel fighter's hurled against the hull of an enemy gunship. Stricken, it flames in descent.

I snap, shaking off shock and paralysis. I fumble out of my restraint. One of Larken's men swings an arm across my chest, but I bat it away.

"Sit down, Phee," Larken orders.

Disobedient, I stagger. At Miyu's side, I stare through the cockpit windshields, straining to see over the next ridge. Our camp. Our precious, protected little valley.

I was right: There's no line Benroyal won't cross.

"Can you get through to base?" I ask. "Is anyone down there? Is anyone left alive?"

Miyu touches the communications screen, swiping through all channels. There's still nothing on the ground-to-air feeds, but the rebel vac-to-vac feeds hum with after-shock screams and panicked squawks.

A sudden blast knocks me on my exhaust, sending me skidding against the back of the cockpit. An explosion in my skull as my head lashes the wall. A second of blindness, then bursts of light—harsh as lens flare—assault my eyes. Voices, muddled and fuzzy, rushing like stale wind in my ears.

"Landlan lellah."

"Lellah, lellah."

A hand at my cheek. I blink. Fahra's hovering over me, speaking in Biseran. *"Lellah,* are you okay?" he asks. "Are you injured?"

"I don't know." My words loll and drag. "Are we hit?"

He shakes his head. "No. But one of our escorts was. Someone shot it down. We caught the aftershock."

Fahra helps get me back on my feet. Nothing's broken, I think, but everything's bruised. We tilt to balance as the ship maneuvers. A parade of seconds crawl by, and I'm disoriented, content to let Fahra guide me back to my seat. The fog in my brain begins to clear, and my hand curls at my chest. There I feel the small roar in my heart, at my fingertips. That voice, the girl I used to be . . . she snaps into rust-flight, let's-fight mode. "Larken, gimme seat number two. I'll man the pulse cannons while you transmit. We have to get through to Hank. Where are the Larssens? Where is—"

Miyu swipes up the volume on a vac-to-vac channel. She's made contact with someone in the air. "Roger, Talon One," she says. "Go ahead."

Talon One. I know that call sign.

And then I hear his voice, coming through loud and clear. "Break low on my signal," he commands. "Broadsword will cover your drop. Keep your nose down, and I will blow them off your exhaust."

"This is Broadsword, copy that," a second voice replies. Hank.

A third rebel. "Target is a go," she says. "Ready in three . . . two . . ."

We sink in a gut-check fall, and I watch the skies. Two friendlies—rebel Tandaemo fighters—split in approach, tag teaming our remaining escorts.

While Hank shields our drop, Bear aims high and fires. Three hits, and the last two parasites are gone.

"Targets dispatched," he says. "Break-break. Broadsword, requesting to provide close air support. Yamada needs cover to fallback position."

"Negative," Hank replies. "I need you back on the offensive. Yamada, get out of here. Break wide, and flank the hot zone. Get behind the Hill of Kings. Rendezvous with remaining forces."

"Yamada?" Bear says.

"Come in, Talon One," she answers.

"Keep her safe," he says.

"Roger that."

We turn, and both Tandaemo peel off, heading back into the fray.

Silent, Miyu threads past the battlefront, and we slip over the burning fields. In the valley, I stand between her seat and Larken's. We scan the terrain and what's left of our camp. No neat little squares or marching patrols. Instead, smoking rubble and the crackle of scattered fire. It's a quiet, burning disorder.

I squint for signs of life, or of death, but there's not much to see. On the ground, only a few bodies. I'm ashamed to feel so relieved, that corpses spell reassurance.

"Where are they?" I ask aloud. "What happened to—"

I glance past my old barracks tent, which, oddly, still stands. But not the infirmary. No, it's gone. The notion lands invisible, a hammer fall at the center of my chest. Hal and Mary . . . no.

"Try every channel," Larken says to Miyu. "Hank mentioned remaining forces. They must have retreated."

I don't like the way he has to convince himself. I don't know where my foster parents are, and Bear is caught at the front. Everything's falling apart in a way I can't manage. Helpless, I watch the daybreak burn.

Miyu picks up a signal. No voices, only the bleating noise of a primitive coded exchange. I toss my flex to Larken, and he runs the hum through my card. The message spools onto my tiny screen. Coordinates, then one word.

Underground.

"Not far," Miyu says. "No time at all if I could pick up speed. Running low on fuel."

We climb out of the valley to soar over the Hill of Kings, scattering the flocks of barden as we pass. Stubborn birds. They won't even leave when the dawn stinks of scorching debris. Incredibly, the tombs stand untouched, as if invincible against all assault. Only time and bird drip have left their mark on the mossy stone of the high ground.

Miyu's freighter hiccups over the last line of crypts and we descend as if we're pulled, drawn by the natural fall of the would-be mountain. Miyu lands much better than I ever could. The freighter nudges the turf and I hardly feel the impact. We power off in a shuttered-down whine, and the pound of our engine's replaced with human whir, the sound of marshaling forces.

We step out of the cargo bay.

It's chaos on the ground. Lines of rebel fighters refuel and take off, firing up into the haze like reversed shooting stars—searing, hissing bodies of energy tossed back into the skies. I recognize some of the vacs, the secondhand aircraft we started with. But there are newer, state-of-the-art birds too, still bright in silver and blue. Our Cyanese friends have come through for us. I owe Larken. A lot.

I turn to him, but he's rushing to meet a towering Cyanese woman who's geared up for flight. We catch up just as her helmet comes off. A flash of recognition, and I see this isn't any pilot. She's the young woman from the Skal, his ally on the council. And apparently, she's also his fellow commander.

Quickly, Larken bows, and she returns it.

"Vilette," he says. "What happened?"

Vilette tucks the helmet under her arm. "You should have been here."

Larken's stricken. He nods. "I know."

"We've no time for a briefing," she says. "I need you in the air."

Larken trails as she heads for a refueling fighter. His guards scatter in their wake, and suddenly, Fahra, Miyu, and I are alone.

"Come on," I say. "Help me find Hal and Mary."

First, we report to what looks like an improvised flight control, a tent near the foot of the hill filled with screens and headsetted officers. They've cobbled together a small communications hub—the servers at base must have been blown to bits. "Explains why we couldn't get through," Miyu says. "They crippled communications first, then swept in to burn everything else."

Fahra's thoughtful. "They came for a small number of rebels, I think. But they had not bargained on Cyanese reinforcement."

Inside the tent, we wait for a break in the rapid-fire lines of ground-to-air squawk. Captain Nandan's here, directing our forces. Finally, I catch his eye.

"Reporting for duty," I say.

"I'm a pilot," Miyu adds.

Fahra straightens. "As am I." That gets Nandan's attention. There's recognition between the two Biseran men, and I can't tell if it's the kind that's bad or good.

I'm about to offer myself as a gunner, but Nandan shuts us down. "Every bird we've got's already manned now. I can't use you up there." He turns away, leaving no more room for discussion.

Miyu and Fahra exchange questioning looks, but I don't wait for them to figure out our next move. To our right, away from the improvised airstrip, there's another hub of activity. Under a stand of balm leaf trees, I spy stretchers and bodies and tents.

"There." I point, then take off in a run.

Inside the medic station, my eyes dart from one face to another. So much movement and frantic exchange. You can almost taste the chaos, the way it hovers, antiseptic and gritty, in every breath. I look for the Larssens, but all of these medics are Cyanese, fresh reinforcements who've arrived since I left for Manjor. Quickly, they separate the injured from the dying. It's a ruthless mercy, and their work has just begun.

Again, I interrupt a soldier's work. "I'm looking for Hal and Mary Larssen," I ask. He's a young medic with too many bags of anti-gel in his arms. I reach out and catch one before it falls.

"They're riding the medi-vacs," he says. "At the front. Picking up survivors."

Don't know whether I'm more relieved they're still alive, or terrified they're still in the air. I can barely answer the medic, my voice a garroted squeak. "Thank you."

"We can help," Miyu adds. "Whatever you need us to do."

The medic nods, but he's already moving away to deliver his armload of remedy.

So we jump in. I show Miyu how to hang plasmatic lines and Fahra how to run a sterilizer. We hustle until there are no more instruments to clean, no more crates to haul, and no more white sheets to drape over the dead.

Until dark. We work until the battle is over.

Not long after dusk, our vacs quit going back to the fields and slowly, the rest of them return. A steady stream of skycraft—some soaring, some scorched and crippled—touch down at our fallback position. I wait at the edge of the action, watching for some sign of the Larssens. Soon enough, they stagger in, their vacs touching down.

First Bear, jumping out of his fire-blown Tandaemo, his copilot Zaide behind him. Then the last medi-vac drops, crowded with stretchers and soldiers. Among them, I can barely see Hal, whose face is marked with ash. In his arms, one of the wounded. As the medics around him break away, Hal sinks deeper into the floodlights, and I see his patient's a corpse. Her head lolled back, blue eyes vacant as glass.

Mary.

Bear sees her too, and he runs to his father. I reach them both as Hal's strength begins to fail. Hal falters, but we help him hold tight. Together, we cradle her body.

CHAPTER TWENTY

THE DAY AFTER THE ATTACK, AN EAST WIND CARRIES WHAT'S left of the poppies, and all morning, they drift—bits of ash and tattered blooms, floating through smoke. Confetti for a hollow victory.

Because that is what they're calling this. A victory. Benroyal's forces were driven back, at the cost of three dozen lives. Already there are scraps of hopeful talk. Surely now, Cyan—a nation of millions—is mobilizing against the enemy. The war, they say, isn't just our own anymore. Now the rebels are part of a larger cause. We will fight to the last, they say. We will win.

But I don't feel like a victor at all. I sit in the grass, in the gray-tasting breeze. Mary is dead because I brought us here. I think of my last race and the day I ran away from

Benroyal. I could've stayed in the Spire, and my family would still be together, a circle of four. Pulled apart by my contract, but in heart still knit tight.

Larken approaches like a spirit conjured up in the smoke. He sits beside me, a small wooden box in his hands. "We're moving as much as we can into the tomb," he says.

I tilt to look back at the rise, eyes fixed on the top. "Up there?" I say. "In those little vaults? We'd be sitting targets."

"No," he says. "Not those tombs. *The* tomb. My ancestor Khed the First is buried under the hill. There's a whole empty warren under there. Strong enough to shelter five hundred. The catacombs are sacred, but Vilette and I convinced the Skal to let us open them."

"Nothing is sacred anymore," I say.

I settle back down, resting my chin on my knees.

"You'll be safer there. At least at night," he adds. "It's cool and dry and made to last."

He puts a hand on my shoulder, and that almost makes it worse. In a second, he's going to say he's sorry, and how deeply he feels for my loss, and then I'm going to shut down or implode or sob. But Larken doesn't apologize. Instead, he puts the box in my hands. The wood's warm and smooth to the touch. There's a sigil carved into it—his ring of nine thrones—but I don't linger over it.

"My father made it for my mother," Larken says. "And now I'm lending it to you."

I pause, staring at Larken, but he gestures me to open it. I do.

Inside, there's a sealed horn wrapped in embroidered cloth. The horn is ornamented with jewels, and there's bright, silky silver in the needlework of the fabric. The sweet aroma of balm leaf and poppy and moss-wood springs from the box. This is an heirloom, beyond priceless. I press it back to him, but he refuses, palms out.

"For Mary," he says.

I wince. I can't bear to hear her name so soon.

"I don't deserve this. I'm nothing, why would—"

"She was a mother to you?" he asks.

"More than anyone else."

"The oil inside the horn must not go to waste. It is fresh, of the same kind we used to anoint my own mother. Blessed in the Skal-rung, the palace in Raupang. Vilette brought it in case I was lost in battle and would need to be buried here. But I'm alive, and Mary is not. Take this and anoint her in peace."

He puts a hand at my shoulder again. This time, I lean in like a caving wall.

He sits with me for a long time.

〜〜〜

We choose a spot at the base of the hill, near the lower entrance to Khed's tomb. Half shaded, the soil here that's not yet overturned is thick with carpet vine and wildflower buds. Mary will rest here, in the cool green.

I've pulled us so far away from Castra, and now she'll never return.

Hal and I stand side by side, and I shift Larken's box, tucking my right arm around it. Hal calls out to Bear, who's avoiding the freshly shoveled mounds. "You'll have to help me," Hal says.

Bear nods, and we make our way back to the medic's tent. It's early; not many are here yet. Exhausted, grieving, asleep under the hill, they're not ready to make their way out of the tomb. But Miyu's awake. She waits for us at the entrance of the tent, a covered pail in her hands. There are others like it—metal buckets, the kind we use in the old mess hall—on the ground.

"Fahra left this," she says. "The water's for you, and the rest."

"Water?" I ask.

"He went to the spring," she says. "You know, the stream that ran by the old armory? Fahra walked all the way to the source. Hauled all those buckets. He wanted there to be water for the bodies, from a blessed well."

I remember the abbey. *Sibat.* The current of souls.

Silent, Hal accepts Fahra's gift.

Miyu moves to leave, but turns before loping off. "Fahra asked me to tell you: He prays for her, and the others too. *Emam arras amam.*"

I nod, a breath away from choking up. My mind whispers the words.

In this life or the next.

In the tent, I put the box down. Hal and Bear lift Mary's body, moving it onto a clean-sheeted gurney. She's still dressed in the same dirty gear she wore during the attack, but Hal's brought a simple white shift for her, salvaged from the old infirmary. Crudely, another sheet's been draped over a chin-high tent cord, and Hal reaches for it, to pull the makeshift curtain closed. He looks at me, and I understand.

I take Bear's hand, and lead him away so Hal can clean Mary up and dress her alone. Far behind the thin curtain, we sit on the ground, which is as littered and dirty as you'd expect it to be. The bloodiest work—the real evidence of battle—has already been disposed of, heaped into barrels and burned away. But there are still abandoned plasmatic lines here, oxygen masks, and crumpled bits of discarded wrap. Small reminders, in case we forgot. As if we ever could.

We wait as Hal struggles with his task. Every whisper of movement is deliberate and gentle. Finally, the pile of her dirty clothes tumbles to the floor, and the movement stirs the air. The smell of death. But then the sound of rippling water. The rainwater drip-drip-pour in the bucket as Hal soaks up a handful of cloth. A burst of something sterile and antiseptic. My eyes are drawn to the pantomime shapes behind the curtain, but I force myself to look away. Barely breathing, I listen. Finally, there's a hitch of breath, a quiet sob.

At the sound, Bear twitches. The grief burns so plainly in his face. It's all I can do to not reach out to smooth it away. Before I can stop him, he bursts up and out of the tent. I want to follow, but a second later, Hal is finished. He pulls aside the curtain.

He's as wrung out as the cloth resting at the lip of the pail.

He takes a step forward, and at first, I think he's going to fall. But he doesn't. Straightening up, he reaches out and hugs me tight.

And then I'm alone with Mary.

Even in death, Mary's defiant. She's supposed to look peaceful, as if she's at rest. But her mouth's slightly parted, and it's as if any second, she's going to wake up gasping and angry.

Sibat, Fahra says. Life after life. One rippling current.

And so I try to imagine a more gentle death, her soul cascading, slipping away like water in a stream. But I look at her pearl-gray face and see that's a lie. No, her life was ripped free in a split-second blast. Every part of her—her smile, her hoarse laugh, her sharp-edged scolding, and her selfless grit—is gone. Scattered like so many bits of poppy ash. I open Larken's box and look at the horn, and the tears come hard and hot. What good is royal incense and oil? What good is water and sacred words, when Mary is gone? How can any of it matter, when I've lost my foster mother?

My sob is a keening, broken cry. No. Not Mary.

She is my *always* mother.

And as my eyes drift back to the box, I finally sense the gift in my hands. This oil was offered to me, not because the ritual's holy or it will bring her back or send her off in peace. The anointing's given as a lasting gesture. One final expression of love.

Hands shaking, I open the horn and pour a measure of oil onto the cloth. Gently, I press it against her skin. I anoint her forehead, the one that touched mine when I was small and sick with fever. I anoint her hands, her hands that threaded stitches and burned toast and cupped my cheek. I anoint the sun-spotted softness above her breast, the heart that took in an orphaned child, the heart that was bigger than two worlds.

I anoint her with Larken's gift and Fahra's water, with all the prayer that is in them. When the horn's empty, I lean down and kiss her temple. I give her what's left, the last of my tears.

We bury her at sunset.

Afterward, I can't bear the thought of spending the night in the tomb. I leave word, then slip back to the makeshift infirmary. It's peaceful here now, just the handful of patients who can't be moved yet and the pair of medics still working this shift. I check in, then claim my own half-curtained spot. Exhausted, I settle near the front, so I can try to fall asleep while watching the stars. But every time I close my eyes, it's not the night I see. I see the flash of battle; I'm caught in the rumble and thunder. Mary and all our fallen—their faces loom. Dead, they whisper to me, but I cannot reach them through the smoke.

My sleep's so uneasy, even the softest tread wakes me. Heart knocking, I wipe the sweat from my cheek and sit up. A split second of confusion, and for a moment, I'd completely forgotten where I was. Not at home. Not at camp. Not in the tomb, but here, in the new and unfamiliar infirmary tent. The lights have been dialed low to let the wounded catch a few hours of actual sleep. Some of them snore, almost as loud as the chugging equipment, but that's not what jerked me awake.

I tilt and focus on the infirmary entrance, between the open tent flaps. A half-lit silhouette. A breeze blows, ruffling the not-quite-as-short-anymore crop of his hair.

"Hey," I whisper to Bear.

He doesn't answer, but he takes a step in my direction.

I can only see his shadow. He is slumped. At first, I'm cautious, like I've lost even the right to comfort him. But then he takes another step and I see his face and read the shape of my name on his lips.

Barefoot, I meet him. I move to put my arms around him, but just my hand on his arm tells me this tower's already crumbling. No tears, but Bear is sinking into himself, like just one gust of wind and he'd tumble and fall. He lets me pull him to the cot, where he falls onto his side.

There, he finally cracks, trembling like he'll never be warm again. I climb onto the little cot and slip next to him. At his back, I put my arms around him. Wordless, he speaks to me. I sense the grief in his breath and his heartbeat and in the lace of his fingers between mine. In answer, I cover him. I'm the wall between Bear and the night.

CHAPTER TWENTY-ONE

WE GET THROUGH THE NEXT FORTY-EIGHT HOURS. I'VE ONLY given the barest report on our trip to Manjor. Word has spread that James and Cash are alive, like an adrenaline burst of hope. But there's been so little time to process the news or plan our next move. No chance to mourn or rejoice or fight back; we're focused on survival.

We move everything we can to our fallback position, settling behind the valley, fitting as much as we can into the catacombs under the hill. All the frantic talk and whispered questions in the air rattle through the rebel ranks. Do we dig in or go? Do we brace for battle or give up the Strand? So much depends on the Cyanese now. They're here for the moment, thanks to Larken and Vilette, but if the rest of the council change their mind, if they decide to back away and cut their losses, we're finished.

Hank and I push through the uncertainty. He rebuilds communications and commandeers a space inside Khed's tomb, the biggest cell in the whole underground hive, a flood-lit operations room filled with screens and micro-servers. Like so many others, I jump in, doing whatever I can.

A hundred times a day, I think of Mary.

But it's different for Hal and Bear. In the tense bustle of retreat, I watch them implode. Silent and flat, Hal mostly sleepwalks. Bear's just as quiet, but a lot more angry. Outside, he helps the Cyanese set up a new flight control. He buries himself in a simulator, flying through missions, shooting down fighters, one after another. For him, there will never be enough targets.

On the third day, Hal and I stand in the center of the war room, at the biggest flex table. Today, I can tell he's so tired, he's edging toward manic. This morning, we finally finished patching things up, with interstellar feeds finally coming back loud and clear. At Captain Nandan's order, we've scheduled a flex meeting with James, to parse intel.

Larken's here, and Fahra too. We're a tight knot, anchored over the table. Hank accepts the call, and James's face springs up on the screen.

A little throat clearing. "Coming through?" he asks.

"Affirmative," Hank answers. "You've already read the briefing?"

"Yes. His Highness is still alive and we're at war, Commander. These attacks . . ."

Hank leans over. "Attacks, as in more than one?"

"Manjor was bombed as well," James answers.

"When?" Larken asks. "What happened?"

"Right after you fled. The summer palace and the harbor."

A gasp ripples between us. For a moment, Fahra crumples, as though kicked in the chest. Slowly, he straightens again. When he does, his nostrils flare and his eyes light up in fury. And he is not alone. My heart is burning.

"No . . ." I struggle against the choke of more bad news. "Are you okay, James? What about Queen Napoor, and . . . what about my mother? Is she all right?"

"I'm still safe underground and Joanna's alive. But she and the queen—Benroyal's now keeping them both in the Spire. He knows you were in Manjor, Phee, and I think he's certain Napoor betrayed him. The queen is now officially under his 'protection.'"

Cash, now his mother and mine. Benroyal has them all. Fahra curses.

"Things aren't looking good for us from afar," James says. "The feeds are boiling over, and we can't risk—"

"What about the feeds?" I interrupt. "What's going on?"

There's a glitch in the transmission, and for a moment, James's answer is frozen, and I'm not even sure if he heard me. Finally, he buffers back in. "Both the attacks . . . they're pinning them on you, Phee."

The room seems to wince. I try to shut out the murmur between Hank and Larken.

James zeros in on me. "In Capitoline, talk of civil war is all but dead now. The feedcasters are reporting that the rebels swarmed and torched the poppy fields. On your orders."

"What?" I take a step back, horrified.

"You heard me. They're saying the rebels fired first, and that the IP rushed in to respond and preserve the Strand. Between that and Manjor, and the news of Cash's 'murder,' it's a disaster. For now, our hands are tied."

"That is unacceptable." Fahra turns on us. Wide-eyed, he's lit like a fuse. "Give me but one squad of your best, and I will lead them."

"You will have it," Larken offers, surprising us all.

Fahra nods. "We will find Prince Cashoman, and rescue Her Majesty. The House of Bisera must be restored."

"It's a noble offer, Captain," James replies. "But I'm afraid your rescue plans must be put on hold. We can't expose Benroyal now. Not while he holds Her Majesty in the Spire and Cash who knows where."

Again, the rage sparks in Fahra's eyes. He looks at Hank, then Larken. There's more urgency in him than ever before. "Send me now. Today. I will take as many soldiers as you can spare. I must rescue Her Majesty and—"

James interrupts, destroying all hope. "You could send an entire battalion, but it wouldn't matter. Capitoline is crawling with Benroyal's soldiers, and Castra's crying out for rebel blood now. You'll find no welcome there, or in Bisera, or anywhere else outside the Strand. It'd be a suicide mission."

"But we have to strike back," I protest.

James shakes his head. "No. You make a move, Cash is dead. And the queen. And your mother. Don't think for a second he'd spare her if you exposed him now. He has us right where he wants us. Silent and on the defensive."

"But we can't just sit here and wait for another attack," I plead. "We do that, and he'll win."

James doesn't blink. The glasses are off. "He already has."

After the briefing, I can't get out of the war room fast enough. Lead-footed and bristling, I head outside. I turn my face up and scowl at the sun. I curse it. I curse everything, guilty or not.

There was a time when the string of cuss words would've

brought relief. Every kick in the dirt and shake of my fist would've cut so easy, like a blade slicing through an invisible knot. But now my shoulders slump. Surrendering, I take a breath.

A rustle in the grass behind me.

"Dull meeting?" Miyu asks.

I turn, too defeated to laugh at her joke. Then I see it— the pinched flush in her cheeks. I'm not the only one who's upset.

"I've been summoned," she says matter-of-factly. "Grace wants me back on Castra. I'm to leave immediately."

I feel the blood drain from my face. I'm turning milk white, right before her eyes. "Why?"

"My mission's complete. I was charged with escorting you to James in Manjor, and now I have."

"Oh," I say. Don't know why the news sucks the wind from my flaps. It's not as if I'd thought Miyu would stick around forever. "I'm sorry. I dragged you into a war zone, so she's probably just worried."

"She's not just concerned about my safety. I'm sure she's irritated that I'm not there, at her beck and call."

I straighten up. "What?"

"Never mind," she says, angling away. "It's nothing. I can promise you, my problems are the last thing you need to worry about right now."

I slip by her side, until we're not face-to-face anymore, but shoulder to shoulder, squinting at the sun. "I'm already worried, Miyu. So you might as well spit it out. What's wrong?"

She grimaces, then finally relents. "Grace is angry and I'm completely unacceptable. And to top it all off, she found out about my girlfriend, Moira. She thinks I'm wasting my time on 'unnecessary attachments.' It's not enough that I'm good in finance and flight mechanics and geopolitical debate. I'm supposed to go where Grace needs me to go and take care of business more 'efficiently.' I'm not supposed—"

I interject. "To date Sixer interns?"

"Moira isn't a Sixer." She shakes her head. "Not really. But that's beside the point. I'm not supposed to date anyone at all."

"It's not a crime to have an actual life, you know."

"I know that, Phee. But you don't get it. You don't get *her*. My mother . . ." She pauses, struggling over the word, her cheeks pinking up with every breath. "My whole life, it's like I've been conditioned to obey. It's just not in me to disappoint."

I risk a smile. "Well then, stick with me. I've been lowering expectations for quite a while now. Watch and learn, and you'll get the hang of it."

Miyu doesn't exactly snort; it's a more graceful approximation. But she's not so upset now, and her half grin is already slipping back into place. "After dinner," she says, "you want me to sift through James's intel? See if there's anything I can think of that we might have missed?"

"Yeah, that'd be great." I frown. "But you're leaving."

"Oh, I never said I was leaving," she says, turning my way again. "I only said she summoned me."

"And you told her . . ."

"Well, I didn't tell *her*. I told her second assistant. I told him I was staying, and then he threatened to call her. So I did what you'd do: I told him to go ahead, and that he could suck a giant cloud of exhaust."

"You didn't," I say, cackling my way back toward the mouth of the tomb. She follows.

"I did," she deadpans. "It was great."

Miyu's grin is so wicked and sharp, it pries more laughter from me. But too soon, the distraction's gone. The breeze dies, and the whisper of battle still taints the air. We stand silent, casting shadows. Neither of us seems ready to go back inside and face whatever comes next.

"He's still alive," Miyu says, as if reading my mind. "It's not too late. We could find him."

My jaw clenches.

"Gimme a couple of days," she says. "I think I may know how to help."

I nod, shielding my eyes. She heads back into the tomb.

CHAPTER TWENTY-ONE

I FLOAT DOWN THE NARROW HALLS UNTIL I FIND MY WAY TO the east barracks, which isn't a barracks at all, but another smooth, stone-walled pocket under the hill, stuffed with empty cots. Hal is sitting on his, alone.

"Hi," I say, landing beside him.

"Morning?"

I shake my head. "Afternoon."

He nods, and I take his hand. When he squeezes, it's like a first sign of life. Such a small thing, but he's barely moved in the last forty-eight hours. The tray of food I'd brought in earlier still sits beside his bed, untouched.

"Hungry?" I ask.

"I'll eat in a while," he says. "I just forgot."

I reach down and grab a packet of dried fruit, tear it

open, and hand it to him. "Lots of sugar-sweet frangi in this mix. Your favorite," I say. It takes a little nudge to get him going, but he finally pecks at it.

"No more forgetting to eat." I'm not very good at forcing a smile.

"Okay, Mary," he slips, mouth still full.

I flinch, shocked. But then I see from the look on his face that it wasn't a slip. It was a hint of black humor.

He chews for a second, then he's the one nudging me.

"Before you left for Manjor," he says. "Mary asked me . . . I promised her I'd get you into treatment."

A tear slips down my cheek. "I promised too."

Hal gives my hand another squeeze. "She had a regimen for you. Counseling and sim exposure therapy. Say when, and I'll help you start."

"Tomorrow?"

"Tomorrow." He nods. "Pass me that protein mix."

Silent, we dig into the rest of his tray. Every bite seems to bring him back. He's here, with me. A little bit closer to alive.

We meet after dinner the next day, outside, near flight control. We'll have to use one of the Cyanese flight simulators to read Mary's program, Hal tells me. He doesn't have to remind me that the others were blown to bits.

Even in the moonlight, I can read the lift in his shoulders. It's not that he's ready to get back to work or that he's any less broken. It's more like he knows therapy's probably good for us both.

Thanks to the battle, with all those fighters roaring in and refueling, the ground out here is a mixture of charred grass and sticky soil. And that's the least of the changes. In the past couple of days, an ever-expanding tent city has sprung up. Every few meters, the soldiers have punched cloaking stakes into the soil, so the IP won't have much luck sending drones in to gather surveillance. Anyone scouting from the air will go back empty-handed, with nothing but non-visuals of an impenetrable blur. Benroyal won't have solid intel on the latest reinforcements; at least we have that. But it's a shame to see so many scars on such holy ground.

We pick our way through them, into the largest tent of all.

Inside, on the far end, there's a bank of simulators, claustrophobic pods just like the one Bear learned to fly in. He's probably here somewhere, closed off and inside, fighting his own private war. I follow Hal into the first one, and we both buckle in.

"Okay," he says, holding up a flex card. It glows, reflecting the low light of the sim. "I have Mary's notes, and a program they sent us from Raupang, in Cyan. Larken says it's a therapy they use with their own soldiers. But it wasn't easy for her to put it all together and customize it for you." When I start to cut in, he stops me. "And I know if she were here, she'd tell you. It's going to get worse before it gets better, and you're not going to like it."

"Will it help?" I ask, jaw already tightening.

"I think it will." He's thoughtful. "The panic attacks may never completely go away, but this'll give you the tools to deal with them. Working the sim, and opening up—it's a first step. Tonight, we'll find out what's triggering the panic attacks. Then, bit by bit, we'll build up your coping strategies. You'll face those triggers. You'll acknowledge your fears. They won't go away, but eventually, you learn to deal with the noise in your head. With help, you can get past it."

I nod. I dig into my pocket. "Wait. Don't start. Just a second."

"What is it?" he asks.

I find Auguste's gift. My fingers close around the racing patch. I focus on the feel of the leather and rough threads. The comfort of fearlessness used to live in every stitch. I pretend it's still there. I take a breath before letting go. "It's nothing," I say to Hal. "Go on."

"Okay then," he says. "Ready or not."

He takes the flex card and swipes it onto the nearest sim screen. Let the nightmare begin.

It starts simply enough. Darkness, a scattering of sound—faraway vacs, distant gunfire. First, flashes of bright light, off and on. Then generic feed clips of battles past, mostly bits from the ground during airborne attacks. And still, my pulse is dead calm. I'm still able to respond to Hal's questions, listing my level of anxiety from one to ten.

"You okay?" he asks.

I nod, but a second later, Mary's sim turns up the heat. It's as if it can read me.

Scattered gunfire gives way to teeth-rattling engine thrum and cannon blasts. The wide camera pans morph into first-person angles, and suddenly, I can't push through the curtain of noise and flashing lights. But it's the human sounds that reach me. Sweat-laced breathing and garroted screams.

An alarm pulses, and Hal rechecks my vitals, but even his voice barely anchors me. The final blitz grinds into my skull; the images loop and swim in my vision. It's the ambush and it's not. The familiar sensation of panic presses in . . . a prickling tightness in my chest, a suffocating flash of heat. I try to shake it off. I close my eyes and swallow. But the flickering light of the screens burns into me, like a heartbeat drumming on my skin, and even with my lids shut tight, I can't un-see this. I can't stop the bullet. I can't stem the flow. Cash's blood . . .

I black out. When I come to, Hal's already dragging me out of the pod.

He's talking, but I can't really hear him. He's nothing but static for the longest time. He presses a canteen of water into my hands. I drink. I sip until the noise becomes words.

"Deep breaths," he says, pressing a cool cloth to my forehead. "You with me?"

Still dazed, I manage a nod.

He reaches out, and I give in. Boneless. Tearless. Pried wide open, I hug him tight.

"She was right," I whisper. "I don't like this."

He nods against my cheek, smoothing my hair. "It'll get easier. In time, I promise. This was the hardest part. Now you know."

"Know what?"

"What frightens you the most. Whatever it is," he says. "It's the demon you have to deal with. But the good news is . . ."

Uncertain, I pull back.

Hal meets my eyes. "You won't have to do it alone."

CHAPTER TWENTY-THREE

MIYU COMES THROUGH IN LESS THAN FORTY-EIGHT HOURS, thanks to her hacker contacts. That girlfriend who interns at AltaGen? Turns out, she really does take on some interesting "freelance work."

Almost no one else knows that her real name is Moira, Miyu warns, and I have to swear never to use it. Only her digital alias, *Thumb*. Thumb, as in the rogue leader of the Fist, a rusting powerful limb of the Castran underworld. They've never worked directly with us before, but more than once, they've passed along news. Clips like the one from Benroyal's last press conference, my favorite, in which one splattered fuel pod—tossed against the security glass in the Assembly House—started a glorious riot.

But all this time, I never knew who these hackers actually were. No one did. We knew they were friendlies, and we knew some of their screen names. That's it. And in a million years, I'd have never dreamed they'd have connections to someone like Miyu.

To list the Fist's exploits is to rattle off every flex hacker's Galaxy's All-Time Greatest Hits. Most folks know this crew best for their harmless pranks. How about the day every single corporate ad was replaced by slo-mo clips of the prime minister picking his nose? How it took the Sixers eighteen hours to stop it and nail down the glitch?

Hands down, best Tuesday ever.

But the Fist isn't just empty snark attack. No, they've landed a few bigger jabs too. Last year, when a billion in Castran tax revenue—earmarked for Domestic Patrol stun sticks and riot gear—just up and magically disappeared? Yeah, you can bet the Fist took credit for that. They always tag their work, yet none of them's ever been bagged or doxed.

So as I stand next to Miyu in the war room and look at this face on the feed screen, I'm a little stunned. I lean in, all the better to gawk. Moira—interstellar hacktivist—isn't what you'd expect at all. No bright pink locks or holo-tats undulating up and down her bare arms. Instead, she's got long dark hair, neatly braided. Dark skin, delicately stained lips. White, high-end shirt, sleeveless and understated, blank as an old-fashioned canvas. She's a little older than I am—just a girl sitting tall in a beige-y, sunlit room. And that's when it hits me. Moira could be anyone, anywhere. A young intelligence agent or even a Sixer.

Or a rusting genius.

"Thanks for doing this," Miyu tells her.

I nod. In truth, I'm a little bit awed.

"Sure, why not?" she replies, as if scheming with rebels is all in a day's work. "We started out tapping the hull," Moira explains. When I blink dumbly, she adds, "You know, looking for anything and everything about Benroyal's system. Access points. Any of the nasty little wormholes his security techs might have tried to bury for themselves. And there were plenty of those back entrances for them to get back in, but every time we'd find one and fish out a little encrypted morsel, we'd get bounced out. Or worse, King Charlie's bot-ware would try to follow and ghost in through our own back doors."

"But you got in," I say.

"Yeah, and I think we've got a couple of good leads for you. Funny," she says, and I see Miyu's not the only one with a killer smirk. "It's always the money. Even the most oblique operations have to keep up their balance sheets. We found all the good stuff buried deep in his financials."

I'm not really sure what she means by "oblique," but if

she's using it to describe Benroyal Corp, I'm assuming it means soul-suckingly dishonest. "Where is Cash?"

"I think we've found him. This intel's pretty fresh. Take a look," she says, touching her screen.

Instantly, a data-deck splays out over our table. Miyu and I reach down to swipe the cards apart. Among the text files are several headshots. I don't recognize most of them, but then . . . the last two images. Blankly, Cash stares ahead, avoiding the camera like a criminal hauled in for a mug shot. It's tough to pull my eyes away, but I scan the picture next to his. An old man, the deep laugh lines on his brown-skinned face no longer aglow. Toby Abasi, ashen and dull. Still alive, but barely.

As a chamberman, he'd publicly opposed corporate abuses. He was the last honest politician in Capitoline. Back when I was racing for Benroyal, after I'd discovered his black sap empire, Abasi tried to help me expose him. And naturally, the old man paid for it. He was arrested right before my big win at Sand Ridge. The Sixers tried him for treason, then reported him exiled, although most of us figured he'd been secretly executed.

But he's alive. Add one more to the list of people to rescue.

Finally, my eyes drift to the text files, but at first glance, they don't look like much. Numbers. Credit symbols.

Expense reports? I swipe them aside and turn back to Moira. "Where'd you find the pictures?" I ask. "And what's in the docs?"

"We pulled them from a black box, a triple-encrypted, self-destructive directory. It's a ledger from one of Benroyal's IP accounts. And there are some legitimately weird expenses logged in the past year."

"What'd he invest in?" Miyu asks.

Moira cocks her head, and I read the delight in her face. "A high-rise in Mid-iron. Checked that out, no secret torture cells hidden there. A chain of restaurants in Belaram—which are probably just fronts for his sap dealers—but then something a lot more interesting."

Miyu and I both lean in, then Moira drops the bomb.

"A space station," she says.

"What?" I say.

"Benroyal acquired it right before you signed your circuit contract," Moira says. "May be a coincidence. I mean, who knows how many far-flung storage facilities he's bought over the years. We know he uses lots of places like this to handle all kinds of old stuff. He uses them like off-planet way stations. Smugglers find what he wants, and they hand it off to Benroyal's men, who ship it back to him. The man's completely obsessed with antiques."

"I know," I say. "He keeps a ton of it in the Spire."

"Yeah, but get this: Not long after buying this station, he outlays a huge expense for renovating it—a ridiculous amount of armed personnel, updated security systems, even a few dozen pairs of detention-grade sync boots. And . . . it gets even better." Moira's bubbling over now. It's a little like listening to elegant gunfire. "We snagged a file with station-bound manifests. First, all this new hardware gets space-freighted there, along with a suspiciously long list of IP personnel. Then two days after your big escape? A smaller vac arrives, with even more security, and last but not least, several unnamed passengers. Finally, we stumble onto those images, in a separate file, but tagged with the exact same code name."

"Code name?" I say.

She nods. "The original name of the space station: U.S.S. *Sweetwater.*"

I fight the sick churn that flares in the pit of my stomach. But Moira's still not finished. "So I keep digging and come up with all kinds of data on the station. Used to be a scientific research complex. They studied combustion, alternative energy sources, desalination techniques, you name it. It's big. It's remote. It's old-world. This clunker's been off the books for so long, it's perfect."

I nod. "Perfect for a secret prison."

"Exactly," Moira replies. "But there's a catch."

"What is it?" I ask. "Did they move him?"

Moira shakes her head. "No, I don't think so. I think he's still out there. But trouble is, your prince is millions of light-years away, in a restricted, heavily patrolled, no-fly zone. That space station?" She pauses. "It's orbiting Earth."

Orbiting Earth. The words spin in my head, like bright, faraway stars. The idea that Cash is out there, just beyond our reach, ignites me. My brain's already firing off a wild hail of directives. *We need a ship, and a mission team . . . pull things together, and leave tomorrow. No. Benroyal's soldiers control every gateway into the galaxy. We'd need our own space bridge to get there. Can we build one? How long . . .*

Miyu touches my shoulder. It's as if she can read my mind. I look up and see the soft plead of reason in her eyes. "Phee, even if we could get there . . . you get that close to Earth, and there's nothing but outlaws and IP. They'd shoot you down the second you jumped into orbit, before you even got anywhere close to that station."

"No," I say. I shake my head. "There has to be a way."

Miyu doesn't let go. "There is none. It'd be a suicide mission." Her tone is gentle, but unsparing. The truth in it drop-kicks the fight out of me.

I look back at the screen, as if Moira might have a magic answer, something to bring back even a glimmer of hope. But there's nothing.

"At least now you know where he is," Moira says, pity written all over her face.

I take a moment, to pull myself together. I'm choking up, but I manage to blink away the burn in my lids. "Thank you for finding him. I don't know how I'll ever repay you."

"You already have." Moira waves me off. "There was a lot more data in those files than docs from this little project, a rust-load of stuff we can use on our own. You ever heard of the Declaration of the Rights of Man? The Bill of Rights? The Cyrus Cylinder?"

I'm frozen, but Miyu nods.

"They're ancient documents," Miyu says.

"Benroyal kept some in his gallery," I say. "I saw something called the Magna Carta, but those others? I'm not sure."

"Yeah? I'd always thought they were legends," Moira says. "Bedtime stories for easy marks. But that's the thing. They're not. Benroyal's created his own personal archive, digitized copies of thousands of pre-Castran documents. My sources say they're legit too. And inventory notes? Don't even get me started. King Charlie's up to his eyeballs in priceless artifacts."

"Yeah," I say. "You should see the display cases in the Spire. It's like he's got a private museum."

"Emphasis on the word *private*," Moira says. "Because half his hoard doesn't align with the history we've been taught, and there is so much we can learn from it. It's going to take a while to sift through all this, but what we've found . . . it's looking a whole lot like long-lost treasure."

She's awestruck at the find, but I can't feel the same joy. What good is treasure, unless it saves Cash? Still, I try not to sink her high.

"I'm glad," I tell her. "Hope you can use it."

I look at Miyu. *Chin up,* her expression reads.

"Someday, I'll buy us all a round," Moira says, touching the screen. "Next time, come here and we'll toast: *Girls, here's to the freedom of information.*"

Then the call screen's blank, and it doesn't matter that I can't manage a grin. Moira's already signed off.

After sharing the news at HQ, I meet Hal at flight control to work through Mary's program. I don't pass out this time, but I do get sick afterward. After cleaning up, I head back into the tomb. By my cot, Bear is already waiting for me. I don't let him hold me. We don't even touch. But when he pulls a bed closer to mine, I lie down beside him.

We're both curled on our sides, eye to eye. Yet in the dim of the cavern, I can't see his face. I have only his breath with the soft promise of his voice, and a part of me clings to the familiar sound. I am so used to hearing him unseen through my racing headset. If only there were static and roadway between us. If we could just talk over the noise, we'd be okay. From here, I can almost reach the old connection, muted words and crackle and hiss.

But when Bear speaks, his voice isn't soft. "Hank's making me squadron leader," he says. "It's a good chance to step up. I can lead." His words spiral out like an invitation. *Accept who I've become, and I'll let you in.*

But I hesitate. I open my mouth to tell Bear to be careful . . . to tell him I'm terrified he'll die in the next battle, that I'm scared of losing him, that I'm already losing myself. That I can't call him best friend or brother anymore, because we've started to become something else: two half strangers hurtling toward something so new and foreign and confusing that I don't know whether to run into or away from it.

I open my mouth to tell him I still dream of Cash, and that, even against the odds, I'm not ready to give him up.

But I bite down and eat the sigh that's struggling to slip away. In the dark, I swallow all these words but two. "I'm scared," I say.

"I know," he whispers. He is so still, his whole body unblinking. The invitation still stands.

But I close my eyes and pretend it's not there. I pretend I don't want him at all.

In my dreams, Cash doesn't die. Tonight, he doesn't come at all. I don't relive the ambush. Instead, I dream of the Spire.

I'm alone, looking at pictures and parchment and books. But there are no walls, and all the glass cases are broken.

The words are scattered. They are everywhere.

They fly from the pages and old paper, rising up like a flock of birds, their soft-lettered bodies sweeping the air in a wave of ink-stained static. It's a bat-winged sound, a building, winding, chaos-twisting cry. The flock spirals around me. They cover me. They blot out the Spire and expand, an all-consuming, black-limbed flutter.

A million words hug the empty space and conquer me. I close my lids and listen. Arms wide, I lose myself in the cresting whir. I fall into the noise.

Eyes open. Take a breath. Surrender.

When I wake, for the first time in a long time, I am calm and clearheaded. It's early, and Bear has already left; my eyes drift to his empty cot. But I know now. I know exactly how to fight.

I flex James.

> PV: SENDING YOU AN UPDATED BRIEFING. READ IT. AND I
> NEED YOU TO DO SOMETHING FOR ME.
>
> JA: ???
>
> PV: I NEED SAFE INTERSTELLAR TRANSPORT FOR ME AND A
> MISSION TEAM.
>
> JA: BACK TO CASTRA? YOU'RE INSANE.
>
> PV: NOT TO CASTRA. I NEED TO GET INTO EARTH'S ORBIT.
> SPACE STATION U.S.S. SWEETWATER.
>
> JA: IMPOSSIBLE.
>
> PV: FIND A WAY.
>
> JA: I'LL TRY.
>
> PV: NO TRY. JUST DO IT.
>
> JA: YES, YOUR HIGHNESS.
>
> PV: RUST OFF. AND THANK YOU. TALK LATER.

Then I ask Miyu to arrange a second meeting with Moira. Turns out, I just might need her help again.

CHAPTER TWENTY-FOUR

I HAVE TO GET TO THE WAR ROOM TO TALK TO NANDAN AND the others. And I'm almost there when the battle sirens begin to wail. The bleat's full-on, droning out a red alert. Hank's coming through the doorway. He catches me by the arm.

"They're coming," he says. "I need to go. But you find Hal, and keep him under the hill. You both need to hole up and wait this out."

"If there's a battle, I'm not just going to—"

He gets me by the shoulders, gripping tight. "Bear's already out there, and Hal's lost enough. *You stay away from the line.*"

He lets go, and he's off before I have the chance to affirm the order.

It's just as well. I'd rather not lie to his face.

I do find Hal, but neither of us stays under the hill. We run to tent city and fill our ears with field orders and secondhand news.

A whole armada this time.

A hundred fighters and a uni-carrier.

We're only seventy vacs, even with the latest reinforcements.

We'll never hold the line.

I dash to the airstrip, looking for Bear, but it's too late. He's already up in the air. No good-byes, and I pray he'll be all right. As for me, I've never wished harder to be more useful. All those wasted days in the valley; I could have trained as a soldier. I *will* train, I swear, if we live through this day, even if I'm only infantry.

Larken won't allow Fahra and Miyu to fly, and Nandan needs Hal on the ground to run the infirmary. So we three jump in to help out.

Miyu and I stand at the infirmary pump, filling buckets for Hal. Hands in the water, I close my eyes and send a silent prayer into the spill. *Don't take Bear,* I beg. *Not this time. Not ever, and I swear, next time, the current can have me.*

Back and forth, we dash between the airfield and the infirmary, tending to the wounded. By late afternoon, the skies become one vast, gray, churning cauldron of heat. My ears are so raw, I can hardly hear the thunder anymore, or the scream of missiles. And the hammer fall blasts no longer knock us off our feet. We balance on the aftershocks, nudging our way through our tasks.

Many fighters refuel. Some don't come back at all. There's talk of soldiers, shot down and trapped on the ground. Inside the infirmary, Hal and Fahra hash it out. They're uncertain what to do.

I hand Fahra a tray of instruments. He runs it under the sterilizer. "But we have one more medi-vac," he says.

"No," Hal replies. "The last one's no good. The accelerant's shot." He pauses, shaking his head. "All those pilots down. Still alive, but no way to get off the battlefield. No one can get through to the line."

"Then we'll just have to get there on the ground," I interrupt.

"How?" Hal says. "We can't just hike up and pick through the crypts. It'd take us hours to make that climb, and we'd probably get blasted to bits before we even made it into the valley."

"No," Fahra says. "There is a road. Just north of here. Up and around, it follows the stream. If it is clear, we can take it."

"Hal, you gather whatever supplies you think we'll

need to take to the line," I say. "We're going to get those survivors. Captain Fahra, Miyu's back at the pump. Let her know what the plan is. Meet me back here in ten minutes."

"And you?" the captain asks.

"Me?" I say. "I'm gonna find us a rig."

I have to lie. I tell Belach, the quartermaster, that we need a vehicle for . . . ugh, we need it for moving stuff. Yes, yes, he agrees. He shoos me off with an ignition code.

I pick the biggest set of wheels in the yard, an armored Nightcrawler, which, if I have anything to do with it, isn't going be doing much crawling tonight. I climb up into the cab and settle into the driver's seat. Just one problem.

My feet don't reach the pedals.

I punch in the ignition code and look for the seat controls. Fully adjustable, my exhaust. They are, if you're a seven-foot Cyanese man. I crank myself closer, as far as I can. When I get to the infirmary, I'll have to find a sheet or ten to roll up and wedge behind me. But what this beast lacks in comfort, it repays in tech. The engine systems are whisper quiet; no chugging roar, which is what I'd expected. And in "ghost" mode, the windshield morphs into full-on, night vision flex glass. Without the least hint of light, I can see every bent blade of grass. Even better, the auto-cloaking system renders this thing undetectable from the air. The additional heat signature detection grid? Just a nice bonus.

Time to roll. One hand on the wheel and one on the console, I kick this monster into gear.

Carefully, I skirt the airstrip and make my way back to our impromptu rally point. Hal, Miyu, Captain Fahra—they're all waiting for me. When I mumble something about grabbing sheets to stuff behind me, Fahra takes one look at my seat and tells me to quit sitting on the edge. I slide back and he reaches over to examine the controls. Turns out I found the seat adjustment all right, but missed the *pedal* controls. One touch and the whole floor panel extends to meet me. With both ends maxed out, it's not a bad fit.

"This is better?" he asks.

"Much better."

"I think . . ." He smiles, then hops back down. ". . . They hadn't bargained so much on a little *gan-gan* like you."

I share his grin, and we help Hal and Miyu load the back end. Hal slides in the last two stretchers and then we're a go. Slowly, we bump our way out of tent city, then pedal to the floor as I sprint for the road.

I can hear it. We're getting closer. The battle's not so far away now. I glance up, where the fighters sweep the gloom. My place isn't up there, in a vac. It's always been here, racing on the ground.

"Watch the tree line," Fahra says. "The road's just beyond them. Sharp curve ahead."

And he's right. The narrow lane—which is barely more than a shepherd's track—zigzags a lot to compensate for the tough grade around the hill. We make it halfway around, just shy of the valley, when Captain Nandan's voice crackles through the Nightcrawler's com.

"What in the name of Bisera do you think you're doing?" he yells.

I cringe. "Sir, with all due respect, we are heading for the line to pick up the wounded."

"No, you're not. The valley's crawling with ground readers and fallen IP. You turn around, right now, get back down here."

I start to argue, but Hal leans between Fahra and me. "Copy that, Captain," he says calmly. "But I'm afraid we're going to have to disregard those orders."

"Listen here, Larssen," Nandan roars. "I'm not having some of my best auxiliaries stranded out there. And we cannot afford Phee getting captured."

I risk a glance at Hal, keeping one eye on the narrow road. The look on his face, it's like seeing him for the first time. Resolute, he looks to Fahra and Miyu.

"We need you, Hal," Nandan says.

Finally, Hal answers. "Yes, Captain. You do need us. And that's why we're here. And if I don't see you at fallback, it's been a pleasure to serve under your command."

Then Hal swipes the volume down on Nandan's pleading. We tune it out, like it's just another roll of thunder.

Even with night vision, it's hard to make out much once we reach the edge of the valley. The air's thick with flash fire and smoke; it takes a second to get our bearings on the downhill. Can't get around the fog, so I gamble on speed to get through it. Teeth gritted, heart pounding, I keep the throttle open. At last, when the terrain levels out, we pothole, then skid, then grind to a stop.

"Visibility's still for sap," I say.

"How will we find them?" Miyu asks.

"Power down," Hal replies. "And I'll show you."

In the hold of the rig, Hal first passes the packs, one for each of us to shoulder. Then he tosses me a bio-scanner. Miyu gets one too. I reach to pocket it, but Hal stops me. "The side screen. Swipe it from 'diagnostic' mode to 'trace signature,'" he says. "And lock it to 'quiet' mode too. We don't know who's out there."

We obey.

"Miyu, you come with me. And Fahra, you go with

Phee," Hal says. "The bio-scanners will ping once when they detect any vitals signature within a hundred-meter radius. The closer you get, the more they'll sound off. If you sense enemy movement, silence and take cover."

When we nod in agreement, he adds, "And if we're going to do this, we're going to do it right. You all wear your masks, and keep your lenses clear. We flex each other if there's trouble. We don't leave anyone behind. Captain Fahra, I've got a pulse gun, and there's another in your pack. Watch out for ground readers; you may need it."

Overhead, another missile meets its target, and the impact shreds the air. Less than a mile east, if I had to guess. Air to ground impact. Another fighter down. A second later, the aftershocks. For a moment, the Nightcrawler quakes. A different tremor moves through me; the sense of doom hits like a tidal wave. In vain, I close my eyes and will it to pass.

We jump out and close the hold behind us.

"Ready?" Hal asks.

"Affirmative," I say.

Hal secures his gun and slings his pack over his shoulders. "Then rendezvous in thirty minutes or less. If you find wounded, get them back here as fast as you can. Stick to our side of the lowlands." He squints into the acrid fog of the eastern sky, where the battle's raging most hot. "Stay west of the old armory. I mean it." He looks at me. "Promise me."

"I promise."

Satisfied, he pulls on his mask. He and Miyu lope off into the darkness.

CHAPTER TWENTY-FIVE

"I'LL LEAD?" FAHRA ASKS, RIGHT HAND ON HIS GUN. A NICE compact pulse revolver.

"Yeah."

We both pull on the masks Hal packed for us. They're snug and uncomfortable, but we'll need the lenses and re-breathers. We take a second to blink and adjust to the claustrophobic view. *"Ay-khan save us,"* Fahra swears quietly, eyeing the endless wreckage.

Ay-khan. The Evening Star. I look up, but it's hidden. I look down at the valley, which is now completely unrecognizable.

It's the first time I've been here since Benroyal's initial attack. The ground, which was once a soft carpet of green grass and poppy-rich silt, is now black and scabrous. Above, pulse and magma fire burst in random, lightning-flash twitches, and it's as if we've stumbled into an apocalypse, into the boneyard under hell's strobe.

I feel a fresh stab of fear, and I can't help but reach for my ribs. Don't know if I'm holding something in, or checking to make sure we're still here, and not already blown apart.

Hoarse breathing and careful steps. Meter by meter, we creep out. No traces of life for what seems like hours. But in the dark, I catch hints of death. A smoking heap of a vac, or the dead-eyed stare of a tumbled corpse, still buckled in or slid under billowing silk, the charred failure of an ejection chute. I force my eyes to glide over the bodies, rebel and IP alike. I'm completely clenched up, braced against the waves of panic. The terror crests as I check the faces of the dead. Every step in the dark seems to steal a little more of my resolve. Rasping, I wade through the gloom. I'm clammy and shaking and gutsick, but I make myself move.

Fahra's whisper pulls me back from the edge, and I latch on to his prayers. *Ay-khan. Ay-khan.* I mouth the words with him. *Sibat, listen and save us.*

I say it and say it until my focus slips within reach. I imagine Mary's face, and feel her hand on my shoulder. She is with me, and I am here in the dark, to serve as she would. There's work to be done; I must borrow her courage.

We press on. Soon I hear the first ping, and within moments, we find two wounded. A man and a woman, both rebels. But a quick roll of the bio-scanner tells me only the woman will live. A wrist and ankle broken, and maybe a punctured lung, but we get an auto-vent on her and prepare to carry her out.

Her copilot's babbling, but it's only shock. Doesn't know his guts are gone and he's bleeding out. I can barely stand to look. There's nothing to be done—all we can give him is compassion and soft words. While Fahra soothes the soldier, I work quickly on the woman. I'm glad she's too weak and out of it to notice her companion's not going to make it. When he's gone, we carry her back, where Miyu's waiting with two more injured rebels. I show her how to sedate them, just enough to keep them stretchered and still. I've never been more glad for Mary's careful training.

"You stay here, while we go back out?" I ask Miyu.

She nods. "Go ahead. Hal asked me to stay with the wounded. He went back out. He'll flex if he finds more."

"Okay," I reply. Fahra and I go after him. On the way, the bio-scanner sounds off again. This time, a chute-tangled IP officer, wailing in pain. One look at both his broken legs and I know the landing could've been better. The second he sees our approach, in a flinch, he reaches for the headset that's gone, then for whatever was once at his hip. The movement plays out on his face like the worst kind of agony.

"Easy now," I say, sinking into a crouch. "Nobody's here to hurt you."

He doesn't look like he believes me. Fahra pulls out his dagger to cut him loose.

"Be still," he orders the soldier. "Or I'll cut you instead of the cords."

The officer nods.

Fahra kneels beside me and we cleave the IP from his chute. As I pull away the last knots, my eyes meet the enemy's. He is so young. "No sides down here, okay?" I say it to him, but also to Fahra, who's looking cautious. But he doesn't argue.

Instead, more gently than the officer probably deserves, Fahra scoops him up and carries him back. But not before I dig into my supplies. I palm a loaded needle and knock the bastard out.

"Merciful," Fahra says, eyebrows raised in approval. "But wise."

"Maybe he has intel," I say to Fahra. "Or we can use him to bargain for our wounded."

He doesn't bother with an answer. He knows the truth as well as I do. I see it in his eyes. Benroyal will not show mercy. There will be no bargaining. But Fahra obeys. He humors me.

As we drop off our injured at the medic-station-slash-rig, my flex buzzes. It's Hal.

HL: HURRY. BY THE OLD ARMORY. I'M GETTING A STEADY READING, BUT I CAN'T GET TO HIM.

I fumble to reply.

PV: WHO?

HL: I DON'T KNOW. CRASH-LANDED TANDAEMO. SURVIVOR, BUT I CAN'T GET IN. NEED FAHRA NOW.

The captain and I take off running. We make it to the rubble of the old mess hall, nearly a thousand meters out, when I hear the wind-whistle rush of the ground readers Hal warned us about. Drones. Flying disks just big enough to put your arms around, that zoom at eye level. Only you wouldn't want to put your arms around them, since they scan for heartbeats, then alert all networked enemy vacs where to land their next missile.

You see them, you run.

I see three, and I bolt. I look behind me.

Not Fahra. He's rooted in place.

He seems to move so slowly, and I'm just about to scream when he finally raises his weapon. Not a split second too soon.

Crack. Clunk. Boom.

Pistol shot. One reader, easily dispatched.

Two more come at him, but this time, he's twice as fast. Before I can blink, Fahra dispatches the remaining pair . . . one shot, then pivot. Fire. Again. Three shots, and they're down. No more whistling in the dark, only the sizzle of burning circuits.

"Nice," I tell Fahra, rounding back and catching my breath.

He opens his mouth, as if to rattle off one of his witty replies, but seems to think better of it. "A hundred more meters" is all I get. We start moving again.

Soon, we lock onto Hal's signal. He's wasn't kidding. There's a great hulking Cyanese bird in our path, tail scorched and yet well-landed, a silver-crowned barden half visible on its sunken hull. The image is a Cyanese fighter symbol, just like the one painted on . . .

Talon One.

"It could be Bear," I say, frantic.

"I know," Hal says, equally panicked. "Help me open the door!"

The windshield's covered in ash and mud, and the rear pilot's hatch is jammed shut. Hal wrestles with it, probably for the hundredth time, but no luck.

"Stand back," Fahra says. We comply.

But when he sees the pistol, Hal nearly bugs out. "Be careful. Don't hit the fuel cells or the core."

"Yes, yes. I know. Stand back."

So we do. Fahra blasts six bolts off the twisted hinges. Under his aim, one by one, they break. By now I know our captain makes no mistakes.

After the dust settles, we three fly at the hatch, Hal and Fahra pulling hardest. Just when I'm sure the door will never give, it groans and snaps out of its fire-blasted perch.

"Back!" Fahra shouts, and we barely clear the fall. The door thuds to the ground and, breathless, I scramble over it, into the guts of the wounded bird. Inside, it's hot and the emergency lights are dead. I feel my way through by chasing the hazy glow of the windshield. The ping of the scanner quickens.

I reach the com seats, where the light's just enough. The copilot's dead, and I shouldn't thank the stars, but I do; because it's a Cyanese man, and not Zaide, Bear's partner. And the pilot's alive. I hear the low-grade wheeze of his breath. I lean in for a better look and see he's unconscious, but alive.

"Survivors?" Hal yells.

"The pilot. He's still alive," I shout back. "It's Larken."

CHAPTER TWENTY-SIX

LARKEN'S THE TOUGHEST PATIENT TO HAUL. HE'S IMPOSSIBLY tall, and it takes all of us to get him into the back of the rig. There, we lay him out, check his vitals, and get him hooked up to a med-monitor before we go back for more. When all is said and done, we've filled the back of the Nightcrawler. Six rebels recovered, and two IP prisoners. Not bad for ninety minutes' work.

After the patients are loaded, I climb back into the driver's seat and buckle in. This time, Hal takes the seat beside me. "I'm game for another trip," I tell him. "If you think we can get back before—"

I stop, silenced by the magma-hot flash in the sky. An explosive blast ripples through the air; it's a wild scream of artillery fire and scorched metal.

"Holy Star of Bisera," Fahra says, ducking into the rig. "Their biggest bird."

I jump out to catch a glimpse. Overhead, we watch the enemy's uni-carrier. This big black beast is their mother ship, and its underbelly has been breached.

I blink, and suddenly, two of our fighters sweep underneath it, gunning again. Another volley of rebel fire, seeded into the wounded carrier's guts. Another white-hot roar, and this time, a fatal hit. At last, the whole monster's lit up and dying.

Blazing, it lurches in the sky, dipping below the highest curtain of smoke.

"Phee," Miyu calls out.

"Get back in the rig," Fahra yells. "Now!"

He's right. We are way too close to this thing. Doesn't matter if the ship's not right on top of us. When it lands, we're all going to feel it.

I jump into the driver's seat. Fahra and I scramble to buckle back in.

"All those stretchers locked in tight?" I ask.

"Strapped down and swaddled," Miyu answers. "I used every pressure cushion we had."

"Better hold on tight," I warn, snapping into gear. We spit up gravel and haul exhaust like there's no tomorrow and never was. I need to get us farther northwest. Out of that battle ship's wake. This pebbled track won't get us there fast enough, so I slide off-road. Running as hard as the Nightcrawler can go, I angle up and cut through the smoothest path of terrain I can find.

Not smooth enough. I pray we don't lose any wounded. Bounce. Skid. Turn.

That beast's gonna hit the ground any second. I rip back onto the road and hit a long stretch of straightaway. The vac's behind us, but we still have to watch out for after-shocks and flaming debris.

"It's coming," Fahra warns. "Brace for impact."

"Masks on!" Hal screams, putting his on.

I'm driving, so Hal helps with mine. I duck into it, and just in time too.

BOOM.

The shockwave comes, and our windshield shatters. High-grade, speed-tempered, armored glass. Smashed to bits. Already it's coming down like molten rain. Around us, beside us. Bits and pieces of the ruined ship. A huge hunk of smoking metal, dropped right in our path.

"Watch out!" Miyu says, but I'm already on it. Swerve. Swing back, and we're still alive.

My knuckles are bleeding, and my lenses are too foggy to see through. After the quake settles, I swipe on the Night-crawler's headlights. Forget ghost mode. Every muscle in my body clenches up, attuned to one fixed point on the fractured nav screen. Just get back. Just make it back. Just get back alive.

An eternity later, we pull into camp. The next few minutes are chaos.

By the infirmary, I rush out of the cab and check out our hold.

One patient gone. The pilot with the punctured lung. I curse myself for driving too hard and not saving her life. But Fahra will have none of it. "The rest are alive because of you," he insists.

A horde of personnel heads our way. The medics sweep past us, to tend to the wounded. Captain Nandan pushes through them. Ignoring me, he's all over Hal. "You disobeyed a direct command. Hank ordered you. I ordered you."

I move between them. "He brought your soldiers home."

"You?" He shakes a finger in my face. "You're lucky—"

Defiant, I straighten under his glare. "You're lucky we found Larken. He's still alive, thanks to us."

That gets his attention. He pauses. "See to it that Commander Larken—and the rest of your charges—are afforded proper care. Then restrict yourself to the infirmary and the tomb, until you are ordered otherwise. I'll let Lieutenant Commander Kinsey and Lieutenant Larssen know you're all right."

"Yes, sir."

"Good night, Van Zant." Stiffly, he starts to turn away, but pauses. "And thank you."

I salute. Silent, he returns it.

We've made it just in time to welcome back the last of the rebel fighters—or, at least, the stalwart few who survived the nightmare barrage. Seventy fighters flew out, and less than half that number have returned. For now, the battle's over. Against all odds, somehow, we held the line and turned away what's left of Benroyal's first armada. But they'll be back. And next time, Benroyal will send five hundred ships. A thousand. Whatever it takes to finish the job. I can't help but wonder: How soon?

I wait at the airstrip and watch the vacs coast in. At last, I see Talon One and Broadsword.

Hank approaches first, looking beat-up. Not surprising, seeing how his fighter's got more patches of blast residue than a wendel has fleas. Behind him limps Bear, whose own Tandaemo vac looks even worse. He and Zaide pull off their helmets and meet for a victor's embrace.

I am grateful to her for flying at his wing and keeping watch over him. Yet a part of me envies her too. I know they're just friends, but I miss being the one he relies on.

"Live another day, brother," she says, and they break apart.

Finally, he sees me.

Bear's eyes tell me he's too tired to run, but I can't get there fast enough, and neither can Hal. He hugs Hal first, and then me. I look up; Bear's face is lit with pride. "Hank and I brought her down," he says. "The uni-carrier. Sent six magma charges right up her exhaust."

"Well done," Hal says. "Mom would be proud."

Bear nods. Another hug and a moment of quiet between them.

"I have to see to our injured," Hal says. He wipes the tears and sweat from his eyes. "But you're not off the hook, son. I want you checked out as well. Meet me in the infirmary."

"I will," Bear replies.

Hal leaves, and we're finally alone, face-to-face, right under the nose of Bear's scorch-marked fighter. He looks down at me.

"We won," I say.

He sighs. "For now."

"Don't think about that. C'mon. Let's get cleaned up. You stink."

"That right?" he says, shoving his pit in my face.

I jerk away from him. "I'm not kidding. You reek like the wrong end of a groat."

"And what . . . you smell like sun-kissed poppies right now?"

"Of course." I shrug.

"More like sweat and engine degreaser."

He sidles and bumps me off balance. I return the favor.

Together, we walk all the way to the infirmary.

CHAPTER TWENTY-SEVEN

AFTER THE BATTLE, I CAN'T SLEEP.

It's four a.m. The war room's packed and everyone's going full tilt. Like me, they're too on edge to slow down. There will be no catching our breath. Not tonight. Maybe not ever again.

I slip next to Hank, who's leaning over the surface of the command table, which is now littered with flex screens and auxiliary parts.

"It's over, Phee," he says to me, without looking up. "Back home, Prime Minister Prejean has already made the announcement."

"What announcement?"

"Queen Napoor is finally abdicating the throne. And of course, Benroyal—Castra's 'humble servant of the people' and 'loyal diplomat'—negotiated the whole accord. Dak is to become king, and Bisera is to be annexed and occupied."

"No," I snap. "She can't just hand everything over. She wouldn't."

Hank sighs. "I'm sure she has no choice. For her, I figure the deal's the same old bargain: Cash's life for her kingdom."

"Then we'll stop him, with Cyan's help. They're not just going to stand around while he—"

"The enemy's already offered a cease-fire. They're asking for a cooling-off period, then formal negotiations with Cyan."

"That makes no sense," I answer. "Benroyal started this. He's the one who—"

"These attacks," Hank answers. "They were nothing. This was a test. To draw out the Cyanese and see where they stand. And it worked. Benroyal has everything he needs now, and all it cost him was two quick strikes."

"So he knows where they stand. They stand with us. So it seems to me, if anything, he just bought himself a whole heap of trouble by messing with Cyan."

Hank rubs his forehead, then casts me a sidelong look. Like he's not sure if I'm naive or just plain crazy. "You think Cyan'll stay in the Strand and back us forever? With Larken, our strongest ally, laid out and unconscious?"

"Well, they aren't just going to lie down and roll over, are they? Benroyal struck first, Hank. He hit them on their own holy ground."

"That's my point, Phee. Benroyal just sent a message: The rules have changed. *There are no rules anymore. There is no holy ground.* And you'd better believe that Cyan got that message. There's already chatter coming in from Raupang. Even among the officers here, there's talk of Cyan getting out while they still can."

"But what about—"

"What about nothing," Hank interrupts. "Cyan's gotten a real taste of war, and no one's eager to finish the meal. They know if they don't come to terms, that next time, Benroyal will send ten times the force. And without Larken to convince the Skal otherwise, all those seven-foot soldiers . . . they'll just go back home and write off the rest of us. No one wants another Thirty Years' War."

I manage one frustrated sigh before Hank cuts me off again. "If we don't pull off some kind of miracle, it's all over for Cash. And not just for him. For Bisera and for Castra too."

"Never. It's not over. We can still fight."

"Who's going to fight?" he barks. "I'm telling you, Cyan *will* sign a treaty with Castra, and then—"

"Cash's people won't stand for this either."

"They will, if an entire IP army rolls in to crack down and make them."

I shake my head, but Hank keeps dropping the hammer. "Prince Dak's already planning the celebration. A jubilee coronation. He's to take his father's throne, on the anniversary of the old king's death. In three weeks, the annexation will be signed. Then Benroyal won't need any trade agreements to secure his hold on the Gap. Once he's got his own puppet king, even the Cyanese won't be able to stop him from sweeping in and taking everything else. Castra. Cyan. Bisera. Soon it will all belong to him."

I stare at Hank and watch him fold in on himself. The defiant edge in his voice, the spark in his eyes—it's all hissing out like a crushed ember. His shoulders slump and he leans over the table. "Know what's worst of all, Phee?" he asks. "Everything all those rebels died for—it's all been for nothing."

Mary, and so many more. I close my eyes and see their faces . . . their lives . . . this cannot be in vain.

"Hank," I plead. "Don't give up. Please don't give up on us."

He picks up a broken micro-server. Pulls out the guts and toys with it, like he can't even hear me. When I open my mouth to try again, he shrugs me off with one last, bitter sideways glance. "Better take a good look, Phee. Everyone who's left to fight—they're all sitting in this room."

I leave the table and find a quieter corner to confirm everything Hank said. And it's all there on the Castran feeds. On a small screen, I nose through a few of them. Not only are there press conferences with the prime minister and statements from Prince Dak, but something else, that leaves me twice as furious.

An interview with Benroyal.

The broadcast starts out harmless enough. Benroyal's lounging in a wicker chair in a garden. Not a fancy artificial one. A real, sprouts-at-his-feet, root-vegetable garden. There are dunes in the background, and King Charlie's not even wearing a jacket or tie. And I have never—not ever—seen him in anything but a sharply tailored, outrageously expensive-looking suit.

But now he's propped in the old chair with homespun sleeves rolled up, like he's a rusting produce farmer. Like anyone's going to buy that image.

But maybe all of Castra already has. After all, they all believe I'm a stone-cold killer.

The interviewer—a slim, focus-group-approved blonde—flies through the script of pre-approved questions. And he answers like the patient and loving father we all wish we had.

"In the past, journalists have focused primarily on your

corporate work," the interviewer says. "Your stature on the Corporate Exchange. Your innovative labor policies. Over the past decade, your very own mark on so many winning circuit rigs. But I have to ask: Is this the work you're most proud of?"

He shakes his head. "Absolutely not, Lara. If you want to know the truth, that's never been my primary focus. It's funny. You mention the Corporate Exchange, and that's not really where my heart is at all."

Like an award-winning actor, he glances at the camera, half bashful. "I'm most proud of—and more interested in—developing products and supporting initiatives that make the galaxy . . . *smaller.*"

"You mean, transportation or fuel technologies?"

"No, I mean my work in the peace-keeping industry. Our Interstellar Patrol . . . the way my company has been able to equip these men and women with life-saving armor and tools, and the speed with which we've been able to deploy these resources in areas of disaster and crisis. Nothing makes me prouder than watching one of our soldiers lift up an orphaned child or take down a terrorist threat. It's a dangerous universe out there, but with the work we're doing—diplomatically, and with honor—we're making it a better, more interconnected place. Not just for Castrans, but for all interstellar citizens."

The feed cuts to a montage of Benroyal Corp's latest "good works." A clean, well-lit lab where Biseran employees smile while quality checking refined fuel sap. A robotics factory where laser-eyed automatons test blast-proof IP exo-suits. In Capitoline, a fresh crop of Domestic Patrol recruits paint over south sider holo-graffiti. The would-be enforcers erase a crude caricature of Castra's most wanted, Phoenix Vanguard, the girl with a sneer on her lips and a gun in each hand. The real me and the imaginary one—both of us are spectators. Silent. Powerless against Benroyal's gleaming lies.

"It's an admirable dream, Mr. Benroyal," Lara says as the feed cuts back.

Again, he glances at the camera. His smile oozes false humility. "It's more than a dream. At least if I have anything to say about it. A lasting peace. Finally, it's within our reach."

I curse, my hands clawed at the edges of the screen. It's as if he's stolen Cash's vision and twisted it into some smiling, nightmare alternative.

"It's not hard to marvel at the prospect of annexation," Lara replies. "Prime Minister Prejean calls it a 'triumph of patient diplomacy,' and he hails this as, well . . . primarily, your personal achievement. Would you agree? Any regrets?"

"I can hardly take credit." He waves her off. "The nego-tiations were straightforward, and Queen Napoor is a rea-sonable monarch who cares as deeply about peace as I do. As for regrets . . ." He stops to rub his jaw, as if it pains him to bring this up. "I would say my only regret is losing Phoenix Vanguard."

My blood boils. At last, some truth.

Lara's pretty good at acting taken aback. "Vanguard? You mean you regret not bringing her to justice?"

"No," he says. This time, the camera zooms in, and I can't stand the way he seems to search me out. "I regret not being able to save her."

"Save her?"

He nods. "You have to remember, I discovered this young woman myself. She was an orphan—living in a ter-rible situation, mind you. And in a way . . . you see, Phoe-nix Vanguard was like a daughter to me. And I know if I'd taken more care and watched more closely, I would've realized much sooner . . . that she was unstable."

"Unstable?" Lara repeats.

Benroyal nods again. "Yes. In this case, we're talking about a troubled young woman who became drawn to the worst sort—terrorists who recruited, brainwashed, and exploited her." He touches his forehead. He seems so con-trite. So very earnest. Then he looks back up. "This is a girl who had so much potential, but in the end, her choices led her down a terrible, tragic path. Even now, when I think about it . . . it's heartbreaking."

"Heartbreaking?" she asks, because apparently, she's incapable of doing anything but parroting back his answers.

"Yes," he says sadly.

"That's a generous assessment, Mr. Benroyal," Lara responds. "But I doubt very many in our audience would share your compassion. And of course, you've spoken with our own Prime Minister Prejean. Unlike you, he has no soft words for Vanguard." Her eyes flick to the left, and I can't tell if she's scanning or avoiding an unseen prompter. "More than once, when asked about the skyrocketing bounty on her head, Prejean's answered, 'better dead than alive . . .'"

When Benroyal pretends dismay, she adds, "You don't agree? Tell us. You'd rather see Phoenix Vanguard brought back home?"

He doesn't answer quickly enough, so she drones on. She's pressing a little too hard; it's almost as if she's going off script. "You mentioned instability. As in mental illness? Are you implying you'd like to see her cared for in a suitable facility?"

For one fleeting half second, his eyes flash cold, his gaze as unforgiving as an ice-water plunge. This one moment is the only thing real the audience is going to get. Quickly, he sits back and folds his hands, a picture of humble serenity. "Oh no. I fear it's too late for that," he says at last. "I'm afraid Phoenix Vanguard is a lost cause, and justice must prevail. *She will have to be dealt with.*"

CHAPTER TWENTY-EIGHT

SHAKEN, I VISIT THE INFIRMARY. I ASK TO VISIT'S LARKEN'S bedside, and Hal takes me to see him. Lying there, so pale and still, he looks like he's just been defrosted. As if at any moment, the color will rush back to his cheeks, and he'll wake up.

"Head trauma," Hal says. "The swelling on the brain's going down, but he hasn't come around yet."

"The anti-gel?" I ask. "It hasn't helped?"

"It has. But our supply's nearly gone. Vilette's flying more in for him, and bringing a team of specialists. They'll arrive soon to decide if he's to be moved to Raupang."

"But he'll be okay?"

"We can hope," Hal says.

I nod, even though hope isn't good enough right now.

You can whisper prayers into the current and beg the stars to look down in mercy, and sometimes, they'll give you a glimmer of it, maybe even a ray of luck. But when they don't, you have to get up off your exhaust and make your own spark. Fate be damned. I'm ready to light things up. Win or lose, I'm prepared to go down fighting.

I stand up. I look at Hal. "I have to go. I've got to take care of something."

"What is it?"

"I need to set up a meeting," I answer, but I'm already walking away. "I'll see you after dinner, at shift change."

"What about our appointment?" he calls. "You still need to keeping working Mary's sim."

"I know. I haven't forgotten," I say over my shoulder. "Tonight, I promise I'll be there."

Outside the infirmary, I look to the skies. It's like I'm dragged back in time, to the day Miyu first flew our way. Again, two vacs in the air, staggered in arrival. One cruising in from the west, and one from the east. The first, a larger medi-vac, is surely Vilette with her team of specialists from Raupang. But the second doesn't look Cyanese at all, more like a small bootlegger's bird, the kind of vac you'd see parked in a launch yard on the wrong side of Manjor.

A jolt of unease roils in my gut, but I strangle the instinct to bolt. I'm able to talk myself down, and that's progress, I guess. Or maybe my brain knows things have finally gotten so bad, they can't get any worse.

Without fanfare, the first vac lands, and sure enough, it's the doctors. Hal and his infirmary crew rush out to meet them. The second aircraft makes its final approach, and all of camp sits up and takes notice.

No sirens, but the on-duty rebels move in, alert and at attention. I can only guess why they let this bird land. Seems a miracle they didn't turn it back, or blow it out of the sky. The pilot must have some kind of high-level clearance. More soldiers trickle onto the yard, and we gather, cautious. We're all itching to know who'd dare cross the border now, in the wake of a cease-fire.

Captain Nandan and his aide—a wiry young lieutenant—march out of the tomb and onto the airstrip, ready to meet the ship. The bay doors of the vac open, and the lone passenger steps out.

It's James.

Nandan steps in his path, but my uncle strolls right past him. An "Apologies, Captain, would you excuse me a moment?" is all our commanding officer gets. Coolly, and oh so casually, James blows past the rest of his aides. It's a move not even I'd have the bolts to play.

The soldiers trail James as he reaches me. "Hello, Phee," he says, like he's fully prepared for a mouthful of sass and a pair of crossed arms. And the girl who last saw him is ready to give it to him. But the one who's standing here now?

I tackle him in a lock-tight hug. "You're okay?"

He nods.

"Then what are you doing here?" I ask. "What happened to skulking in the underground lair?"

"You didn't expect me to skulk forever, did you? Not with this 'new era of peace' rolling in. Naturally, in light of recent events, I thought it'd best to clear out, while I still could." He glances around. "But if you ask me, it doesn't look so well here either."

I don't tell him he doesn't look so great himself, what with his whiskery jaw and rumpled shirt. I should probably be worried about what that might mean, but the broken-down spitfire in me is relieved I'm not the only one completely undone. We're all on the same slippery edge. And if we're falling, we might as well tumble together.

"Yeah," I answer. "We've seen better days."

Captain Nandan interrupts our not-quite-happy reunion. At his nod, his aides take a step back.

"Welcome to base, Mr. Anderssen," Nandan says, sounding slightly annoyed. I'm starting to think that's his default.

"We've prepared accommodations, at your request. I trust your flight was uneventful?"

I raise an eyebrow at James. "Hold on here. He knows you're coming, but you left me in the dark?"

He shrugs. "What can I say? Things were a bit . . . rushed."

Nandan clears his throat, to catch my eye. "I'm sure you won't mind if we have a quick word with your uncle, inside headquarters."

"Yes, of course." James steps back, to let them lead him away for debriefing.

"Wait," I say, catching his arm. "Did you come with good news? Did you get what I asked for?"

"That depends." Weary, haggard, yet still sly, he winks. "How do you feel about zero-g space travel?"

The next morning, I check in with Moira in the war room, to confirm everything's ready on her end. She'll be linking up with us virtually, using an avatar on her screen. We have a plan. Now it's time to share it. I meet with James, who talks me through the scheme we'll have to run to rescue Cash. Then I gather everyone else. We'll need to recruit as many people as we can for the final gambit.

I haven't been able to find Bear all day, and now his absence leaves me feeling strangely untethered. Tonight, more than anyone else's, I want to see his face in the crowd.

I flex him one last time.

PV: NEED YOU TONIGHT.

No answer.

"Everyone's here," Hank says.

I look up. The room's too quiet, and as I scan it, I'm gutted by the looks on so many faces. The hopeful spark of rebellion's gone, and frozen in their expressions, I catch something worse than fear. Everyone here—they've already slid past panic. Now all that's left is resignation.

I'm nothing but sweat and sick knots pulled too tightly. Reluctantly, I begin. "I've asked you all here tonight because I still believe there's a chance that we can . . ." I trail off, paralyzed by the weary stares. "I know you've been through battle after battle, and you've fought so hard. I want you to know . . . you have a choice. No one's holding anyone hostage here. You're all free to stay or to go."

I brace for a wave of resistance—sarcasm, indignation, anything—but it never comes. Another beat of stillness. Thank the stars, Fahra rescues me.

"Well, I am not leaving," Fahra says, crossing his arms. Fierce as ever, he looks over us all, as if rooting out unbelievers. "I stand with you."

"Hear, hear," Zaide says quietly. She steps forward. I'm grateful for her courage. She nods, as if sending some my way. Thankful, I accept and turn back to the crowd.

"If you decide to stay . . ." I take a deep breath. I dig deep, curling my toes in my boots. "I'm not here to peddle false hope. But I'd like to talk about what we can actually *do* to turn things around. Before it's too late."

"Haven't you heard the news?" comes a voice from the back. It's Nandan's quartermaster, Belach. At his word, a whisper of life—the smallest murmur of uncertainty—moves through the room. "It's already too late."

Fahra curses under his breath, and I can tell he'd like to share a few more choice words with Belach, but I shoot him a quick glance and a shake of the head.

Hal puts a hand on my shoulder, and I take the cue. I drop two hands on the table to nail down everyone's attention. I have to rekindle the fire. I have to. "Maybe he's right," I say. "Maybe I'm wrong, and it *is* too late. Maybe all that's left to do is to watch while Benroyal snatches up the last bits of our worlds. There's probably still time. You could pack up and hitch a ride to Raupang." Slowly, I turn to meet each pair of eyes. "You could do that. There's no shame in survival."

No one answers. Instead, all around me, the pilots and cooks and medics and builders look to one another. In the quiet glances, I still catch uncertainty, but gradually, something else begins to bloom: a silent, steadfast promise, built on the bonds forged right here, in the Strand. We are no longer just Castran, and Biseran, and Cyanese, looking out for our own. After all we've been through . . .

We are family. All of us.

Now, in this moment, so many faces wear the same pledge: *I will go where you go. You are my people. You're all I have left.*

I meet their eyes. I say it out loud. "We are more than rebels. We are brothers and sisters—not by blood, but by choice. And if it's all the same to you, I'd rather fall at your side than live to see King Charlie take what's left. We have one last shot to rescue Cash and take down Benroyal. So if you're game for one more fight, stay and listen. Otherwise, you're free to go."

My heart beats in my ears.

But no one makes a move, not even Belach. I'm shocked when he finally uncrosses his arms. Along with everyone else, he's cast his lot. We are in this together.

"All right then," I say, straightening up. "Let's talk about the war we can actually win."

That buys me more than a few blank looks, but I press on.

"Not the war over the Strand," I say. "We need to win the battle for hearts and minds."

Still, they are quiet. Willing to listen, but not yet convinced. I squeeze out the waver in my voice. "Right now, Benroyal's beating us on every front. His propaganda's turned everyone on Castra against us. His lies have allowed him to occupy Bisera and burn down Manjor. Gave him the power to blow a hole right through the Strand. He burned your own fields and desecrated your most holy ground."

On the opposite end of the table, a rebel leans forward. "And we answered him. In blood."

At his words, the crowd comes to life.

"And we paid with blood too," I answer calmly. "And the whole time, what about the rest of the planet? The rest of the galaxy? No one stepped up to support us. And they didn't because we're fighting the wrong way."

The room's buzzing. I raise my voice. "We have a plan. An attack on all three fronts: Castra, Bisera, and Cyan." I look at my uncle, who stands on the other end of the table. "James? Help me out here."

He leans forward, splaying his hands on the table. "One of the ways the Sixers consolidate power is through the careful management of information. Benroyal owns every satellite and data compressor on Castra. From Mid-iron to Capitoline, official feeds keep the pipeline filled with pro-Sixer propaganda. Everyone else's transmissions are closely monitored, scrubbed and filtered. And that's where our allies come in. We've got an army of flex hackers, ready to help."

On the screen, Moira's avatar nods. "The Fist's prepared to hack into every sky server, and we've aligned ourselves with the largest coalition of flex net hackers on both planets. Together, we're more than well equipped to hold off any Sixer interference for at least twenty-four hours. On the day of Dak's coronation, we'll send out a message."

"What message?" Belach asks.

Moira smiles. "A nice little breakdown of Benroyal's dirty little secrets, to be transmitted on all feeds. We've made counter-propaganda, using all the best bits from his files. You name it, we've got it—financial records, illegal interrogation transcripts, black sap lab blueprints, dealer distribution routes, payout lists for bribed public officials. We've even got footage of IP soldiers executing sap miners in the Gap," she says. "And all of it's perfectly packaged and ready for delivery in super-compressed unstoppable files, which will be pushed to every single networked screen, banner, wall, and flex device on the planet."

The war room seems to expand, filled with rapid talk.

"But our work won't end there," James says. "Once this gets out, Castra will boil over. We're counting on every ally we still have there to help redirect the chaos. We've already got one Sixer company on our side, Yamada-Maddox, and we're hoping at least one more will follow."

Another rebel speaks up. "You won't be able to control

this. Think of Capitoline. This'll tear the city apart."

Around the table, others chime in. I catch snatches of conversation.

"—*mobs in the street.*"

"*Blood on our hands*—"

"—*no way to contain the violence.*"

James reins everyone back in. "Yes, it's a gamble. There will be riots. But this time we're planning something greater—a widespread, organized response. And once the message is out there, the soldiers won't be able to contain it. Even the Domestic Patrol will waver. Many of them believe in what they do and simply don't know the truth. Once they do, I believe they will come to our aid."

Belach cuts in. "If you're betting on their good nature—"

"No, we're betting on *human* nature," James says. "We're out of time. The people have to know. After that, it's up to them."

"And it's up to us," I say. "Bisera needs our help too. We have a plan to rescue Cash, just before the network attack. We'll only have a short window to save him, so we'll work quickly. If he's still Benroyal's hostage once everything hits the feeds, he's dead. But we're going to try. If the people see Cash is alive, they won't accept Dak's rule."

"And what about us?" Belach asks. "What about the Strand?"

"The Strand is the last front," I say. "Benroyal is poised for battle. At any moment, he may attack. Here, we'll make our final stand." Unblinking, I sweep the room one last time. "If you're still with us, stay. If not, find a transport west, to Cyan. Your choice. It's no tread off my wheels either way."

At first, nothing. But then the first crisp flutter of movement, as the first rebel steps forward. Then another, and another and another, until we're standing inside something new. An impossible home surrounds me—every wall built strong, made of clear-eyed, straight-backed rebels. At last, the words come. They curl like a closing fist. A hundred fists, held over fast-beating hearts.

Bidram arras noc.

Someone calls from the war-room doorway. From my chest, the voice pulls a deep sigh of relief.

"Cash's rescue mission. I volunteer," he says.

I look up. It's Bear.

CHAPTER TWENTY-NINE

EVERYONE'S ALL IN. NO ONE EVEN MAKES A MOVE FOR THE exit until Nandan dismisses them. Even then, countless soldiers check in at the table, pledging to stay and hold the Strand, no matter the odds.

Walking in, I had been prepared to go it alone, or to manage with a handful of stalwarts. But now we're a hundred strong, no matter what the Skal decides to do. It may not equal an army, but on the heels of our darkest hour, it feels like a miracle.

Now the room's mostly cleared out. Bear asks me to meet him after I'm finished.

James and I tidy up while Miyu says good-bye to Moira.

"You okay?" James asks me.

"I think so. Everything went well, right?"

"I didn't mean that. I meant . . ." He eyes the doorway, where Bear was just standing. "Is everything *else* all right?"

"We're . . ." I nod, course-correcting my answer. "I'm fine."

James raises an eyebrow but doesn't press. Instead he slips beside me and pulls a flex card from his pocket. "I need to show you something."

"What is it?" I ask.

He swipes the card against the table to sync an image. "Just take a look."

I glance down at the screen. The picture, it's . . .

"Amazing," I say aloud. And it is.

A flame-tailed phoenix glides in the sky, one wing spread against the wind and the other curled around a constellation. Four stars—one red, one silver, one gold, one white.

"You had this made," I say. "For me?"

"It's an emblem. It seemed . . . right. She's soaring against the storm," he adds. "Part of her's always flying. But see the way she shields her own?"

And then I catch on. The artist gathered stars from our own banners. The red star for Bisera. Silver for Cyan. Gold for my home, for the sun-gilt flag of Castra. "Why the white star?" I ask.

"Maybe I picked that one for Earth." He shrugs, his grin buttoned up and lopsided. "Or maybe for peace. Or . . . okay, I admit it. I just like the symmetry."

Without thinking, I reach for my shoulder, the right blade where Benroyal's racing logo is still etched. The driver's mark is ugly and scarred; the phoenix crest is cleaved in two. I still remember the finish line wreck, the one that left my ribs bruised and my shoulder slashed. Benroyal's doctors wanted to fix the mark, but I wouldn't have it. For me, it wouldn't matter if they stitched or rebranded; the cut would always be there.

I look at the phoenix on the screen, and it's as if the artist plucked her unscathed from my skin. I trace a forefinger over the bird, from the fire-lit feathers to the small ring of stars.

James leans over the image, as if inspecting it one last time. "It'll go out with Moira's message, like a watermark, embedded in all the files and tagged on every image. Every revolution needs a symbol, you know. So what do you think of ours?" he asks, looking up. "Do you like it?"

My hand drifts from the screen and curls at my chest; the heartbeat I find there is both mine and the bird's. I smile. "It's perfect."

I look for Bear, but he's not anywhere in the tomb. Hank tells me he's already off duty for the night, so I walk down to Flight Control. He's there, alone.

In the doorway, I watch him as he hauls a bundle of

parachute to the center of the room, then billows it out. The silky chute flutters and undulates before coming to rest. Carefully, Bear walks its perimeter, spreading the cloth for inspection. If there's any fault or tear, he'll find it. And he does find something, sure enough. I'm too far away to see the rip, but he seems to consider it, as if he's not sure it's worth repairing. He sighs. With a shake of his head, he walks to the other end of the chute. He pulls out a knife to cut something small from its edge.

Whatever he's taken from it, he tosses it aside.

I walk to him. "You asked me to come."

Looking up, he nods, then puts away the blade.

"Repacking chutes?" I ask.

Another nod.

I tilt my chin at the one on the floor. "This one's no good?"

"Nope," he says.

"What'd you take from it?"

"Oh," he says, then reaches into the pile of metal rods near his feet. They're tiny, polished Pallurium cylinders, about two inches long. He picks one up and hands it to me. The coppery tang of battle still clings to it. "These? They're just beacons. Every chute has them. They stitch a few into the edges, to aid in search and rescue."

He takes the one in my hand and snaps it in two.

Apart, both ends blink. "See? If you jump in somewhere and lose your bearings, you just take one half with you and leave one half with the chute. Each piece transmits its location to the other. Doesn't matter if you're six miles away or six thousand. The power cells on these things are damn near infinite, and the range is almost as good. If one half's anywhere on the planet, the other will find it." He snaps the pieces back together, and the light grows steady, then dies.

"That way," Bear adds, "when your squad comes to get you, if you aren't with your chute, they know where to go."

"Pretty handy," I say.

"Yeah. Even if we trash the chutes, we save the beacons. A lot of pilots keep one on them all the time. One half for themselves, the other for their copilot."

"Do you?" I ask.

He doesn't answer, but he puts the beacon back into my hand. "Keep it," he says.

He holds on to the beacon. I wait for him to break it apart, but instead, he closes my fist around it, then suddenly he takes my face in his hands.

Eye to eye we stand, and when I open my mouth to say something, he stops me. "Don't," he says. "I know what you're going to say."

"I still—"

"I know you still love him," he says. "But I know you love me too."

I nod against the cradle of his fingertips.

"And I know what's going to happen. We're going to rescue him, and when he returns, you'll be with him again, for always."

"Bear, stop—"

He strains. His voice deepens, thick with refusal. "But I don't care, Phee. Be with me. Be with me just for tonight. Just for now. It's enough."

Our foreheads touch, and I can feel myself teetering on the edge. Against Bear, I tremble. I could fall so easily, so fast and so far. But if I fall for him tonight, there will be no return. A breath passes between us. His lips brush mine, but I pull away.

"No," I say. "I can't do this. I can't."

The boy I used to know would've retreated in anger or silence. But that boy is long gone, and the man before me won't back down so easily. Bear slides his arms around me and knits us together. One hand reaches for mine; he presses my palm to his heart. "Don't tell me you don't feel this."

I close my eyes and imagine what's next; the future unspools in my mind. He'll bring my hand to his lips and then mark me with kisses under the billowing silk of the chute. I'll stay with him tonight and tomorrow and forever and always. Always warm. Always happy. Always safe. Always loved.

The only price for our always is a future with Cash.

I see him, even now. The honor in his face. The fire of his touch. Giving him up—it would destroy me. I can't live a life split at the seams, my love torn into pieces. I have only one path; I cannot choose two roads.

I open my eyes and look into Bear's.

He is so close, like a blade at my breast, yet it's agony not to give up and lean in. "I love him, Bear. I can't stop loving him, no matter how long he's gone or how much it hurts. I won't give him up. It's too late for us."

"No." He shakes his head and shuts out the truth. "It's not too late. I'm not asking you to choose."

"You are," I say, accusing. "There is no just tonight. Just tonight will never be enough. What you're asking me . . . you want me to cut my heart out, and give you the half that's yours. Don't you understand what that will do to us?"

He tries to back away, but I reach out and cradle his jaw. Fire curls in my chest; it burns the tears as they fall from my eyes. "I love you," I choke, wide-eyed and desperate. I grip him hard, by the scruff of his collar. "Don't you understand? I love you, but that love is tearing me apart."

When our eyes lock, at last, I watch our always die. It

slips from his sight. He stops fighting, he understands. I let go.

"I love—" he says, before stopping himself.

I stare back, unblinking. "Our love is another life."

I leave the beacon in his hand.

CHAPTER THIRTY

THE NEXT MORNING, I REPORT TO THE LAUNCH YARD FOR
mission training. I've convinced myself Bear won't be
here. He'll back out of the rescue mission and leave word
with Hal.

I am wrong.

Bear falls into line right next to me. Side by side, we
wait for Captain Nandan. Bear stares straight ahead, but I
risk a glance.

"Good morning, Phee," he says, still avoiding my gaze.

I nod. The rest of the morning he's perfectly cordial,
and there's no trace of longing or anger or disappointment
in him. As we work with Hank and Fahra, Bear even goes
out of his way to help Miyu slip into her exo-suit. I watch
the interaction like an outsider, too afraid to interrupt.

"Just pop this lever," he tells Miyu, punching the left collar plate of her exo, "and your shields lock into place."

Sure enough, a clear, retractable hood arcs over her head and slips into the gutter of her collar, and suddenly Miyu's self-contained in her own atmosphere, behind the clear flex glass of her helmet and the dull, gunmetal skin of her suit. Lights dance on the visor as her screens read and assess us as friendlies. "Hey-o," she says. Her voice comes out foggy, as if distilled in a jar. She touches the small weapons port on her forearm. "Is this loaded?"

"No," Bear says. "Stun guns are disengaged. This suit's not yours anyway. It's just for training. You'll get weapons when you've learned to use them."

"Mine will have them," she says, no question.

I catch Bear's sideways glance. Just a flash of pain—a one-second stumble in his gait, and then his gaze is calm. He's taken his loss and quietly put it away. Unlike me, his eyes aren't red-rimmed and he isn't pale with grief.

I straighten and take a deep breath. If he can endure this, so can I. I will make it as easy for him as I can. No more talks. No more bunking together. No more quiet exchanges. Civil and cordial and nothing else. Bear's shown me the way it has to be.

Miyu pops the helmet switch again, and her visor retracts with a hiss. Gingerly, her finger hovers over the opposite lever, the one on her exo's right collar plate. "What about this one?" she asks.

"Careful," he answers. "That's the quick-lock. Punch it, and every bit of your plating flies off. You'd be left standing around in nothing but liner."

She cringes, and I don't blame her. The tight black liners we wear under the suits are like glorified underwear. If underwear were thermo-woven and nearly bulletproof.

"There," Bear coaches, pointing to a spot a few meters behind her. "Back up, then punch out."

"Punch out?" she says.

He nods. "Hit the quick-lock."

She eases away from us, then manhandles the switch. There's a loud magnetic click as her armor breaks loose from her suit. Clearly repelled by her liner, the plating hovers in the air, and the hang time's unnerving. When Miyu takes a step forward, at last, the spell breaks. My jaw drops as the armor finally clanks to the ground.

Miyu's a little less impressed. "Isn't that a critical design flaw?" she asks Bear. "A switch that leaves you vulnerable?"

"Not necessarily." He says. "Punch it again."

She does, and the exo resurrects itself. Bit by bit, the plating flies up and leaps into place over Miyu's liner. Just as quickly as it came off, it all clicks back on. Again I gape, but Miyu still doesn't look sold. I guess her standards for next-generation exos are higher than mine.

"If I can punch myself out so easily, then so can my enemy." Miyu asks, "Why would anyone use it?"

Bear's answer is less than patient. "You really want to wear an extra hundred pounds of armor bolted down on your back all the time? You'd prefer a solid exo that doesn't come off so easily? You'd use the quick-lock if the suit malfunctioned, or the power cell was leaking or corrupted, or the plating jammed, or maybe you'd punch out after pulling a double shift, because you just want to get the damn thing off."

"Oh," Miyu says. "Good point."

And after we spend the next six hours in an airless, simulated zero-g freighter hold . . . I can't help but agree. We can't punch out fast enough.

Larken wakes up the day before we launch the rescue mission, thanks to a little stim therapy and a *lot* of anti-gel. The doctors insist he still needs rest, and I only get a few minutes to sit at his bedside in the infirmary. As I walk in, I see I'm not the only one vying for his attention. Larken's propped up, talking into an oversized flex screen.

He sees me, then quickly wraps up his conversation. He signs off and puts the screen down.

I sink into the chair at his bedside. "How are you feeling?"

He ignores my question. "I hear you're leaving soon. The rescue mission."

I nod.

"Is Hal going with you?" he asks.

"I can't convince him *not* to go."

"Good. I'm glad. You'll need him. And when you're both out there, trust no one—not completely, at least—but Bear and Miyu and Hank."

"And Captain Fahra," I correct.

Larken doesn't quite frown, but he doesn't answer either.

I think of Fahra and the first moment I laid eyes on him in the wellspring abbey. If you'd asked me what I thought of him then, I'd have said he was a cutthroat for hire. But after everything that's happened since Manjor, all the sap we've slogged through together? No, there's no way he'd knife me in the back.

"He saved your life, Larken. You still don't trust him?"

"I'm just saying . . . be careful. I'm not saying he's a traitor, but don't forget: His allegiance isn't to you. It's to his queen, who's now aligned with Benroyal, in case you've forgotten."

"She doesn't have a choice. She's just protecting Cash."

He cocks an eyebrow, and lets it go. "Fair enough. Just keep your eyes open, then. That's all I'm asking."

Again I nod.

"I wish you were going with us," I say.

"Why? You've already got the rebellion's best on your mission team."

"Except for you, Commander."

"I'm no good to you out there," he says. "You need me here."

I sigh, sitting back. "We need something, that's for sure."

"I'll do what I can," he adds. "Vilette tells me cease-fire negotiations are already under way between Castra and Cyan. But I'll speak to the council. I may be able to slow things down, at least."

"If that doesn't work . . . if the Skal calls you back to Raupang, what will you do?"

He squints, nursing the faintest smile. "I'll try to convince them I need to stay . . . with a few 'peace-keeping advisors,' of course."

"Peace-keeping advisors?"

"Absolutely. You know, it can take a lot of soldiers to tidy up this sort of thing. We'd be very busy, preparing *not* to engage in armed combat. But if the IP happened to show up again at the border . . ." The smile on his face turns into a full-on sap-eating grin. "Maybe we could figure something out."

"Thank you, Larken," I say. "For not abandoning us."

"It's me who should be thanking you. You saved my life, Phee."

A few seconds pass by, and I don't know what to say. So I settle on the truth. "I'm just glad you're okay. And I had help, you know. If it weren't for the others, who pulled you out—"

"I know. Hal told me." He pauses. "He also told me you're in therapy. That you've been working hard on Mary's sim, showing up every night."

"The sim's not that hard to deal with. It's not really the sim at all. Doesn't even raise my pulse anymore. It's the talking part that's hard."

"Talking with Hal?"

I hesitate, and suddenly, I have to glance around—at the ceiling, at the floor, anywhere but at Larken—just to keep going. "Group counseling."

His raised eyebrows might as well be question marks, so I add, "Takes the edge off. I don't have to run around so much now. Just as well; it's not like I can hike up to the poppy fields anymore."

"So it helps."

I nod. I don't tell him how much it hurts.

"It helps," I answer quietly.

"I'm glad," he says. "If it didn't, I wouldn't want you to

go on the rescue mission. I wouldn't think you were ready."

"I'd still feel better if you were going with us."

He sits up, until we're eye to eye. "I know. But my place is here, on the line. As for you . . ."

I try to lower my gaze, but he holds it. "You were meant to do this. To go and rescue that prince. So get out of here. I'll stay and hold my ground. You go and hold yours." Just when I think he's getting too sentimental, he adds, "Like a flock of stinking barden, hold it well."

One smile, one scrap of laughter, and now it's time to go.

I hope it won't be the last.

CHAPTER THIRTY-ONE

WE LAND NOT FAR FROM RAUPANG. I'M TOLD IT'S A BEAUTIFUL city, the glittering, ice-kissed heart of Cyan, a citadel built of three-thousand-year-old stone and timber. But we see next to none of it. Our vac touches down in the lowlands, south of the Cyanese capital, which towers above the fjords. From a distance, looking up, all we see is a glimmer of polished gray—the very tip of the Skal.

No. We won't be visiting Larken's snow-capped home during this trip. Instead, we're prepping for launch, in the foothills far from Raupang's gates. In a matter of hours, my team and I will buckle in, blast off, then drift toward a giant calibrated ring—a gateway through folded space. In an eye-blink, we'll charge it, hurtling out of our galaxy and into Earth's orbit. Then, millions of light-years from here, we'll find a different kind of ring. A forgotten space station. The U.S.S. *Sweetwater*.

For now I sit alone in the flight master's office planted on one end of the yard. It's cozy and spare, a glorified glassed-in box that trembles at every takeoff. Through the windows, I watch the many vacs in the yard, launching and landing in the shadow of the not-so-distant peaks. The Cyanese Mountains are cold and strange. But the ice and snow are beautiful enough. In a way, their endlessness speaks to me the way the Castran Desert does. One hand on the windowpane, and the chill bites my fingertips. The frost reminds me: I'm a long way from home.

I shiver as the side door swings open. It's Hal. Windblown, he walks in and it clangs shut again. I know why he's here. We're squeezing in one last session before the rescue mission.

He sits down in the opposite chair. A heating vent grumbles between us.

There's no space to run a sim. Here, at the end of the road, there's only room for quiet talk.

Finally, Hal takes both my hands.

Mine are trembling.

"It's going to be difficult up there, Phee," Hal says at last. "You're going to have a hard time."

My gaze drops, but it's not a dodge. It's a giant, gut-swooping nod.

"And that's all right. Whatever happens . . ." he adds. "It's okay to bug out and lose it and be afraid. It's okay to fall down."

"I . . ." I trail off, uncertain. But Hal jumps into the gap, squeezing hard. There is no more softness in him now, only unfailing strength.

"Every time, all we have to do is get back up."

We launch.

Hal gives me something to ease the trip, and mercifully, I doze off. Now there's a split second of disorientation as I finally wake. I look up. Fahra's still sitting across from me, and he's saying something, but I can't make it out. The sound is low and sluggish like syrup in my ears. And then my hair slithers by, and everything spins back into place.

We're in an unlicensed, obsolete orbital shuttle. I'm still buckled in, weightless under my seat restraint.

We made it through the gateway.

The last time I ripped through folded space like this, I was in one of Benroyal's vacs, jaunting from Castra to Cyan-Bisera for my final race. *That* ship was state-of-the-art, with inertial dampers, gravity drivers, and a mass-condensing core. Then, I made the trip in air-conditioned luxury, and still threw up. So now? In this zero-g tin can?

Even with Hal's best meds, I don't have a prayer.

I look out the tiny side window. There is no sideways, or up or down; there is only spinning. Lots and lots of spinning. Ugh . . .

"Take it," Fahra says. "Take!" He thrusts something in my face. And just in time too. Before he can shout a third command, I latch on to the valved air-sickness bag.

After . . . well, I'm sure we're all thankful the bag's opaque. I rock against my tethers, limp as a wrung-out rag. Fahra laughs.

"You know what that is?" Fahra says to Hank, pointing at me. "Freshly squeezed gan-gan."

I think my face must turn a deeper shade of green, because Fahra quits grinning. He reaches under Hank's seat. "You need another one?" he asks.

Slowly, I shake my head. I try to answer, but burp instead. The belch clears my head, and the past twenty-four hours slam back into it. I see everything in rapid playback mode, and marvel: We're finally here, in another galaxy. *Here* being something like eight hundred kilometers above my ancestors' burned-out planet. I angle toward our window again, and there it is, slowly crawling below us, a sun-rimmed swirl of churning gray storms.

Earth.

I am mesmerized by the light, the way it hugs the surface of the planet, slicing through the surrounding darkness like an unstoppable glimmer. There's no end to the shine, no matter how far the shadows reach.

Hal passes me the necessities. A dose of motion antisickness meds, mouthwash, and a small bottle of water. Eager, I take them. By the time I look up again, there's another patch of Earth meeting the dawn. The gray storms still swirl here and there, looming like threats, but there are pockets of dull blue and deep brown and even a bit of green scattered in the gloom.

Up here, in orbit, the stars belong to IP ships and bloodthirsty smugglers. Below us, on Earth, I'm guessing it's worse. There are two kinds of folk down there. First, the people who were left behind, after Castra was colonized. Second, all the criminals Castra's dumped here over the years—the worst sorts, the ones they won't even put to work in the sap mines. To these luckless herds belongs a half-shadowed planet. The burned-out, used-up world my father once called his home.

I turn away from the window. We wait.

Finally, Miyu touches my arm. "Almost there. Feeling better?"

"I'm okay. How much longer?"

"I see it," Hank says, looking out. "Come look."

We all unbuckle, then float toward the glass. Weight-less and jostling, we crowd around the tiny window. And sure enough, there it is. Our ride to the space station. A big black decommissioned IP vac, its bay doors yawning wider by the second. The crew manning it does business with Benroyal, but they aren't soldiers. This outfit? Apparently, they were recommended to James by a friend of a friend of a nefarious friend. Because there are no legal ways to get out here.

"Buckle in and gear up," Hank says. "Docking in five."

He doesn't need to repeat the warning. We know the score. That fast-looming freighter's our ticket to Cash. Our last hope? A ship full of no-account, credit-stealing, vac-hijacking, black-marketeering, antiquities-hauling, inde-pendently contracted space pirates.

We dock inside the pirate freighter.

The first thing I notice is how awkward and off-balance I feel lumbering out of our vac. The moment we touch down and depressurize our doors, the free-floating sense of weightlessness . . . gone. Now I can't quite adjust to the artificial gravity of this new ship. It's as if I have lead in my bones, and more in my boots.

Second, there's no escaping the gray, grimy dim of the industrial space, or the low-grade static of wall-to-wall chatter. Inside the landing bay, the burly freighter crew stare us down. A second later, they flash their weapons. I read the warning. *Easy now. Don't do anything stupid and we'll all get along just fine.*

Cautiously, my eyes search the bay. But the smugglers don't make a move. They just stare. Casually they grumble and snicker amongst themselves.

I touch my right arm. I'm prepared to fire at will, ready to tap the trigger pad of my glove. My thumb hovers over it, just in case. I can stun the first sap-hole who makes the wrong move. One of the crew—a hulk of a man with silvered dreadlocks and matching whiskers—leans against a half-shadowed stack of crates, his arms folded. After sizing me up, he damn near laughs. When Fahra answers with a fast draw of his dagger, he whistles.

At his signal, the rest of his mates back away. As they part, I see who's standing behind them.

One look and I gasp. I know those sly, deep-set eyes and that gold-toothed, sap-eating grin. I've faced down his ugly mug a thousand times in his own tin-roofed garage, and rust all if he hasn't cussed me out half as much. Here comes bad luck and trouble.

Benny Eno.

Or Fat Benny, if you're asking for him on the street. Toughest crew boss in Capitoline. The fierce hard-nosed crook who was inexplicably kind to me. The muscle-brained tough guy who gave me my first rig and backed me on the streets. At the sight of him, Bear's eyes flare in anger, and I can't even try to hide the mixed-up grimace on my face.

"Got nothing to say to your old boss?" Benny huffs, his hands up and his shoulders bunched in mock surprise. He walks my way. Short, thundering steps, just like always.

A jolt of nostalgia tempers the shock. "Benny," I say, clumsy and a little breathless. "What are you . . ."

Then it occurs to me. I'm standing here, looking at the man who sold me out. Who set me up to race the night Benroyal first had me arrested. And now he's probably selling me out again. In my mind, I see it all slip away. Our plans. The rescue. Cash's life. Selling us all out, right now. I should be bugging out. I should be wetting my exo.

I should be landing a punch.

Instinct kicks in. My right hand curls into a tight, trembling fist.

"You know this man?" Fahra asks.

I ignore him, closing in on Benny. My old boss doesn't even flinch. He looks me up and down, appraising me as usual. It's a familiar tic; he measures every knuckle-cracking, bone-breaking, odds-making move. When his eyes narrow, I can't tell what he's thinking. The uncertainty's enough to raise the hair on the back of my neck, and if I were wiser, this one tingling whiff of caution would stop me.

"*You snake,*" I hiss. "*You slithering, two-faced, double-dealing—*"

Bear lunges at Benny, but a handful of freighter crew jump in. They look to Benny, who tosses a dismissive wave. "Bear's a good kid. Keep him off me; don't rough him up."

The smugglers laugh. Bear struggles against them.

"Benny, you're a clown," I spit. "And I will make you pay for this. For everything you've done."

He looks at me, drinking in my alarm. His mouth goes a little slack, as if he's actually surprised.

"Hey now," he says.

I'm still shaking. "When my uncle finds out you're here, and that you've double-crossed us, he will spend every last credit he's got to hunt you down and—"

His hands fly up again. "Wait a second. If you think I'm here to sell you out . . . Look, I took this job to help you. I'm not here to double-deal you."

I can't believe what I'm hearing.

"I'm not heartless, am I?" he pleads. "Sure, I gave you up to Benroyal. I had to. But hey, I figured King Charlie'd make you famous. How was I supposed to know he had it in for you?"

"You betrayed me," I growl.

He looks away for a moment, then jerks his chin at the gray-haired smuggler. The man answers with a nod, and the whole room seems to relax. The rest of the crew—they back off and holster their guns. A little less than gently, they let go of Bear. Without so much as a stumble, he shakes them off and moves back to my side.

Benny looks back at me. "Didn't I give you a start? A spot in my garage and a shot on the circuit? Don't you remember nothing about the good I did for you?"

A little hand-wringing—that sparkle in his beady eyes—and it's like I can't help it. Already the scorch in my cheeks is fading. "Benny," I say, sighing. "What are you doing up here?"

"I'm here because I said I'd be here. I promised I'd get you to the station."

"Right," Bear snaps. "I'm sure that's the only reason."

"Promised who?" Hal squints at Benny. "You made a deal with James?"

"Hey," Benny answers. "Mr. Anderssen came to me, thank you very much. I know the guys who run antiques for King Charlie, and he hit me up to broker the deal." Benny scratches his left eyebrow. Another tic. "So I'm involved in a lot of . . . enterprises. What can I say? I got a lot of connections."

He shrugs. "Look, maybe I owe you one. For handing

you over to King Charlie. This'll square things up. And if it knee-caps the bastard, I say all the better. So I'm here. We're here. To get you to the station."

"Liar," I say. "You're here for the money. How much are you getting for this? Tell the truth, Benny. We know James pays well."

"I get ten percent for picking you up, and your uncle's agreed to keep paying out until you're all nice and safe, back in Cyanese airspace. But we don't get nothing if something goes wrong. Your uncle's a sharp guy, just so you know." Benny pauses. "Some banker's holding the money. We double-cross you, we get nothing. And since you insist on being crass about it, yeah, I'm getting a nice piece of the whole deal."

"And these guys?" I say.

"You're looking at the best independent contractors around." Benny grins. He jerks his chin at the crew. "They run a lot of King Charlie's antiquities and such. Find it on Earth and deliver it here." Benny pauses, as if reading the skepticism in our eyes. "Look. You don't gotta worry. Like I said, this outfit's independent, they got no love for King Charlie, either. I'm telling you, these guys are solid."

There's a flicker of unrest in my team, a collective crossing of arms and a whole lot of sidelong looks. Even Miyu looks rattled. I know what they're all thinking. *Yeah, sure. They're solid. Whenever it suits them.*

Hank shifts. "And you expect us to take your word on that, Mr. Eno? That you're only here to help?"

Benny's smile twists into something sharper—a wolf's grimace. "Hey, I don't give a rusting piece of dried-up drip what you believe. I don't welch on deals."

"Is that so?" Hank snaps.

"Look, wisecracker . . ." Benny moves in. He raises a fist, and if Hank knew better, he'd duck. Most fights with Benny don't last too long. I run interference, slipping between them. "Benny . . ."

Fahra pulls at Hank. Wisely, he steps back.

"Yeah, that's right. That's better. Just remember: I owe her one," Benny says. "But I don't owe *you* nothing."

Amused, the dreadlocked smuggler sidesteps toward the bay's inner door. With a mocking flick of the wrist and a hand-waving flourish, he bows. "Welcome aboard. Right this way, if you please . . ."

CHAPTER THIRTY-TWO

DOUBLE-CROSSED OR STRAIGHT DEALT, WE DON'T HAVE MUCH of a choice. Either we trust a bunch of criminals or we scuttle the mission. For just about everyone else on the team, it seems Benny's our biggest concern. But for me, he's the only known variable.

Yes, he's a crook. But he's a crook I can read, and there's a part of me that's glad my old boss is here. If there's one thing I've learned about Benny, it's that he knows how to land on his feet. If things go south at the station, he'll figure out how to get himself back alive. Maybe even all of us.

At last, Benny ushers us into the cargo hold, which is a tethered maze of tightly packed crates and black-market goods. Old books and statues and rugs and furniture—treasures from Earth, to be smuggled into Benroyal's hands.

We stash ourselves wherever we can, crouching amongst King Charlie's plunder. When we're all settled in, they seal us in the hold. We power down our weapons. Alone, we wait in the dark.

I'm crushed between Miyu and Fahra.

"This place reeks," Miyu says. "It seriously smells like dirty feet."

"Why did we let them lock us in here again?" I ask.

Fahra doesn't answer but hums quietly. Minutes crawl by, and soon Miyu's breathing sounds begin to match the slow tempo of his tune. I'm pretty sure Captain Fahra just lulled her to sleep, which is amazing, considering we're squeezed between two crates. In the dark, in the quiet, I risk a question. One that's been rattling in my brain since the night we left Manjor.

"At first, when we met, you said your name was Fahrat," I say. "Why? What happened? Why do you let them call you that?"

He replies with a sharp inhale, and I wish I'd never interrupted his song. "I'm sorry," I say. "I shouldn't have asked. It's rude, and you don't have to—"

"Because I am dishonored," he says. "Because I failed in my duty, and that failure cost my king his life."

There's a wince in his words. The pain's still there, so I

don't press. Fahra begins to hum again. At the refrain, he stops. "I do not expect to survive this mission. We all may die here—as likely as not—so I will tell you what I have done."

"We're not going to die here," I say.

"Perhaps. But listen to my story, and judge for yourself. After, I will accept any name you would give me."

He pauses, then takes a breath. "It was the twenty-fifth year of His Majesty's reign, and the king and the queen and Prince Cashoman spent their summer in Manjor. There was to be a great celebration at season's end, but Prince Dakesh would not come. Dakesh was twenty-one, just barely a man, and determined to stay behind in Belaram. I should've known. It should've sounded the warning in my head.

"On the eve of the feast, Prince Dakesh sent his regrets, wrapped in an elaborate gift. An entire company of monks. Red-robed performers who dazzled the court with music and story and song. A play, it was. An original production based on the king's life, with all of his bravery and good works set up on a stage. And all of it sent with greatest regard, from the first son to his father. But, in truth, the monks the prince had hired never made it to the palace. On the way to Manjor, they were waylaid, and their costumes stolen. The attackers were curiously prepared. How is it that they were so well-versed in the monks' work, the very play they were to perform? How could they have lain in wait, at the right place, at just the right moment? But we did not know. Not then. No, we let the impostors through the gates. And that night, so late that even the merriest guests were passed out and dreaming, the performers traded their red robes for black." He growls. "Assassins, sent by the prince, but paid by—"

"Benroyal," I finish.

"Yes. This was their gambit, most carefully planned. And when the murderers slipped from the throne room into the royal quarters, one of our men raised the alarm."

"You were there."

I hear the nod in his voice. "I was not yet captain then. I was a King's Guard, and though I'd spent many years assigned to Prince Cashoman, I was bound to His Majesty. And that night, I patrolled the walls and watched the gates, looking for an enemy we'd already welcomed inside. When the alarm sounded, I knew my charge. *Fly to His Majesty's chambers. Go and protect the king, at all costs.* This was my oath and duty. I was halfway there when I heard Her Majesty scream. I abandoned my orders and ran back to the nursery. There, I found her with Prince Cashoman. I rushed in. They were cornered by assassins.

"Prince Cashoman was only a boy. He held a dagger in

one hand, and a footstool in the other. If you had seen him, you might have laughed; so full of blind courage, he was. 'Back, back,' he snarled at them. 'Leave my mother alone, or I'll cut off your ears.' There were three black robes closing in . . . I didn't hesitate. I opened their throats with my knife."

"You saved them," I say. "You saved the queen and if you hadn't run into that room, they'd have been murdered too."

"I saved the boy I'd known from the day his mother bore him, the boy I'd taught to fight and shoot and swim. I saved the son, instead of his father, the king." He pauses. One last, heavy sigh. "And for that, by many, I'm called *dishonor*."

I don't get the chance to tell Fahra I'm grateful for his choice. Groaning, the ship seems to lurch. Miyu startles, and Hank orders everyone to be quiet. We brace ourselves against another jolt of movement. Then, one last rumble of noise as the freighter skids to a stop. Doors are opening. The ramp is descending.

It's time. We've landed at the station.

Our destination's an enormous satellite wheel, gleaming sterile and white against the cold darkness of space. The station rotates swiftly, and for good reason. Miyu says this thing's like a giant centrifuge; the movement generates a crude sense of gravity. A primitive feat of engineering, but hey, it beats filling up another air sickness bag.

For the longest time we hold tight, still crouched in the dark of the freighter's hold, but nothing happens. The smugglers are supposed to lure a squad of Benroyal's personnel inside, to unload the usual shipment of plundered treasure. The IP stumble in, and we'll catch them by surprise. Then the crew holds the landing bay while we rescue Cash. A few pods of dozing gas dropped into our enemy's path, we pull down our masks, and King Charlie's guards take a nap. Get in, get out. *Fast.*

Our intel says there are between sixty and eighty guards here. For us, the odds are worse than terrible, but they're the only ones we've got.

The hold door begins to creak, and I reach for Auguste's patch. I hold it close and breathe in a little bit of spitfire. *Give me one last shred of fearlessness. Help me get back up and see him one more time. If I live or die, just let everyone else make it back home.*

We're all poised and ready to spring when Benny walks into the hold. I stare at him for the longest time, waiting for footsteps, voices . . . anything. Some sign that Benroyal's men are trailing.

Cautious, Hank inches toward the door and peers

through it. "What happened?" Hank asks. "Where are the guards?"

Benny shakes his head. "There's no one."

"What do you mean there's no one?" I ask. "They won't come aboard?"

"I mean there's nobody to bring aboard," Benny replies. "It's a ghost station. They're gone."

Unbelieving, I rush past him and dash down the landing ramp. I shrink against the bright lights. The station's landing bay is dazzling white, but completely empty. My brain hums in alarm; I was prepared to white-knuckle it against the chaos of combat. I wasn't prepared for silence.

No. I run toward the inner doors and slam my fist against the command glass. The doors open, but there's nothing to see on the other side. A long hallway. Windows looking in on other rooms of the station. All deserted.

By now the rest of the team have caught up. Hal, Fahra, Miyu, Bear, Hank, and I stick together and nose through the rooms. Nothing. No one. There's a blast door at the end of the hallway. When I put my hands on it, it's as if I can almost feel a presence on the other side, like a buried heartbeat.

Hal touches my shoulder.

"He has to be here," I say, more to myself than anyone else. *"He has to be."*

I reach for the door, but Hal won't let go. "No. We're not going any further. We're not rushing through that door without a new plan."

"And if you're thinking about taking off alone, forget it," Bear warns. "Not on my watch."

Fahra is silent, but the look on his face tells me he'll do anything I ask.

Miyu steps beside us. "We will figure this out. We won't leave without searching every inch of this station," she says. "If you think I'm going back and telling my mother we failed," she adds, "then think again. This mission isn't over."

We make our way back to the freighter, where Benny and the crew are waiting. They're lounging around the nose of their ship like they've got nothing better to do.

"Let's go," Benny says.

I don't move.

He tries again. "Come on, Phee. We'll get you back home. It'll be all right."

"We need to check out the rest of the station," Bear says. "This place is huge. Maybe they left something behind."

Benny shakes his head. "Kid, you're just asking for trouble. Quit while you're ahead."

I snap at Benny. "You said you came to help. They could be hiding on the other side of that door. Or maybe they're just waiting to attack. This could be . . . a trap." The second the word passes my lips, a bead of cold sweat curls down the nape of my neck. Every breath of the air in the bay grows thicker in my lungs.

"I knew you were smart, kid." Benny nods. "You see now?"

Glassy-eyed, I stare at him. "Benny, I can't leave without searching . . . I have to find him. I have to know."

"Look, you don't wanna know." At first he huffs and rolls his eyes, like he's ready to wash his hands of me. Then something in him shifts, and when he looks back, the flare of impatience is gone. "Listen to me. I've been cracking skulls for over twenty-five years, and you know how I've survived so long?" he says. "I'll tell you how. By not asking questions like *What's behind that door?* Many a scrape, Phee. I've gotten through a lot of tight spots just by avoiding the answer. I never walked into no place blind, and I'm not about to start. Not even for you."

"But what if Cash is—"

"Your boy is dead, and I smell a trap. Nothing but rotten luck left here."

I look to the crew, but find no help there either.

"We will take you back," Benny adds. "Or if you insist on searching the place, we'll wait for you. But don't think I won't light out of here and torch this whole station on the way out if things get violent."

"I understand," I say, unblinking. "I'm going. Wait for us."

Benny sighs, disappointed. "We will. As long as we can afford to."

"Try leaving anyone behind," Bear says, slipping beside me. "And you'll learn what you can afford."

Benny ignores the warning. Instead, he reaches into his jacket. He pulls something out and presses it into my hand. A pistol. By the looks, more than a common pulse blaster.

"I already have weapons."

"You got stun guns," Benny says. "Not good enough for this little adventure. Take it. High-caliber exo-rattler. Only ten shots, but at close enough range, even armor won't spare the chump who gets on the wrong end of your barrel."

I look down and feel the weight of it in my hand. Its grip is a bad dream. Benroyal's picture of me. But when Benny closes my fist around it, I take it.

CHAPTER THIRTY-THREE

A PANEL CONTROLS THE BLAST DOORS, AND WE PUNCH THEM open. There is nothing behind the first threshold, or the one beyond it, or the one beyond that. For an hour, behind the fog of our visors, we crawl through lab after lab but find no sign of life, only motion detectors and automatic lights. There are tools and made-up bunks and dead flex walls. It's unnerving, the way every cold white surface blends into the next.

What few windows we find hang like dark patches. Looking through, I sense the slow spin of the station in the silent void of space. We stand on a false star, bright but cold and hollow.

By now we must be halfway around the wheel. I check the safety on Benny's pistol, then nose it into the utility pack at my hip.

"Shh . . . I hear something," Miyu whispers, lowering her blast shield. We're in what looks like a kitchen when she bolts for the hall. We follow.

Visors down, we gather around her. I close my eyes, straining for sound. And then I hear it too. A rhythmic, muted noise. Machinery. No . . . the pattern falters. This isn't equipment. It's something else.

Hank cocks his head. He hears it too, and runs toward it. The rest of us are fast on his heels, sprinting to follow the commotion. The hallway narrows, and we reach a row of holding cells. Someone's here, beating against one of the doors.

Knock. Knock.

Knock. Knock. Knock.

I stop, cocking my head. Just ahead. On our right, the last cell. A beat of silence, then the pounding starts up again. Pounding, then finally, a muffled cry.

We round on the door, and the first thing I see is the tiny window inset at eye level. A hand. A face. A hoarse and desperate voice.

Abasi.

We punch the lock and open the door. The old man collapses into Fahra's arms.

〜〜〜

Toby Abasi's eyes are cloudy and jaundiced, and his face is a pale, bruised map of misery. He is so weak and gaunt, he can barely stand.

He sees me and reaches out, his hands little more than brittle claws. "Is it really you?" he asks. "Am I dreaming?"

We embrace, and I tell him, "It's real. We're here to rescue you."

He sobs. "I don't know how long . . . the soldiers stopped coming . . . I can't believe it's really you."

"Believe it," I say.

Toby stumbles, but I hold tight. Bear pulls him off me and props him up. "Should I carry him?"

Abasi shakes his head. "I can walk. Do . . . do you have any water?"

Hank pulls a canteen from his utility case and holds it to Abasi's lips. Abasi sucks it down, then coughs and chokes and heaves. Nothing less than sheer will plays across his face as he struggles to hold it down.

"I'll get him back to the ship," Bear says, taking over. Carefully, he puts an arm around Abasi and steers him toward the landing bay. When the old man stumbles, Hal jumps to his other side. Together, Bear and Hal shoulder Abasi. Halfway down the next narrow stretch, Bear calls back. "Don't go any farther. Wait until we make it back here."

"We will wait," Fahra answers. He and Miyu stand sentry with their weapons at the ready. In turn, Hank moves quickly from wall to wall. His eyes sweep over every surface, as if he's taking in the details and analyzing our position.

I am less useful. I pace and pace, for what seems like forever.

And then I hear screaming.

It's him.

His cry cuts like a scythe. I sprint into it before anyone can catch me.

Hank and Fahra and Miyu clatter after me, but I'm barely aware of them now. I'm too focused on the guttural, teeth-clenched howl. I've heard it before, on the clip Benroyal sent Queen Napoor. Cash's cry is unmistakable. I have to find him. I have to pull him from the jaws of whatever trap Benroyal's laid here.

The screaming stops and starts. I keep chasing the echo.

Doorway after doorway after doorway, and the misery in Cash's voice is growing louder. Ten more feet, and another gated threshold. A blast door slams down behind me. Hank and Fahra and Miyu fly against it, but they can't get in. I can hear their beating fists and muffled warnings.

Come back, Phee. Come back.

Ahead, the doorway on the right. I race through it into a white room.

He is here. Trapped in a nightmare.

I run to the table where Cash is lying. His bare chest is slick with sweat. His jaws are clenched and every muscle is tight and twitching. He'd fall from the table if he weren't strapped down at the ankles and wrists. The stim wires attached to him dance, pulsing at an agonizing pitch high enough to drive an animal mad. I reach for one of the leads, but the moment I touch it Cash flinches, and I'm afraid I'll electrocute him or worse.

I glance up at the flex screen behind the table. It's a control panel, with levels and readings. The largest bar's at eighty percent; the others are climbing. I gamble, swiping them all down to zero, and the pulsing squeal dies. The wires stop dancing. Cash thuds against the table. A shivering groan melts into hard, sucking gasps. Frantic, I detach the wires and peel the leads off his body.

There are dozens of them, fastened over his arms and his neck and his chest. He flinches as I pull. His sweat's loosened the adhesive under some of the leads, and it's a small mercy.

He's quieter now, but even as I fumble and unbuckle

his restraints, his eyes roll back and forth behind his lids. When he's free, I'm desperate to scoop him into my arms, but the way he's trembling, as if every nerve ending's been plucked to fever pitch . . . my touch might be torture. Instead, softly, I call to him.

"Cash . . ."

He convulses, but less violently than before.

"Cash . . . I've got you. I'm here."

He blinks. His eyelids flutter against the light. I keep trying. I keep calling his name, over and over, until his pupils remember to focus. He looks at me.

"Phee," he croaks, shuddering harder. Tears leak from the corners of his eyes. Now I'm crying too. I can't breathe. I'm covered in plating and gloved from chin to toe, but I need to get skin to skin, just to know the moment's real and not an illusion. Cautious, I lean over. His hand rakes the back of my neck, but he's weak, and can't hold me for long.

I want to tell him he doesn't have to. He doesn't have to work for this. Still, he tries to pull me in. Our lips brush, but I can see even that's too much, so I turn aside, and rest my cheek against his. And it's enough. He's here. He's alive.

Finally, he lets go, still shivering and worse than exhausted. I straighten and suddenly, I'm full of anger and disbelief. "How could they leave you like this?"

Cash struggles, shakes his head as if to clear it. Blinks

and swallows. He tries to sit up but can only manage a lopsided elbow lean. A second later, fear kindles in the dark glimmer of his eyes. "You have to leave," he warns. "You have to get out. Right now. You shouldn't have come."

As a wall slides back, I understand why.

CHAPTER THIRTY-FOUR

I LEVER MY BLAST SHIELD INTO PLACE THE SECOND I SEE THE hidden door opening. I leap in front of Cash. My exo-suit will have to protect the both of us now. Benroyal personnel pour in, dressed in white uniforms. They look more like orderlies than IP, but I don't wait to find out. Forearms crossed and locked, I lean back and hold both thumbs over the trigger pads of my gloves. Voice control. "Weapons on."

The sound of my guns charging halts their advance.

"Stay back," I snap.

The uniforms hesitate. There's a half dozen of them. They fan out, keeping their distance. A suit walks in behind them. The sight of him pries a hiss from Cash. I'm almost certain it's the man from the clip I saw at the palace. The torturer.

The man steps through the line of white shirts.

"Stay back or I'll shoot," I say.

"Miss Vanguard . . ." he soothes. There's a needle in his hand.

It is him. I recognize the bastard's voice.

"Don't try me," I growl through the panic. "You make a move, and I'll clear this room."

"No need for threats, Miss Vanguard. Just safety your weapons, and let's discuss this. If you come with me now, then I'll put this away"—he gestures to the needle—"and all is forgiven. Mr. Benroyal's offering a generous deal. If you agree to surrender, he'll allow you both to live."

My vision swims, and I blink to anchor it. My aim's shaky, but I pretend it's only the laughter. "You'll put that away if I surrender?" I mock. "You'll have to do better than that."

He takes another step toward us. "No one's going to hurt you, Miss Vanguard."

"You're right," I say, caressing the triggers. "Not anymore."

The stun catches his neck; the whiplash jerks his chin. As he drops, the scrubs try to rush us. I shoot left and right, crossing streams from both weapons' ports.

I don't have to be the best marksman. I just have to spray the room.

I brace against Cash as the kickback hammers through us. I tap the triggers and keep it coming in an ear-piercing rain of rapid stun signal. Cash shifts behind me. One arm reaches for the pack at my waist. Cash finds Benny's pistol. Sluggish, he angles around me, aiming for the two goons I manage to miss.

"No," I rasp. "Not yet."

He nods against my shoulder, and I take the last two down. Seven bodies on the floor, all stunned. The ones who hit the ground hardest are waylaid and bleeding. Don't know if they're still alive or not. Either way, they're not getting up.

Terror washes through me, and I can't shake the knock of dread and adrenaline hammering in my chest. Wildly, my mind reaches for everything Hal and Mary taught me. *Focus. Stay focused. Count down in deep breaths. You can't make this go away. You can't deny it's happening. You can't pretend it isn't real.*

But you can get back up. You can get through, if you learn to ride it out.

I have to get us out of here. Now. But Cash is still weak. Lit up and panting, I wait for more personnel to rush through the door. Five . . . four . . . three . . . two . . . more sharp exhales and they come. This time, a pair of IP soldiers, geared up in exo-suits just like mine. At last, I'm outmatched.

Cash aims for the first one. One pistol shot, and the bullet tears into the plating at his ribs. Not deeply enough, I guess. Stumbling back, the soldier recovers. If anything, all we've done is rip his armor and scorch him off.

"At close range," I say to Cash. "You have to—"

Furious, the IP yanks me away from the table and tosses me into the arms of his partner. But I kick out of the second's grip and lunge back at him, just as he's barrel to barrel with Cash. Cash rolls off the table and fires; the second bullet rips into the guy's shoulder. I leap on the wounded soldier's back just in time. His weapon misfires against the wall, and the errant pulse fire smokes up the room.

My dance partner growls and tries to heave me off. We slam into the wall, and I'm caught behind him. A third pistol shot. I glance up. Cash shot the second IP in the thigh, but the bastard's getting back up. He lunges at Cash, and they crash into the side of the table. Again, the first IP slams me against the wall.

Breathless, I fumble and rake my hands over the front of his visor. He slaps my gloved hand away, but not before I hook two fingers around both his collar levers. A quick, knuckle-breaking pull and I let go completely, swinging out and landing hard. I'm back on the ground. But now so is the sap-hole's armor. His visor snaps back, and his plating shoots off, clattering to the floor.

Before he can react, I stun him right in the face. He drops, and I grab a piece of his exo—a right breastplate. I stumble through the tangle of bodies to get to Cash. The second IP's got him pinned against the side of the table. They're grappling for Cash's gun.

In an eye-blink, Cash takes an elbow to the jaw, and then a fist. The pistol flies from his hand, but he scraps his way up as it clatters against the floor. Snarling, Cash rallies. He reaches for the soldier's collar. But this goon's wiser to the game. He blocks Cash's offensive, and goes for the throat. His hands find Cash's neck.

Frantic, I leap, heaving the breastplate at the IP's head. The hit isn't good enough to crack his visor, but it buys Cash a breath. It shakes the soldier loose and sends him sprawling. I drop him, but not for long.

The IP's back on his feet. He raises his wrist, aims his weapon's port at Cash, but I slide in front of him, to shield him. Pulse fire hits me square in my chest plating. It's enough to knock me off my exhaust, and I tumble. Groggy, I try to get back up. Cash dives for the gun and comes up fast. Straining, he lunges forward, until it's in close enough range.

Boom. Boom.

Cash lowers the pistol. The last IP won't be getting up. Cash stumbles back and sags against the table. It took everything he had to make that shot, and now he can barely stand. Exhausted, we lean on each other.

Suddenly, footsteps and shouts and weapon noise. More figures run through the door.

Bear, Hank, and Fahra. Benny's with them, plus four of the smugglers.

The cavalry is here.

They gape at the bodies at our feet, but don't bother asking what happened. The soldier I stunned in the face begins to stir. Ever efficient, Bear stuns him again. Twice.

"C'mon," he says. "Let's move out. They'll all start waking up sooner than later."

"Not all of them," Cash says, the pistol still in his hand.

Fahra moves between us. "Allow me, Your Highness," he says, reaching out. "I will carry you."

Cash shakes his head. "I can walk."

"Then I will help you," Fahra replies.

Cash nods wearily, and I take back the pistol. Still good for a few more shots. I stuff it back into my hip pack. Quickly, Fahra and Hank commandeer a few essentials from one of the soldiers. Cash gears up, taking a gun, a jacket, and a pair of boots.

"Everyone else okay?" I ask.

"Hal and Miyu stayed back at the ship, to take care of

Abasi. And we need to get there now," Bear warns.

Fahra and I flank Cash. We make it to the door, but Hank stops us. "We'll cover you. Stay behind Bear and me."

"And we'll bring up the rear," Benny says.

"So what happened to not risking the crew?" I ask.

Benny nudges the dead IP with the toe of his boot. He grins. "Yeah. Well, I guess I shoulda told you. I'm kind of a liar."

"Thank you," Cash says. "We're indebted."

"Yeah, yeah," Benny replies. He reaches out and helps Fahra shoulder his weight. "You can thank me later. Let's get out of here. I'd like to keep you all alive long enough to collect my cut."

We head for the door and I slip next to Bear. "What happened?"

"You were right. They were hiding on the other side of the wheel, waiting to attack. After luring us in and cutting you off, the IP swarmed us. We had to fight our way through to you. Now we'll have to fight our way back."

Bear turns to me. "Listen. No matter what comes at us, just keep going. Keep running, until you get back to the ship."

I nod, but it's not enough.

"Promise me," he says. "I mean it, Phee. Whatever happens, you keep moving. You get out of here alive."

Benny's calling from the hallway. Telling us to hurry up.

I jerk Bear by the arm and get us going. I don't answer him.

Thirty yards from Cash's room, we stop at a blast door. On the other side, you can hear the pulse fire and shouting. Ahead, there's a war.

I look at Benny. "Is that our crew?"

He shakes his head. "They're holding the bay."

"Who's fighting here, then?"

"It's guards versus inmates now," Hanks says.

"Inmates?" I ask.

"The rest of Benroyal's prisoners," Hank answers. "At least a dozen. We let them all out. No telling how long they've been interrogated and tortured here. I'm guessing the guards moved them to this part of the station, then left Cash and Abasi as bait."

"How are we going to get through? Can we gas the hall?" I ask. "Put everyone to sleep?"

Bear shakes his head. "There's no gas left. The crew shot most of it at the first wave of soldiers in the bay. We used what was left on our way here to drop the officers in the command center."

Through the door, yelling and gunfire. By the sound of it, the fighting's getting more intense by the second.

"Get ready to run," Bear warns.

We nod. Bear hits the command glass.

The blast door rises, and we plunge, guns out, into the chaos.

Sirens blare. A full-on riot's broken out, and it's ear-piercing anarchy. We pass a group of inmates jumping a guard. Behind them, a fellow prisoner huddles at the threshold of his room. I can't exactly blame him. Another detainee bursts past us like a gust of wind. Hank levels a gun and drops the IP who's hot on her tail.

We stick together, a tight little squad, but it's slow progress. Fahra manages to fend off a pair of guards as we make our way down the hall. Out front, Hank's armor catches some bullets, but he keeps charging, giving worse than he gets. Cash is weak, but he's hanging in there.

At the next blast door, a cluster of holdout IP have made a makeshift barricade, keeping up a steady rain of pulse fire. Bear shouts back at me, "Stay behind me. You hear me? No matter what happens, stay behind the line."

I nod, but I can tell it pains Cash to obey. He shrugs off Captain Fahra and tries to stand on his own. The pain and exhaustion play out on his face. I put my arm around him.

"I've got this," I tell Fahra. He joins Hank and Bear as they make a run for it, rushing the barricade.

Cash and I limp behind them, struggling, while Benny's crew brings up the rear. Cash's breathing shallows up. With each step, I feel the twitch of spent muscle and the tiny tremors rippling through his body. It's like holding on to an earthquake. We both stumble, falling against the left wall. Rallying, he pushes off, and we keep moving.

Fahra's just ahead, flanking the rest of our group. His marksmanship drops the gunner at the far left corner of the barricade. It also draws enemy fire, and he absorbs a volley of hits. We scramble to pull him back, but Benny's already on it, moving in to cover him.

Bear and Hank keep pressing toward the barricade, taking hit after hit after hit. Each one lands like a hammer fall, crippling their gait. Over and over, they recover. Just one blast of pulse fire nearly knocks me over, and I'm barely able to shield Cash. More than once, he is almost hit.

Bear's aim takes out two more of the shooters. Only three more gunfire streams coming from the chest-high barricade. Almost there. Almost . . . there.

Benny's the first to breach it. He kicks a section of the barricade down. Too close for rifles now. Around me, pistols fire and fists fly. My mind and my reflexes tunnel down for one purpose. *Get through this. Protect your people. Keep Cash alive.*

Cash is drained. An IP unloads a hot mess of pulse fire at Bear, but Fahra manages to take out the shooter. Bear's exo-suit is smoking, but he's still alive and the last IP's dispatched. Bear stumbles up. He can barely move.

I call out to him. "Are you hit? Are you okay?"

He takes a second to catch his breath. "I think my plating's nearly done for. The load system's glitching out . . ." An inch at a time, he seems to buckle under the suit. Without the magnetic control, the plating's a hundred extra pounds of dead weight on his back.

"You need to punch out," I tell him. "We can cover you."

He shakes his head. "I'm fine."

Our crew kicks aside the last bits of the barricade. They close the blast door behind us. The hall begins to quiet. For now, there are no more guards to fight.

"How far away is the ship?" I ask Benny. He doesn't answer. I turn, and he's kneeling on the ground, someone lying at his feet. I collapse beside the body. A trickle of blood runs from his nose. His suit is powered down, fireblasted to hell. His hazel eyes blink, unfocused.

Hank.

"He's in a bad way, kid," Benny says. "Took one shot too many."

Hank coughs, then closes his eyes. Another rasp, then nothing. My clinic training kicks in, and I check for a pulse. It's weak, but still there. He's barely breathing. I look up at Bear.

He moves in to lift Hank's body, but Benny shakes his head.

Together, he and the crew shoulder Hank's weight. "It is not far to the ship," Fahra says. He glances back. "Perhaps a hundred more yards."

We follow. Another stretch of silent hallway, past the sealed command center, then a double set of blast doors. We open them and step into a bay, one much smaller than the main landing area. Lined up against the walls, there are many small capsules, about the same size as the simulators at flight control.

"Escape pods," Benny says. He tilts his head toward a few empty spots between capsules. "Looks like a few prisoners already lit out of here."

The room begins to shake. Debris rattles against the floor, and I feel a change in gravity, something only my stomach recognizes. "Hurry," Bear says. He runs toward the opposite blast doors and punches them open. The doors lead to the landing bay, where our ship is waiting. Where our ship is *firing*.

Benroyal's remaining guards are in the bay. They're trying to take out the ship, but Benny's crew is firing back. I spy Miyu among them, manning one of the turrets. *Boom. Boom.* Another violent shake. The cannons are taking the station apart.

Bodies litter the bay's floor, like fallen chess pieces on a scorched and bloodied board. There are maybe forty or fifty IP gassed asleep, some gutted by cannon blast. The handful left standing finally begin to retreat. Thank the stars, they don't see us. They take the opposite way.

"Go, go, go!" Bear yells, and the team obeys. Ducking low, Fahra takes Cash while Benny and his men carry Hank and hustle him back to the freighter. Miyu must see them too, because her barrels swivel away, then adjust. She lays down a line of fire, behind them, to cover their run.

There's no more time to waste. We have got to get out of here.

Just as I take Bear's hand, there's a crushing volley of cannon fire. An explosion at the other end of the bay, and the station groans. We rise, shuddering into the air, as the gravity systems begin to fail. Weightless and stranded, we launch ourselves from the threshold of the small bay. I hear the snap of a smaller round. Pulse fire. I glance behind, and a lone IP's lunging for Bear. "Bear!" I scream. Weightless, he spirals just in time. He grapples with the exo-armored soldier.

Frantic, I reach for Benny's pistol. The cannons swing in our direction, but hesitate. Miyu must realize she can't hit the IP without hitting Bear. Bear and the soldier hurtle through air, spinning and twisting and fighting. Over and over, the guard tries to raise his right weapon's port in my direction, but Bear keeps knocking it up. Pulse fire sizzles over my head.

I level the rattler. I squint and aim. I take a breath and aim again, waiting for just the right moment. One shot. The bullet rips into the IP's gut. He tries to cling to Bear, but Bear shakes him off. I try rotating toward them, but with nothing to propel me, I'm painfully slow.

We're jerked sideways as a tremor runs through the bay. The station is failing fast.

The shift nudges me toward Bear. I'm almost there, when I see it from the corner of my eye. The wounded IP drifts behind Bear, and he's already reached into his pack. The soldier has a rattler of his own. And the barrel's already raised. I scream.

Boom. Boom. Boom.

Three shots, and the world shatters like glass.

CHAPTER THIRTY-FIVE

THE STATION FALLS APART AROUND US. TIME SEEMS TO expand, and an ocean of seconds fall between Bear and me. The ship is still firing. The wounded IP is hit. The pistol falls from his hand. The soldier's head lolls and he floats away.

Moments later, the cannon falls silent. I look around. The battle is dying down. We're alone, drifting among the weightless corpses.

I reach for Bear and pull him to me. Our eyes lock, and for a moment, I think he's okay. "Phee . . ." he gasps.

But then I look down, and see the holes in his plating. The trickle of blood under his breastplate. The space below his heart is weeping. I press my hand over the wound, as if I could make it stop. "You're all right, Bear. You're all right." I say it and say it and say it. I can make it so.

"Phee," he says again. Slowly, he reaches for his pack and grabs something from inside it. He holds it in his hand.

Voices are calling to me, but I can't really hear them. Because I'm looking at Bear, and the quiet in his eyes drowns out everything else.

Bear rakes his fist over his heart. I won't let go. I'm just going to stay here. We can stay here forever. *Just for tonight. Just for now. It's enough.*

This is our always.

"Take it," Bear says. He's trying to put something in my hand. It's smooth and small. Without thinking, I palm it. I have so much to tell him, but I can't break the quiet, where our always still lives. Far away, I hear an engine.

"You have to go." He sighs. "Phee . . . I can't go with you."

And that's when it's finally real: He's dying.

"No," I choke, shaking my head. "You can't leave, Bear. I won't let you. You can't."

His breathing grows more rapid and shallow. He pulls me tight, and for a moment, I think he's trying to keep me for good. But then he whispers in my ear, and with one final force of will, he pushes me away, as hard as he can. I hurtle backward toward the freighter, half our beacon in my hand.

I carry his last two words.

Another life.

CHAPTER THIRTY-SIX

THE BAY QUAKES AS I SAIL BACKWARD. THE SHIFT SENDS
Bear flying, far from my reach. Lifeless and drifting, he
vanishes into the smoke as I tumble into a pair of strong
arms. *Hal.* He's tethered to the freighter, and behind us,
Benny and Fahra work to reel us in.

I twist in Hal's arms. There's something terrible in his
face, in the bright blue shine of his eyes.

His son's eyes.

I bury my head against Hal's shoulder. When he cries out,
the sound sharpens in my chest. In my hand, the little cylinder
blinks and blinks and blinks and suddenly, I'm pushing away.
No. No. He's not gone. He's not dead. He can't be dead. I kick and
struggle, but Hal won't let go. Finally, I surrender, and his hold
loosens. His strength fails, and broken, he sags against me.

The shudder in him is the deepest cut of all.

"*Oh god. Phee . . .*" he wails. "*My son . . . My son.*"

In that moment, part of me disappears. Cleanly bladed, it falls away and follows Bear into the smoke.

The landing bay groans. The massive doors are gasping open and Benny's vac is blasting off. On the end of the cord, we're pulled into the closing mouth of the freighter. Into the ship. Into the darkness. Into Cash's waiting arms.

I'm stripped out of my exo and liner. I slip in and out of consciousness, waking up to gravity, to Cash's body curled around mine in the infirmary, to the sound of engines churning in the dim. He is warm, made of steady heart-beat. Against him, I'm burning up. Every cell smolders into nothing until I black out or fall asleep. I feel it in my lids and limbs. I'm heavy, ready to drift again. *I don't want to wake up anymore.*

"Shhhhhh," Cash says, his cheek at my shoulder. "Rest now. Stay."

Strong arms pull me closer. A hand reaches for mine. I take it, the dead beacon in my other palm.

There is no end to our tears.

I wake up a hundred times. Then I wake up for real. In cotton scrubs, under thin sheets, shivering. My lids flutter and my eyes adjust. I'm lying in a berth snug-tight against a wall. Cash is gone. I turn over.

Hal is sitting beside me; there's a bio-scanner in his hand. He's checking my vitals. Gently, my hand closes around his wrist. I can't quite find words yet.

"I had to give you something." He sighs. "Hell, I had to give myself something."

I remember how to talk. I remember everything.

"To get through the trip back," I say. "To get home."

He nods, even though there is no home.

I nod too. We both start crying. But there's something else in Hal, even in tears: a hard, bitter edge. It's like looking at Mary, and I see what we've lost. We won't be the same. Nothing will.

I force myself to ask. "Is Hank—"

"He had a stroke," Hal says. "A pretty good one. But he's alive."

Relieved, I embrace Hal.

"We landed in Cyan, had him flown to Raupang," he says, letting go. "We don't know if he'll make it. It's too soon to tell."

I let out a breath.

"Let's go home," Hal says. "I'm tired."

I don't ask him where home is. He's forgotten too. Or like me, in his mind, he's already burned the place down and is ready for anywhere. Just someplace safe. I take the bio-scanner from Hal's hands and check his vitals. His blood sugar's a little low. "Have you eaten?" I ask.

"No. Have you?"

"We should eat."

He nods. Together, we take care of us.

It's early morning. Way too early.

I missed saying good-bye to Benny. I missed the shuttle boarding, and charging the bridge to Cyan-Bisera, and touching down at Raupang. I even missed saying good-bye to Hank when the medi-vac took him. Delirious and sedated and exhausted, I slept. Cash recuperated. Hal did very little of both. He lies down, but doesn't rest. He walks around, still asleep. I worry for him, most of all.

I do remember boarding this boat—a sap-stinking, wave-hovering bluefin hauler. We are running hard now, bound for Nankennan, Queen Napoor's childhood home. Near the northern coast of Bisera, the little village is still a hotbed of rebel defiance. Like Manjor, Nankennan has no love for Benroyal's Interstellar Patrol or for Prince Dak, and right now, it's the only harbor we can sail into without running headlong into the Interstellar Patrol. It's the best James and Grace could do, and the only place left. From there, we'll race to Belaram, the capital.

It's Coronation Day.

Miyu walks into my little stateroom. She hands me a stack of clean clothes. On the bottom, a neatly folded bolt of red, a robe for me to wear later. I put it aside and opt for the rest—cargos and a tee, boots, and everything I'll need. Miyu lays something else on the end of the berth.

Benny's pistol.

"He wanted you to have it," she says. "Be careful. Still loaded."

Gingerly, I pick it up.

I check the rattler. Three shots left in the chamber. I safety the gun and tuck it into my pack. I get dressed. Tuck my flex into my pocket. I sit down and pull on my boots.

Miyu sinks next to me as I tug the laces. She doesn't talk, or throw an arm around me or try to cheer me up. She is quiet, and it's just what I need. I double-knot the ties on both boots, but what I'm really doing is silently saying, *I'm glad you came to the Strand and stayed with us to the last. I'm really, really glad.* I stop, and look at her.

She knows. I've learned to read her half smiles.

My flex buzzes. I take a look. It's Larken.

KL: HEARD YOU MADE IT BACK.

PV: YES

KL: I ALSO HEARD ABOUT BEAR. I'M SORRY.

I don't want to get into it. I'm leaden as it is. It's an effort just to sit here. I ignore his last reply.

PV: HOW'S YOUR END? HOLDING GROUND?

KL: MASSIVE TROOP BUILD-UP. THIRTY THOUSAND IP AT THE BORDER.

PV: YOU OKAY?

KL: I'M FINE. NO MOVEMENT YET. EITHER HE'S GETTING READY TO THROW EVERYTHING HE'S GOT AT US, OR HE'S BLUFFING.

PV: BENROYAL DOESN'T BLUFF.

KL: I'M NOT EITHER. NEITHER IS THE ARMY AT MY BACK. ONE HUNDRED THOUSAND CYANESE SOLDIERS, FRESH FROM RAUPANG.

PV: WHAT??? ARE YOU SERIOUS?

KL: VERY SERIOUS. CYAN'S AWAKE NOW. THEY'RE READY TO FINISH KING CHARLIE, WHATEVER IT TAKES. AND THEY'RE NOT ALONE. SO IS CASTRA, I HEAR. YOU TALKED TO JAMES YET?

PV: NO. THANK YOU, LARKEN. I OWE YOU ONE.

KL: BIDRAM ARRAS NOC.

I put the flex away and look at Miyu. "What's going on?"

"Cash is waiting for you," she says. "I promised I wouldn't spoil the news."

"Good or bad?"

"The best," Miyu says. "The revolution. It's begun."

Miyu sits with me as I watch the incoming feeds from Castra. I hear my people in every grainy clip. I hear their shouts as they pour into the streets. So many voices, more than ever before. They won't be quieted this time.

Larken was right. We're all awake now.

CHAPTER THIRTY-SEVEN

FIVE MONKS, RED-ROBED AND HOODED, ASCEND THE STEPS OF the palace. They trail the queen's personal guard, Captain Landalau Fahra. Each of the monks carries a jar of water, drawn from a sacred well, specially blessed for a king's coronation. The monks are solemnly welcomed. Quickly, they are ushered past soldiers and servants, through the throne room, up the grand stairs, and into the hallway outside the royal chambers. There, they are met by two dozen of the queen's most loyal guards, and by the doors, they wait to be announced and presented. All are impostors.

One is an old politician.

One is a rebellious pilot.

One is a grieving father.

One is an exiled prince.

And one—the last—has been many things. Street racer. Corporate circuit driver. Sixer heiress. Suspected terrorist. A girl who was once fearless, then frightened, and now . . . almost free. Inside the palace, she's nearly there.

Not Phoebe.

Not Phoenix.

Just me. Phee.

Behind the next set of doors, Prince Dakesh and Her Majesty are waiting for us, their ceremonial attendants. Along with their servants and advisors, and a couple of special guests—Prime Minister Prejean and, of course, Charles Benroyal. The great peace-maker. Castra's earnest, forgiving, ever tireless savior.

Or he was, forty-eight hours ago.

Fahra steps forward. His men open the doors. They announce us. On the threshold, we wait to be summoned in.

I scan the chamber. To my left, gauzy curtains sway in the breeze. Morning light shines through the transparent bulletproof barrier between the balcony and the screens and cameras and the teeming crowd. You can hear them—a hundred thousand subjects packed in the courtyards and streets below. A low-level hum, like steady crackle on a far-away feed. To my right, archways to other rooms. My eyes don't linger there. They're pulled straight ahead.

Before us, an empty cistern rests on a pedestal. It's

perched between us and the royal entourage. They stand opposite us, a wall made of splendor. Jeweled fingers and silken gowns and sharp suits shadowed by a few bodyguards and many, many more IP.

Dak—the preening, would-be king—sits in the middle of it all, trussed up in full regalia. He's brooding in his gaudy, gilt chair. His mother stands at his right, sober-eyed and subdued, draped in a dark shade of crimson. The look on the queen's face tells me this day's something to endure. My gaze slides over her, moving to the man on Dak's left.

Benroyal.

I look at him, then Prince Dak. Their expressions match. I guess news travels fast; looks like today doesn't taste as sweet as it should.

Impatient, Dak barks something in his own language, but it's obvious he's scorched that we're late for the party. *Hurry up,* he's probably cursing, *let's get through the formalities.* Fahra bows to him and steps aside.

We walk in. One by one, we empty our jars into the cistern. As the scent of balm leaf drifts from the splash, I suck in a breath to savor the fragrance. Holy water to anoint a king. We put the jars down and they ring the pedestal. After, we kneel before Dak's clumsy throne.

Cash rises first and pulls off his hood. "Hello, brother," he says.

His smirk is sharp as a knife. It carves the glower from Dak's face, which pales, melting from shock into fear and then anger. Cash's eyes darken into something far more steely. He jerks his chin at Fahra. Cash's command comes low and steady. He's still weak, but he's not letting it show.

"Captain," he says, tearing off his robes. "Clear the room."

The whole room snaps. A few of Benroyal's men try to make a move, but the royal guard takes care of that quickly enough. In seconds, they've disarmed his personal detail and the scattering of IP soldiers. Fahra's done his job well—he packed the chamber with his most trusted sentry. Some in the entourage are shocked, like Prime Minister Prejean. Some are fussing, like Negendra, Dak's thick-necked foreign minister. Others struggle and fight, but it doesn't matter. All the extras, they get swept out of the room.

Finally, one of Fahra's men moves on Benroyal. I stop the guard before he can drag him out of the chamber. "Leave him here," I say. "We're not finished with him yet."

The guard obeys and forces King Charlie into a chair. I shrug out of my robe and reach behind me, where Benny's gift is tucked in my waistband.

"This is an outrage," Dak says, springing up. "Treason! I will have you all—"

Cash rounds the cistern, and with one vicious, straining punch, he lays his brother out. Dak crumples. He scrambles to get back on his feet, but Cash grabs him by the collar before he's even halfway up.

"You want to talk about treason?" Cash snaps. He drags his brother to the bowl and forces him over it, toppling three of the empty jars around the well. They shatter against the floor. Dak trembles; his face hovers an inch over the surface of the water. "You want a coronation? This is as close as you get. I should pour it all out and drown you in our father's blood."

"Cashoman!" his mother cries out.

Her voice is the only thing that reaches him. He growls. "She just saved your life," Cash says to Dak, before tossing him to the floor. Disgusted, he turns away from his brother. "Get him out of my sight," he tells Fahra. "I don't want to see him again, until we can call a tribunal."

"Yes, Your Highness," the captain says. Dakesh kicks and spits and curses in Biseran as half a dozen sentry drag him from the room.

Under the shouting, there's a softer voice. I turn and catch the tail of Benroyal's words. ". . . Joanna. But of course, it's not too late to discuss your mother."

In the space of a breath, I'm right up in his exhaust,

pistol raised. "Don't you say another rusting word about my mother, or I will end you right now."

He smiles. "I could be persuaded to strike another deal. For—"

But then he stops. Looks behind me. Quiet-eyed, Toby Abasi limps another step closer. He touches my shoulder, peering down at Benroyal. "And what kind of deal have you to offer now?" he asks. "Now that the Spire is burning?"

King Charlie doesn't pale the way Dak did. His mask slips only an inch. Just one small twitch of the upper lip. "It's of no concern. Capitoline has always—"

Now it's Abasi's turn to smile. "You believe the Domestic Patrol will suppress the riots. How many officers have you there? Enough for the half million protesters lining the Mains?"

Benroyal tries again. "But of course, the Interstellar—"

Abasi pretends surprise. "Haven't you heard? The IP abandoned defense of the Exchange and the Chamber and Assembly houses. Revolutionaries have taken them all, and are commanding a good number of your men now. I expect to join them after we are finished here. You wanted peace, did you not?"

Benroyal's frozen. He can't bring himself to nod.

"Peace is coming, yes," Abasi says. "But not silence. The

people have seen the truth. And it is too late to quiet them now." Another knowing smile. Abasi pauses. "But I suppose you're probably thinking of the Strand, and your forces there. Ease your mind on that account, my friend. Your admirals have already sensed the shift in the wind. I hear they are set to offer terms of surrender to the Cyanese this very hour. And so I have to wonder, Mr. Benroyal . . . exactly what kind of deal are you offering now?"

Benroyal lifts his eyes to me. Rage is quietly blazing behind his crumbling grin. "My life for your mother's. I leave, of my own accord, and I'll let you—"

"She's being held in Cashoman's chambers," the queen interrupts. "In the suite next to mine."

Fahra makes the call. For a tense line of seconds, we watch him, his flex to his ear. Finally, after a minute or more, he turns to me. "We have her."

Benroyal's last card. He knows it's been laid bare on the table. He opens his mouth and tries to stand, but I shove him back in his chair, pushing the unforgiving end of the pistol against his forehead. "Don't. Say. Another. Word," I tell him.

I sense everyone closing in, but I shut out their pleading. I don't want to stay calm. I don't want to stop and think about this. "Stay back," I snap. "Nobody move." Then I slide the safety off and savor the warmth of the trigger.

Three shots left.

One for my father. One for Mary. The last one, for Bear.

Gods and stars, I see his face even now. I watch him drift away.

One pull of the trigger and it'll be over.

I take a deep breath and look into Benroyal's eyes. But there's something so astonishing and alien in them that it puts a shake in my grip. He is . . . *afraid.* The cold-sweat panic strikes me like a forgotten wave, and I see myself through Benroyal's twisted lens. I am the sneering monster of his propaganda. The stone-cold killer. The crazed, unstable girl they've made me out to be. I shoot, and he wins.

"Phee . . ." Hal says. "No. Not like this."

I don't answer. I'm still locked on Benroyal.

I imagine lowering the gun and backing away. I fantasize about taking the high road. About letting King Charlie face whatever courts are left, back on Castra. But I'm not as disciplined as Cash. And my mother—my *real* mother, Mary—is not here to stop me. So I'll have to compromise, and steal a little justice for myself. Just for now. Just for one moment.

I look at Benroyal again. He's practically quaking now. I circle his chair. Behind him, I lean over his shoulder and hover at his ear. "You see, there's no need for a new deal . . . *I fear it's too late for that, and justice must prevail.*

You will have to be dealt with. In prison, you sap-sucking bastard."

Safety on. Pistol whip to the back of the head. Lights out.

I win.

After Benroyal slumps forward, the tension breaks, and all the fury drains out of me. The guards haul him out and I'm left frozen, all shivers and chattering teeth. Cash takes a breath and finally relaxes, too exhausted for words. We embrace each other. He runs his hands down my shoulders, and I'm glad for the warmth. Hal hugs me. No more tears tonight. We've got nothing left.

As Hal backs away, Captain Fahra clears his throat. "Your Highness," he says to Cash. "Perhaps it is time . . . ?"

Softly, Cash smiles at me. He straightens once more. "Are you ready for this?"

"Ready for what?" I say.

He turns toward the balcony. As Fahra's men pull back the curtains, there's a fresh wave of noise and expectant shouting. The people wait for a new king. I step back and try to let go of Cash's hand. "Go to them," I say.

He shakes his head and gently reels me back in. "Together," he says.

The guards part for us, and we step out and onto the

343

riser. For a moment, the light through the bulletproof glass is so blinding, I have to shield my eyes. Cash's face appears on the flex screens below. And that's when they realize he's not Dak at all. Finally, they recognize Cash. To them, he's larger than life. Stronger than the fiercest lion. A roar erupts, and the air trembles with their cries.

At first, their shouts are nothing but ecstatic clamor. But then, their voices knit together and thunder as one.

Ay-khan. Ay-khan banat bakar. Eb banat bakar.

I know these words. They're the same ones the people chanted when Cash last entered the city.

The Evening Star. He returns.

But this time, their prince—their all-but-anointed king—is lit up a thousand times brighter. Tears shine in his eyes like unfallen stars. He is here at last. He is theirs. He is home.

I lower my hand and lose myself in the rhythm of their joy. Cash turns to me. His arms reach out and he pulls me close. And when his lips find mine, I yield. Before the crowd, we share the sweetest, tenderest kiss. Finally, we break and I see my face on the screen, next to his. The people cheer more wildly than ever before. Soon, they begin a new chant.

Beharu. Beharu. Ay-khan. Beharu.

"What are they saying?" I ask Cash.

He shakes his head; he can't hear me.

I shout to be heard. "What are they saying?"

He laughs. "*Beharu.* You have a new name."

"Behar-what? What does it mean?" I say.

"Never mind what it means. They love you." He smiles, then kisses me again, then once more for good measure. "As do I."

Laced tightly, we turn back to the crowd. We wave for a long time, and drink in their roar.

〰〰

It should be raining right now. It shouldn't be this perfect, cool, cloudless day. Days like this aren't made for good-byes. They're not made for letting go, and it will probably be a long, long time before we're all together again.

But it's time, and James and Miyu have already spent an extra week with the rest of us in the Strand. And already Grace is impatient to see them. Since the mission, she's hardly left Miyu alone. All those flex chats and plans and special arrangements to meet up in Manjor . . . seems Grace cares a lot more about her daughter than either of them realized.

I'm glad for her. And, I suspect, she is too. It's not something we've talked about, but you can read it in the way she's started spitting out the word *Mom* instead of *Grace*.

Now we stand in the launch yard, and trade embraces.

"I'll miss you," I say.

"Likewise," she replies.

Oh, how I've come to love that half smile.

"Better take care of yourself," I add.

She nods. "I will. But only if you promise to stay out of trouble for a while. I mean it. And don't be getting any crazy ideas about skybrids. I swear, if I hear from Cash that you've fixed up some old Lucky Star and are flying around in it, I will come back here and kick you in the teeth." She pauses. "Or maybe not in the teeth, but somewhere."

We laugh, and before I can get in the last word, she ambles up the ramp and disappears into her vac. I'm left standing with James. We turn at the same time. Face-to-face, both of us uncertain and awkward and unprepared for this.

"You're sure you don't want to . . ." he says. He takes off his glasses and tucks them in his pocket. He squints into the sun. "I wish you and Joanna were coming with me, or that I was staying, or . . . I don't know what I wish."

I don't finish for him, but I'm pretty sure I know what's really on his mind. For the first time, I'm stepping out on my own. I'll be splitting my time between Castra and this world, at least for a while. For now, I've decided I'm not cut out to handle billions of credits. I've asked him to manage the family fortune, and I think, in different ways, it both satisfies and disappoints him. But, I suppose, James walked away from his old life too. I've abandoned my street-racing ways and he's let go of his corporate goals. We've both found a middle ground between rebel and Sixer. I will work alongside Cash, and James will start up the galaxy's most powerful nonprofit. Rebuilding Castra for all . . . that will be the Anderssen legacy.

I tell my uncle I am proud of that. I am proud of him, and what is to come.

As for me, for the next three months, I'll be traveling with Cash. In Bisera, we'll take stock and address the damage to his kingdom. And with Larken's help, we'll begin to repair the Strand. The Hill of Kings will stand sacred again; we will see to that.

And then there's home. I have a few loose ends to tie up on Castra too. We're breaking ground on a new project, right in Capitoline. Hal will oversee it for James and me—a new hospital for recovering addicts and post-traumatic stress survivors, built in Mary's name, on Mercer Steet. For her sake, I am proud of this too.

I look up at my uncle, who's waiting to board Miyu's vac. We'll be apart most of the time, but we'll still be on the same crew. I like to think of it that way, at least. It makes it easier to let go.

"I know what I wish," I tell him at last. "I wish you well."

He smiles, his gray eyes brightening up like morning light after a storm. "Wherever the route takes you."

I nod. One last hug, and he walks away.

〜〜〜

Most of the time, my mother doesn't remember my name. If it's a bad day, she doesn't even remember my father. On a good day, she calls me Phoebe and can tell me stories about the great Tommy Van Zant. About the time they first met, or the time he flipped a rig at Sand Ridge. But thankfully, not about the last time they said good-bye. The stories come in tiny gulps. They make her smile, and ease her pain.

The stim treatments seem to help a little, but Hal frets that it's not enough. After eighteen years of addiction, the black sap's taken too much from her. She's so far gone. There's no telling how long we've got before she slips under for good. Maybe we've just got right now.

Today is a good day, and I'm glad.

Hal, Hank, and I sit beside her cot under the pavilion. A little makeshift celebration before I leave for Castra with Hal. A reclining chair for my mother. Another for Hank, who's getting his late-afternoon snooze. He's perking up a little more each day and almost walking now, so I suspect his napping days are numbered. I smile. Blankets under our feet, and a modest spread of cool drink and good food. Above, the white tarps stretched over us.

We lounge on the eastern crest of our little valley, and I drink in the warm breeze. After months of whirlwind traveling, from the Gap to Belaram to Manjor, I've got one more night in the Pearl Strand, and I'm going to enjoy it. For the past few days, we've been hard at it. Sunup to sundown, we've worked. In a way, it's been a little like sewing up an old wound. Even Larken and Fahra get along now. Together, they've welcomed a thousand civilian volunteers—some Biseran, some Castran, some Cyanese—to clear out debris, turn the soil, and renew the poppy fields.

Right now, this particular field is still its own brand of graveyard—an endless stretch of charred, shriveled petals and ash-covered ground. Not for long. This morning, I spent a few hours driving one of the tillers, while the crew ahead of me cleared out the most stubborn stalks.

Cash is out there now, just beyond the next rise. I can hear him—or rather the tiller—churning the soil. At dawn, he promised he wouldn't rest until he'd prepared me the best patch of land up here. As soon as he's done, we'll get the drill and replant. Not just poppies, though. Not for this sun-kissed bit of earth. Fahra's getting me a special mix of seeds for this ground.

And here he comes, motoring in a ridiculous little flatbed rig, with a miniscule seat and an open top. At the moment, our captain's four wheels of funny-looking, but I don't dare laugh, even though he's way too big for the thing. He parks beside our pavilion and heaves himself off his tiny perch. I finish giving my mother another sip of watered-down nectar before getting up to greet him.

"Have a look," he says. "I trust it will be enough?"

I nose through the various buckets of seed on the bed of the rig. "What'd you find?"

"Slipwood," he says. "Some ice-leaf, some bleufleur, and a few buckets of beryl-bud. A good balance of ground cover and climbers and creeping vines. Is that satisfactory, *Beharu*?"

I nod. I guess at least Fahra's stopped calling me a *gan-gan*. But this *Beharu* business . . . I really need to drag it out of someone what it means. If I knew exactly how to spell it, I could look it up myself. I make a mental note to flex Miyu and ask her.

I hear another engine rolling up. I look out and see Cash's tiller chugging along to meet us. He's sitting high in the cab, and after catching his eye, I cover my ears, then put a finger to my lips. Quickly, he eases on the brake, then shuts the rig down. He understands.

Noises sometimes startle my mother. I glance back at her, but thankfully, she's still resting, and Hank gives a reassuring wave. She's all right for now. It's still a good day.

I turn back to the tiller. Cash jumps out of the cab and lands on the black-mulch ground. But he takes his sweet time getting to me. Impatient, I put a little hustle in my step. We meet between the tiller and the tent.

I start to ask him how it went, but he tackles me, silencing me with a long, sweaty kiss. He's breathless and rank, but I don't care. I let him melt into me. No shame, don't care who's looking, even when we're a tangled knot of thirsty lips and sunburned limbs.

Finally, Cash pulls away. "The field," he says. "It's ready. Fahra came through with the seed?"

I nod.

Cash waves at Fahra, who's blushing and averting his eyes. Most of the time, Cash can't keep his hands off me, and I think it embarrasses the poor captain.

But when you've been through what Cash has endured—months of torture and half as many days of stim therapy to ease the nerve damage—it leaves you hollowed out and hungry for better times. Cash seems eager to erase the memory of the white room and its marionette wires. He wants to *feel,* to drink everything in too hard, too fast, too soon, even when it costs him. Some days, Fahra's the only one who can fuss enough and force him to stop and rest.

But I don't begrudge Cash. I understand. It's the way

he's wired. My Evening Star . . . like me, he's all spark and energy, made to burn. I know what he needs.

I take pity on Fahra and pull away from His Majesty. Just a little breathing room, for the captain's sake.

"*Ay-khan*," Fahra says. "If it pleases you, I could send for a team and a second drill."

Cash shakes his head. "Please, Captain. Go and enjoy the rest of the afternoon. Phee and I can take it from here."

"*Ay-khan* . . ."

I raise an eyebrow at Cash.

Cash relents. "Thank you, Captain. Please send for the drill."

"Yes, *Ay-khan*." Fahra bows and backs away.

After he's out of earshot, I tease Cash, rolling my eyes.

Cash crosses his arms. "What is it?"

I face him, and drape my arms around his neck. "*Ay-khan*, this. *Ay-khan*, that. Someday, I swear, you'll turn into a royal monster. It's all going to go to your head, and you'll be completely insufferable."

He laughs. "Wait. You're not jealous, are you?" He tries to kiss me, but playfully, I turn aside. "Is it *Ay-khan* that bothers you so much? Or *Your Majesty*?"

"I am not calling you *Your Majesty*, Your Majesty."

"You've got your own special name, you know."

"Yeah, and you won't even tell me what it means."

He sighs, leaning in. "That's because it's complicated."

"How is it so complicated? Just tell me."

"*Be*haru means little flame, but . . ."

"But . . . ?"

"Be*har*u means beloved, and finally . . ."

I raise an eyebrow. "There's more?"

"One more," he says. "Behar*u* means deliverer."

I wrestle with the different pronunciations, and Cash laughs even harder. "See?" he says, capturing me. He laces his fingers at the small of my back. "That's why I just call you Phee. Because I don't need a special name for you. If I had to list all the things you are to me, I would need a hundred names. And then every time I looked at you, I would have to choose one, and honestly, that is time much better spent kissing you. For example, right now, I could be kissing you."

He grins, and I surrender. "You're right," I say. "Let's just stick with Phee."

We finish at dusk. The field's planted, and after turning everyone else loose, Cash and I lope to the pavilion. It's late, and they've already driven my mother back to camp. I sigh. Good thing they left some of the food. I'm starving, and we've already worked past dinner.

Cash and I collapse onto the blanket and rest on our

elbows. I break a loaf of bread and pass Cash the larger half. There's a little cheese left, and I peel a sweet, sticky-hearted frangi, and we share that too.

We stuff ourselves. Then we lie on our backs, under the greater pavilion of the night sky. It's early, and just waking up. The land's rimmed with red and gold light, but way up there, the twilight's turning out its pockets, scattering stars above the horizon.

I settle in the crook of Cash's arm. I close my eyes and take a deep breath, but the almond-sweet haze of the poppies is gone. I miss it. Every day, I wake up and expect it. I forget it's no longer here, and then I long for the new buds to push their way up. Especially here, in this field.

"How long will it take?" I half whisper. It's so peaceful and quiet here. "For the flowers to grow?"

"You'll see a little green, some pale shoots in a few weeks, but the blooms . . . they'll come back in a year, and this place will be bursting with them."

I look out again, and imagine it. A sweeping field of blossoms, swirling in the middle of the snowy white hill, like a bright sapphire eye. Yes, blue. All of them blue, every bloom a beacon. For my best friend. My partner. My pacer.

For Bear.

For him, I will tend this place and keep it holy. For

Mary, I will live a life that's worthy of her death and deal out relief to as many as I can. For all that we've lost, I will never stop replanting and rebuilding and defending this ground.

I will remember Bear. I will honor his name. I will teach it to my children, and they will know the price he paid for my life and theirs.

For him. For them.

For always.

CHAPTER THIRTY-EIGHT

I PULL UP TO THE RED LIGHT.

James doesn't like that I'm coming here, without a pack of bodyguards, but I'm doing it anyway. I get it. I really do. Half of Castra's pegged me as some kind of figurehead—"Phoebe Van Zant, Hero of the Revolution," while the other half—die-hard circuit fans—still pine for "Phoenix Vanguard's triumphant return." They want me to race again, keeping my alias. And let's not forget the Sixer holdouts, who're still beating the drums for my arrest. To them, I'll always be the worst kind of criminal.

So yeah, I know I need to be careful. But I can't be inconspicuous with an entourage. And I promised I'd be here. How could I not be?

This is my town.

The rig James let me borrow isn't too bad. It's small and black and sleek, like my old Talon, but the engine's standard, so it doesn't have much get-up-and-go. And rust if the accelerant driver isn't delayed. It's knocking in late, and a little too weak . . . I'd roll it into Benny's shop and see what they'd make of it, if I could. But I don't really think my uncle would appreciate that.

At the signal, I ease down the right lane, then pull up to the curb.

The rig powers down in a whine as I park across the street. There's a good deal of traffic today, a ton of people on this stretch of the Mains. At second glance . . . a lot of DP. But they aren't hassling anyone or barking orders. They're just managing traffic and keeping an eye out for the horde of pedestrians. Even their uniforms are different. As public officers, they wear the Castran flag on their badges, instead of King Charlie's lion. But I'm a south side girl, and I am used to badges spelling trouble. I have to tell myself not to wince.

I zip my jacket, pull up my hood, and climb out. Head down and hands in my pockets, I move into the herd of people crossing the Mains. I am short enough. I can almost disappear.

But one of the walkers seems to notice me. And I suppose I can see why. I'm not that much taller than this small brown-eyed girl whose hand's in her father's as they rush the crosswalk. He doesn't look like he's paying attention to anything, let alone me. The two of them pass quickly, but she looks back. I can almost read her mind. The spark of recognition flashes in her brightening pupils. Her mouth rounds into a great big O.

Under my hood, I smile at her. Her stubby little legs almost misstep, and she has to turn around again to right herself and keep walking. Her father pauses for half a beat to let her catch up, and then they move on. I lose them, and I'm anonymous again.

On the other side of the street, I make for the steps. The long parade of wide stone risers; it's a punishing climb, but worth it for the view.

I pass through the crowded sculpture garden, pausing amidst the tallest statues, the giant obelisks that once taunted the sun. I read the scorched, black shadows clinging to their bases, where only a few months ago, riot flame left its mark. Not so many riots now. For the most part, there's more talking around tables than tear-gas and screams. Between passersby, I notice the new patches of life—spindly scrubroot and my favorite—fragrant, yellow hackweed—that have been planted in a few bald spots.

I find a bench and stand beside it, a step back from the swarm. I look for my friends, but I guess they haven't arrived yet. It's been a long time since I've seen my former circuit crew. Gil and Goose and all the rest . . . word is, they just want to "catch up and grab some lunch," but I know the score. They seem to think I'm not done with racing, that I should get back behind the wheel, this time on my own terms. Yet every time I imagine one more shot on the track . . . one more rally, for old times' sake, I can't quite nail down my answer.

Absolutely not. Never again. No way. *Maybe?*

I banish the thought. Craning hard, I look up, but the Spire won't quite loom over me anymore. It simply stands, quiet and still, hollowed out of all its stolen power. Abasi says they'll turn it into a national museum. After he's sworn in as prime minister, he'll make sure of it. So many lost treasures . . . so much forgotten history. Everything Benroyal hoarded for himself will belong to everyone once more.

I check the time, then I scan the garden again. Any minute, I'll see my friends. I'm startled, not by a tap on my shoulder, but by a tug at the hem of my jacket. I wheel around, and amidst the patter of footsteps, there she is. The little girl.

The cheeky thing, she's given her dad the slip. He's standing around about fifteen feet away, watching a couple of quarreling birds. Between us, there's a handful of people. The girl stares at me. I stare back.

She's still inspecting me when I snap at the sound of a familiar voice. I look up. My friend is here, and he's walking my way. Behind him, I see the old gang, assembling at last.

I spy Navin, who detailed every rig. Dev, who hauled our tires. And Billy and Arad and Gil and so many more. Even Banjo. Sweet Banjo, who faithfully loaded our fuel. Beyond a hundred unfamiliar faces, they stand near the obelisks, and I'm pulled back in time, to the night of the gala. They stood there . . . *right there* . . . at dusk. They posed for photographers.

Arms linked, we posed as a team.

"Ma chère!" Auguste calls, a storm of wild, wiry hair and gangly limbs. He's going against the grain, slipping through the throng. The sight of his brightly tailored suit is the happiest jolt. But the crew behind him looks so different. No crimson and gold. No uniforms or tuxedoes. No Benroyal crests stitched over their hearts. I ask myself . . .

What colors would they choose now?

Again, the little girl tugs at my jacket. Bold as anything, she puffs out the words. "Are you the . . ."

She stops herself, and I wonder how she'll finish, whether she'll ask for the circuit star or the renegade.

The girl's father finally glances our way. He sighs, then crooks his finger at her. There's no time for her to finish her question, but I decide it doesn't matter anyway. I don't have to wait on expectation. I don't even have to choose.

I glance back at the crew. *My crew.*

"Yes." I nod. I glance down and meet the girl's eyes. "I am."

Then she lets go. And I push through the crowd. I walk into Auguste's wide-open arms.